Retribution

David Lee Corley

Table of Contents

Quote

"Yesterday's enemy is today's friend, and today's friend is tomorrow's enemy."

\-   Ancient Vietnamese proverb

Prologue

The seeds of war were planted long before the first Chinese soldier crossed the Vietnamese border. In the years following their victory over American forces, Vietnam had grown strong, had forgotten its place as China's little brother, had begun to see itself as a major power in Southeast Asia. The Americans, who had once fought against Vietnam, now found themselves sharing China's concerns as Vietnamese troops pushed into Cambodia, toppled the Chinese-backed Khmer Rouge, occupied ground that had known too much blood already. In the twisted mathematics of power, America chose to support Pol Pot, the very leader whose genocide they had once condemned, chose to arm rebels fighting against Vietnamese occupation, chose to turn blind eyes toward past atrocities in favor of current necessities.

China watched from the north, watched its influence in Southeast Asia shrink, watched Vietnam grow too proud, too independent, too dismissive of proper hierarchy. The Soviets had signed treaties with Vietnam, had promised support, had given their ally weapons and supplies, but geography made their promises hollow, made their support symbolic, made their treaties worth less than the paper that held their words.

In the halls of power in Beijing, the Politburo counted costs, measured distances, calculated how many sons they would spend teaching Vietnam its place in the order of things. They gathered their forces quiet as storm clouds building, 300,000 soldiers who would carry empire's judgment south while Vietnam kept its strength in Cambodia and along the western border, kept its armies occupied with holding conquered ground, kept its eyes turned away from the thunder building along its northern borders. The leaders in Hanoi underestimated China's resolve.

The Americans, who had once fought alongside these mountain people against Japanese invaders, who had once trained these hill tribes, who had once seen firsthand how this ground drinks blood, now gave their silent permission to China's plans. When Deng Xiaoping told American President Carter that the child needed spanking, Carter's studied silence spoke volumes about how powers shift, about how alliances change, about how yesterday's friend becomes tomorrow's obstacle.

In the northern mountains, where ancient borders meant little to the tribes that had outlasted emperors and colonizers alike, the Chinese army gathered while Vietnamese forces stayed south, while Soviet promises rang hollow, while American diplomats looked away, while all the pieces of tragedy aligned themselves like stars coming into fatal conjunction. The ground waited, patient as stone, waited knowing it would drink deep, waited remembering when all wars were fought for simpler reasons with simpler weapons with simpler ways of counting the dead.

In Hanoi, the generals who had survived French steel and American bombs, who had outlasted two empire's attempts to claim this ground, who had learned to fight with patience and fury in equal measure, did not see, did not know, did not understand that 300,000 Chinese soldiers stood ready to teach them why some powers cannot be challenged without cost, why some lessons must be written in blood so deep no army can wash it clean.

The River

Northern Vietnam

The river ran cold through black stones that had seen three wars. The morning sun glinted off the water, turning ripples to gold. Granier stood thigh-deep in the current, teaching the village boys how to feel the fish slide past their legs in the shadows. He spoke little, letting his hands show what words could not.

Spitting Woman walked the bank barefoot, watching the boys spread out in the shallows with their bamboo poles. She called out in her harsh mountain dialect when they crowded too close, when they forgot to mind the deeper pools. "Mind the deep water," she called to a boy edging toward a dark pool. "The big fish will pull you in if you're not careful."

It was good here. The war had not touched this bend of the river. The boys still laughed without looking over their shoulders, still splashed the clear water high into morning sun. They had not yet learned to scan treelines or count the seconds between mortar rounds.

The smallest boy, Duc, saw it first. His pole dipped

forgotten in the current as the baby elephant waded into the shallows fifty yards upstream, its dark wrinkled hide glistening wet in the morning sun. "Look," he whispered, but the word carried across the water like a stone dropping in still water. The other boys turned, their fishing forgotten as the baby elephant's trunk swayed above the surface, testing the air like a curious snake. It snorted, sending up a spray of water that sparkled in the light.

"It's just a baby," Little Cadeo whispered, his eyes wide with wonder. He took a step toward it, then another. The baby elephant didn't startle, didn't run. Its eyes held a playful gleam that drew the boys closer, their feet splashing through the shallows. "I can ride it," Cadeo called over his shoulder, pride making his voice crack. "My uncle rode an elephant once, in Hanoi. He showed me how."

"Me too," Hien shouted, dropping his pole to splash after Cadeo. One by one, the other boys abandoned their fishing, drawn to the baby elephant like moths to flame. They crowded around it, hands reaching to touch its rough hide. The baby elephant seemed to welcome their attention, its trunk gently exploring their outstretched fingers.

Spitting Woman had been helping young Binh untangle his line when she noticed the silence spreading across the water. She saw the abandoned poles floating downstream, watched the boys clustering around the baby elephant. Her heart seized in her chest. Years of war had taught her to read silence like others read books, and the jungle had gone still as a held breath. Even the cicadas had stopped their endless droning. "Granier," she called, her voice carrying the edge of urgency that three wars had honed sharp as a blade. "The boys."

Cadeo had both hands on the baby elephant's back now, trying to pull himself up. "Help me," he called. "I just need a boost." The other boys cheered him on, their voices too loud in the unnatural quiet.

Granier felt it too - the wrongness in the air. Birds had stopped calling. Even the insects had gone quiet, as if the jungle itself was holding its breath. Then came the sound that made his blood run cold - massive footfalls, deliberate as destiny, coming from the treeline upstream. The mother elephant emerged from the shadows like a nightmare taking form, her head low, ears spread wide as battle flags. Something in her stance spoke of mindless fury, of rage that knew nothing of peace or mercy. She took one step into the sunlight, then another, her eyes fixed on the cluster of boys around her baby.

"Cadeo," Spitting Woman's voice cracked across the water like a whip. "Get away from it. All of you. Now."

The boys scattered, water spraying. But the smallest one stumbled, fell. The mother's charge began, her feet striking earth like thunder. Granier's hands found his rifle. The oilcloth fell away and the weapon came up smooth as breathing. Through the scope he saw the elephant's eye, saw the muscle in her shoulder that would tell him when she would turn. His finger found the trigger. He would kill her before she reached Spitting Woman.

But Spitting Woman was moving toward the beast, her arms raised. Granier kept the rifle trained on the elephant's head. One wrong move and he would send the round through the elephant's brain. The woman would not die here, not after surviving three wars.

The elephant slowed. Her trunk swayed, testing air. Her front foot struck earth once, then again. She trumpeted, the sound shaking leaves from trees. Spitting Woman did not flinch. Her voice came steady in a dialect Granier had never heard her use before, words that seemed to reach past the beast's rage into something deeper.

The elephant's head lowered further, but now it was different. The fury drained from her stance. Her trunk reached toward Spitting Woman, questioning. They stood that way for a long time - woman and beast, each taking measure of the other. Granier's finger stayed on the trigger. He had seen elephants crush men to paste in Cambodia, had seen them tear trucks apart like paper. This one could kill Spitting Woman before anyone could stop it.

But Spitting Woman knelt slowly, her eyes never leaving the elephant's. Her hand found river grass, pulled it free. She held it out. The elephant's trunk explored the offering with terrible gentleness. Behind her, the baby splashed through the shallows toward its mother, water streaming from its sides.

For a moment longer the elephant stood watching Spitting Woman. Then something passed between them, something Granier could not name. The great beast turned away, her baby following. They disappeared into the jungle's shadows as silently as they had come.

Granier lowered his rifle. His hands shook as he wrapped it again in oilcloth. He had been ready to kill. Would have killed. Some things you could not unlearn.

The smallest boy still lay where he had fallen. Spitting Woman helped him up, spoke soft words that made him nod. The other boys crept back to the shallows. Their laughter did not return quickly.

Granier waded back into the current. The fish still moved in the shadows below. The river ran on through black stones that had seen both death and life. But his eyes kept finding the rifle on the bank, and the place where the elephant had stood, and the woman who had chosen a different way than his. They had built something here in this river bend, something worth protecting. But they knew better than most how quickly peace could shatter, how close the old ways lurked beneath the surface of things.

The muddy path wound through bamboo shadows while cicadas screamed their endless chorus. The boys walked ahead, their voices still trembling with excitement as they relived the morning's terror. Granier and Spitting Woman followed behind, close enough to watch but far enough that their words wouldn't carry.

"Sometimes I don't understand you, woman. Why risk your life for a beast?" Granier asked, his voice low. He kept his eyes on the path, on the boys, on everything except her face. "The rifle would have dropped her clean. One shot. No risk."

Spitting Woman walked silent for several steps, her bare feet finding earth. "The boys needed to see," she said finally. "Needed to learn there are ways to face death besides making more death."

She touched a bamboo stalk as she passed, her fingers reading its grain like braille. "My grandmother taught me that song, that old elephant song. Said it came from times when people knew how to speak to mountains, to rivers. To great beasts."

"Songs don't stop tusks, don't turn rage," Granier

said, but his voice carried a question.

"No," she said. "But that mother, she wasn't full of rage. She was full of fear. Fear for her baby. Like I was fearful for the boys." She looked at him then, her eyes dark as mountain pools. "You see only beast. I see mother. Same as any mother who'd die to protect her children."

Ahead, the boys had stopped to watch a snake cross the path, their voices rising in excitement. Spitting Woman called out sharp words in her dialect, making them back away. "Life answers life," she said softer, to Granier. "Death only makes more death."

Granier touched the rifle slung across his back, feeling its weight like old sins. Three wars had taught him that death was often the surest answer, the cleanest solution. But something in her words reached past that knowledge, touched something he'd thought war had burned away. "You could have died," he said, but the words carried less certainty now.

"Yes," she said. "But I didn't. And now those boys know something bullets could never teach them." She walked ahead then, leaving him to think about mothers and beasts and ways of answering death that didn't involve more dying.

Red lanterns swayed in the evening breeze while Mai knelt before the ancestral altar. Her homemade dress gleamed like fresh snow in the candlelight. Behind her Tuan stood straight as a young bamboo his hands steady his eyes fixed on the burning incense. The smoke rose in spirals toward Heaven carrying their prayers to those who had come before.

The village had gathered since dawn. Women cooking sweet rice and roasted pork, men bringing rice wine in clay jars and children weaving palm flowers into garlands. They had built the young couple's house in three days. The walls rose clean and straight from red earth the thatched roof tight against rain. Inside the bed waited carved from ironwood that Tuan's grandfather had cut. The villagers had given everything that makes home from wood and palm.

Grandfather Vu touched Mai's forehead with fingers stained red from the marriage papers. His voice carried soft as temple smoke. "You come to us from the river village. Now you are ours. Now you belong to this ground." Mai bowed her head while behind her Tuan's breath caught sharp as a knife.

Spitting Woman brought forward the tea tray her movements precise as ritual. The cups had belonged to her grandmother small as thimbles delicate as bird bones. Mai's hands did not shake as she poured. Did not tremble as she passed the cup to Tuan's mother. The older woman's eyes softened at the girl's grace.

"They will do well" Granier said. He stood with the other men passing rice wine in bamboo cups. The night air carried wood smoke and incense and the sound of women singing old songs. Songs about love lasting longer than mountains, about homes built from heart-wood, about children carried like precious jade.

The feast began then. Pork crisp as autumn leaves, sweet rice sticky with palm sugar, bitter melon soup that Tuan's mother had seasoned with ginger and memory. The villagers ate and drank and told stories about other weddings, other homes, other times when peace walked these hills.

Mai and Tuan sat together their shoulders touching through silk while elders offered blessings. Each blessing came with a gift. A cooking pot black with age and use. A quilt sewn from fabric older than the givers. A water jar that had stood in three houses. Things that carried weight of years, things that made home from more than wood.

When night deepened the music began. Old men with bamboo flutes, young men with drums, women singing in voices clear as mountain streams. Mai and Tuan danced then. Their feet found earth's rhythm while around them the village celebrated. Children scattered palm flowers in their path while lantern light painted everything red as luck red, as fortune red, as love that outlasts war.

Later when the wine was mostly gone, when the songs had grown quiet, when the lanterns burned low Mai and Tuan walked to their new home. The house rose clean against stars while behind them the village slept. Inside everything waited. The bed with its carved posts, the cooking hearth with its first wood, the water jar by the door. Everything that makes life from simple things.

Spitting Woman watched them go. Her eyes held knowledge of what comes after celebration. Of what it means to build a home in hills that remember blood. But tonight was for joy, was for hope, was for everything young love promises. The lanterns burned red against dark while somewhere far to the north China gathered its strength like storm clouds while the village slept, while the new house held its first dreams.

Morning would come soon enough with its own demands. But tonight belonged to Mai and Tuan. Belonged to a village that built homes from heart-wood and hope. Belonged to love that grew like bamboo through whatever ground fate offered.

The temple stones held the days heat like a furnace. Incense rose in coils while old women moved between carved pillars that had stood when French guns first spoke in these hills. Their bare feet made no sound against floors worn smooth by 10,000 prayers. They carried brass bowls of rice wine and dried fish and set them before wooden faces black with age.

Granier watched from the doorway. The women worked in silence, knew their places, knew the order of things. Mai brought fresh yellow flowers; laid them at the feet of gods whose names he did not know. Her daughter followed with water in a clay jar that had survived three wars.

The Buddha sat above them eyes half closed in eternal contemplation. Knife scars marked his wooden chest where Japanese soldiers had tried to burn him. The villagers had saved him carried him into the hills while their homes turned to ash. Now he watched them with the patience of mountains.

"The harvest comes soon," Tu said. She knelt beside a wooden bowl filled with last year's rice. "The spirits must be fed before the fields." Her fingers moved through ancient patterns as she prayed. The other women followed her lead their voices rising and falling like wind through bamboo.

Children played in temple shadows; their laughter echoing off stone walls. A boy kicked a ball made from wound twine. It rolled beneath the altar where brass cups caught morning light. His sister retrieved it, bowed to the Buddha before running back to their game.

Spitting Woman appeared beside Granier silent as smoke. "They remember the old ways," she said. "Even the young ones. Even after all that came before." She watched Mai light fresh incense, let the smoke wash over her face. "Some things bombs cannot break."

The day moved slow as ceremony. Women brought food shared it on woven mats spread before temple steps. Rice and fish sauce dried meat carried in leaves. The men came in from the fields, sat in age order, spoke of crops and weather. Children served their elders then ate their own portions squatting in the shade.

Old Binh brought out his zither began playing songs older than any man present. The music floated through temple air mixed with incense and prayer. Women sang words that had survived French guns and American bombs. Their voices carried weight of generations who had knelt on these same stones.

When evening came they lit lanterns strung and them between pillars. The light caught carved figures that had watched this village live and die and live again. Shadows danced on walls like memories given form. The Buddha smiled his eternal smile while below him people who had survived three wars celebrated simple peace.

Peking, China

The black limousine moved through the streets of Peking, headlamps cutting yellow paths through darkness. Police escorts flanked it fore and aft, their red lights washing across marble facades. General Chen sat motionless in the rear compartment. A leather portfolio lay heavy in his lap while the city passed outside like something viewed through fever.

The summons had come at midnight. They always came at midnight, these messages that changed the world. The motorcade passed beneath stone dragons and into the circular drive where Party guards stood rigid in their green uniforms. Security lights caught the dull gleam of rifle barrels.

Chen's boots echoed through marble corridors. The building held power in its bones, in its high ceilings and polished floors that had seen revolution rise from peasant fields to presidential palaces. Behind these walls waited men who had never held rifles, never felt the earth shake with artillery fire, never watched young men die in mountain passes. Yet they held Asia's fate in their soft hands.

The general straightened his collar before the great wooden doors, his father's words echoing from decades past. "Never show them fear, boy," the old man had told him, touching the bandage that covered his missing eye. "Fear is how mountains eat soldiers. Fear is how empires fall." His father had learned that truth fighting Japanese in these peaks, had watched good men die because fear made them step wrong, made them hesitate. "What of courage, father?" young Chen had asked, watching the old man clean his rifle with hands that never stopped shaking. "Courage?" His father's laugh had been bitter as snake venom. "Courage is what frightened men call it when they're too proud to admit they're afraid." The general touched his collar again, feeling his own hands steady as stone. His father had died in these mountains, had given his bones to ground. The doors opened.

They sat before him, twelve men arranged around a mahogany table while overhead lights cast shadows sharp as knife blades. Chairman Hua Guofeng sat at the head, his face carved from the same stone as Mao's, his presence carrying weight of a man who'd survived revolution by learning when silence spoke louder than words. He had taken Mao's seat when the great helmsman fell, had steered China through waters dark as prophecy.

The Minister of Defense, Tang Wei, sat rigid as bamboo in his black suit, his hands folded over reports that told how Vietnam had grown too bold, how their troops had pushed into Cambodia, how they dared to claim territory China saw as its own sphere. The Vietnamese had forgotten their place, had forgotten how China had armed them against the Americans, had forgotten that small nations lived or died at empire's whim.

Next to him General Wu of the People's Liberation Army watched with eyes that had seen Korean snow turn red, his face bearing scars from battles the others only knew from maps. He had watched Vietnam grow stronger with Soviet weapons, had seen them take Cambodia like wolves taking sheep, had measured their army's strength and found it greater than any dared admit.

The rest were party men, bureaucrats who'd climbed to power on papers and promises, who'd never heard bullets speak war's true language. They had spent years watching Vietnam align with Moscow, had seen them sign treaties with Russia, had watched them become Soviet dogs in China's own backyard.

Smoke from Hua's cigarette hung motionless around him while he studied the maps spread before him like fortune teller's cards. The Vietnamese had grown arrogant with their victory over America, had started believing their own legends, had forgotten that China had ruled these lands when Vietnam was still learning to walk. His voice came dry as autumn leaves falling. "General Chen, you will not take territory. You will not take prisoners. You will bring them pain such as they have never known. You will make their children scream and their old ones wail and their women curse the day they were born Vietnamese." His fingers traced paths through mountains. "When you are finished they will know what it means to defy China. They will know what it means to think themselves our equals."

The other members watched while Hua spoke destruction's dialect, while he measured distance between pride and punishment. They had watched Vietnam sign military pacts with Moscow, had seen them take Cambodia from China's ally Pol Pot, had measured their growing strength with increasing alarm.

"You have thirty days," Hua said, crushing his cigarette into an ashtray that cost more than a farmer's yearly wage. "Make them days that history will remember. Make them days that mothers will speak of in whispers. When they withdraw their forces from Cambodia you will withdraw our forces from their north." His hand moved across the map like death's own shadow. "Leave nothing standing that can be toppled. Leave no village unburned, no field unsalted, no well unpoisoned. Let them learn what happens when small dogs bite large dragons."

General Wu's scarred face twitched. He alone knew what such orders meant in soldier's flesh, in village screams, in the equations war writes with blood and bone. He had watched Vietnam defeat three empires, had seen them bury French pride and American power in jungle graves, had learned why some nations refuse to bow no matter the cost. But he stayed silent. The time for debate had died with Mao.

General Chen bowed, understanding in his bones

what demons they were unleashing, what dark gods they were waking, what price Vietnam would pay for defying China's will. The men around him had planned this like accountants planning an audit, had turned suffering into spreadsheets, had mapped out atrocity with pens. But somewhere in his soldier's heart, a small voice whispered that Vietnam had buried greater armies than this, had learned war's lessons in French blood and American brass, had taught three empires why some grounds kill those who dare claim them.

Outside, the limousine waited in the dark. Somewhere south, young men cleaned their rifles and checked their equipment, not knowing they were about to become instruments of historical retribution.

Chairman Li lit another cigarette. In the brief flare, his eyes showed the weight of watching empires fall and rise again. Around him, the other members gathered their papers, tucked pens into pockets, already thinking of other meetings, other decisions. To them, this was policy. They would sleep well tonight in their comfortable beds.

"That is all," Li said. "You have your orders. Make it hurt. Make it last. Make them remember."

The general bowed again and withdrew. Twenty divisions waited in the southern provinces – 300,000 men with tanks and artillery and aircraft that would turn Vietnamese sky black with smoke. The largest army China had assembled since revolution painted these same halls red with landlord blood.

In the mountains of the north, children slept in their beds while their mothers dreamed peaceful dreams. Soon those dreams would turn to nightmares. History held its breath, waiting to record what would come.

Through Peking's dark streets the limousine carried

its cargo of sanctioned cruelty, while behind steel doors and marble walls, twelve men had signed death warrants for thousands they would never meet, never see, never have to watch those people die. The city slept on, unknowing, while somewhere far to the south, war gathered like a storm.

Northern Vietnam

The sun pressed hot against earth while water ran cool around their ankles. Mai splashed Tuan once laughing while her hands planted rice quick as thought. "Too slow, farmer. The birds will steal our crop while you dream."

He splashed back, caught her waist, pulled her close. The rice plants dropped from her fingers made ripples in the paddies mirror surface. "Maybe I dream of you," he said. She tried to pull away, but he held her while around them mountains watched young love paint itself across morning.

"The rice won't plant itself." But she stayed in his arms while water moved against their legs, while sun turned their skin copper, while everything simple and good wrote itself in mud and memory. Her fingers found his chest pressed against muscle made strong from working earth. "You've grown stronger since we married."

"Strong enough to carry you home." He lifted her, spun her once while she laughed, while water flew from her feet, while birds rose startled from nearby trees. When he set her down she kept her arms around his neck. Their faces came close enough to share breath.

"First the rice," she whispered, "then carrying." She kissed him quick as dragonflies touching water, then broke away grabbed more shoots from her basket and began planting again. Her movements ran fluid as the stream that fed their field.

They worked through morning heat sharing the rhythm they had learned from parents who had learned it from ground older than war. The rows grew straight as prayers behind them while overhead clouds wrote their names in simple shapes. Sometimes their hands touched beneath the water and the touch carried more than accident.

When the last row was planted they stood together in their field that would feed them, that would remember their feet, that would mark seasons turning by how green grew against blue sky. Mai leaned against him while water ran around them, while mountains watched while everything worth having wrote itself in mud and memory and the spaces between heartbeats.

"Now," she said, "you can carry me home." He lifted her, held her close, carried her from the field while she laughed, while birds sang, while the day turned sweet as rice wine. The jade pendant she wore caught sunlight turned it green, as hope turned it bright, as promise turned it into everything that made young love outlast empires.

Dawn broke as Granier and Spitting Woman walked the dirt path to the nearby town's market, their shadows long against the red soil. They carried baskets of smoked fish from yesterday's lesson.

"More rumors of Chinese troops from the north," she said, shifting the basket of fish. "Always rumors in spring. Like the ravens coming."

"This is different," Granier said. His eyes held that distant look she knew too well, the one that meant his mind was walking old battlefields. "The Chinese don't move hundreds of thousands men just to make a point."

"They want us out of Cambodia. Nothing more. Threats without teeth. China has stood with us through three wars, fed us when the French blockaded us, armed us against the Americans. They are our brothers in revolution."

"Cain still killed Able."

"Who are Cain and Able?"

"Never mind."

She made that sound in her throat again, the one that wasn't quite a laugh. "You see armies in morning mist. The party chiefs in Hanoi say it's just theater, just politics. They remind us how Chairman Mao supported Ho Chi Minh when all others abandoned us."

"Party chiefs don't dig graves," Granier said. "They don't know how earth smells when it's covered in blood. And Mao is dead. Chairman Hua is not Mao."

"Even if you're right, they won't come this far north. These mountains mean nothing to them. We share a thousand years of history, of culture. They are our teachers, our allies."

"Mountains mean everything. You cut the head, the body follows. They'll come for the high ground first." He touched the rifle scar on his forearm, an unconscious gesture she'd seen a thousand times. "They'll come hard. And when they do, a thousand years of brotherhood will mean nothing against one day of empire."

"Then they'll learn what three armies learned before them," she said, but her voice had lost its certainty. "That these mountains have teeth."

"Yes," he said quietly. "But at what cost?"

"You can't relax and just live life, can you? You always have to look for a fight."

Granier grunted in response.

The market stirred to life around them, vendors arranged their wares with practiced motions, the air thick with wood smoke and the scent of morning fires being stoked.

Locals bowed slightly to Spitting Woman as she passed, a gesture born of respect earned through years of healing both beast and man.

A mother pushed forward through the growing crowd, her sick child fevered and limp against her shoulder. "Please," she whispered. Spitting Woman paused in her stride, touched the child's forehead with fingers that have known both warfare and medicine, spoke words in her hill dialect. "Gather purple mushroom caps from the north slopes," she told the mother, "brew them with river mint when the sun sits highest." The mother clutched her child closer, watching Spitting Woman with eyes that have seen her heal too many times to doubt.

Granier moved among the market stalls with military precision that years of village life haven't softened. He traded their fish for supplies with the economical movements of a man who has learned efficiency in three wars. Behind him a group of village children trailed in formation, their small backs straight as boards, tiny feet matching his measured stride. He ignored them as he would ignored any potential tactical weakness, focusing instead on the business of supplies and survival.

A vendor called out, offering mangoes. Granier selected three without haggling, knowing the price of being foreign even after all these years. The children continued their game of mimicry, but he paid them no mind.

Spitting Woman watched it all, her dark eyes missing nothing, cataloging every movement, every exchange, every shift in the morning air.

They finished their trading as the sun climbed higher, the day's heat beginning to press down. The baskets now held rice, dried pork, spices, and the small necessities of village life. They had built something here, in this place between war and peace, but neither of them forgot what lies beneath the surface of their quiet days.

A breeze stirred the market awnings, carrying with it the scent of coming rain. Somewhere deeper in the mountains thunder rumbled. Granier studied the darkening sky. "Storm's coming," he said, and in his voice is the echo of other storms, other rains, other times when dark clouds brought more than just water to these mountains. Spitting Woman nodded once. They turned toward home, leaving the market's morning bustle behind them.

An old woman called out for healing, her joints swollen with the changing weather. Spitting Woman stopped, spoke quietly in her dialect, telling her which herbs will ease the pain. The woman grabbed her hand, pressed a small bundle of dried flowers into it. Payment, though they both know Spitting Woman would heal without it. This was the way of things. Small kindnesses. Exchanges. The delicate web of village life that they had woven themselves into, though never completely. Never enough to forget what they were, what they might need to be again. They walked in silence, each step measured, each movement precise.

The weight of the baskets was nothing compared to other burdens they had carried.

At the proposed building site by the river Spitting Woman walked the ground in bare feet while storm clouds gathered above the mountains. She spoke of privacy, of being closer to the water's song, her dialect mixing with French in the way it did when she wanted something from Granier. "Here," she said, marking the earth with her toe, "the morning sun will warm the walls."

Granier watched her movements, saw the warrior's grace time had not softened, but his eyes kept returning to the nearness of the river. "The bank has eroded since spring," he said. "Another season of rain..."

She cut him off. "The river has always been here. The village has always been here."

"The river was lower then. The rains came different."

She turned to him, her face set hard as mountain stone. "You think I don't read the water? Don't see its moods? This is where we belong."

"I'm not so sure. Le Duan knows what I was," he said, his voice dropping low. "Who I worked for. He has known since the beginning. But men like him can be pushed from power." His hands worked unconsciously, testing a bamboo pole's strength. "New men come. Men who won't understand why their people harbor someone like me. The village would pay for that misunderstanding."

Her face softened for a moment. "These are my people," she said in her dialect, then switched to his French. "Our people."

"You're all I need," he said. "We could go

anywhere."

She touched his arm the same way she did years ago when they found each other after the war. "We need this place. These people. This is where we found peace."

Mai sat in her home singing softly to herself and she prepared the afternoon meal. The storm came without warning. Thunder split the air and Mai looked up from where she knelt grinding herbs. The pestle stopped mid-stroke. Through the open door she saw clouds black as smoke pile against mountains. The wind changed then carried a scent like wet stone.

The storm rolled in with sudden violence. Lightning lit up the sky, thunder followed without pause, and Granier and Spitting Woman ran for the village through the heavy drops.

A bolt cleaved a towering ironwood, sent it crashing through Thanh's hut. Inside they found the mother Le pinned beneath centuries-old wood. Spitting Woman ran to a nearby chopping block and grabbed an axe. She ran back to the collapsed house and handed Granier the axe. He went to work on the fallen tree pinning the woman. Granier's axe strikes echoed the thunder while the woman's family watched, their faces lit by each lightning flash. Moments later, the wood broke and she was free. He family rushed to her side and helped her up.

Then came a sound Spitting Woman had not heard since the war. "No," she whispered. "Not like this."

Tuan burst through the door and found Mai on the floor surrounded by herbs and half-filled bowls. "The river," he said. His clothes were soaked from checking their rice field. "It's rising fast. We need to move things higher." They grabbed what they could. The marriage quilt, the ancestral tablets, the cooking pots still warm from breakfast. Mai's hands shook as she wrapped her mother-in-law's teacups in clean cloth. "There is no time for that. We have to go," said Tuan as he pulled her out the door.

The first surge took their pig pen along with most of the chickens. The water came black and angry, swallowed the wooden walls like they were nothing. Tuan and Mai dropped what was in their arms and ran to help Old Hai whose hut had caught the full force. They dragged the old man free while behind them the ancient ironwood tree gave way. It came down across yards of ground, took three fences with it. Frightened animals scattered fleeing the rising water.

"The house!" Mai screamed. She stood in rising water and watched their new home shudder as the river rose. The walls they had built together, the bed they had shared, the hearth that had cooked their first meal. The water took the foundation first. Chewed the posts like hungry teeth.

Tuan ran toward their home. The water was at his waist, then his chest. "The strong box!" he shouted. "The papers. Our money." He reached the door as the first wall fell. Mai screamed his name, but the river ate her voice.

The current caught him at chest level, but he lunged through his shattered doorway. The flood came like a black hand. Took their house whole, turned it sideways, showed its belly to sky. Tuan went under. The current had rolled him like a leaf. He came up once arms striking out for anything solid. The house broke apart around him, sent splinters and precious things into the churning dark.

Granier saw him go under. Saw Mai trying to wade deeper, saw her grief already starting. "Grab Mai. I'll get Tuan," yelled Granier. Spitting Woman waded into the dark water and pulled Mai out. Granier ran along the bank calculating angles and currents. Found a place where the river bent. Where its fury made mistakes.

He went in up to his chest. The water tried to take him too, but his feet found purchase in mud that wanted to swallow everything. Tuan came past like wreckage. Granier caught his shirt hauled him sideways out of the main current. They fought the river together while on the bank Mai's scream cut through thunder.

When they dragged themselves out Tuan coughed river water fell to his knees tried to turn back toward where their house had been. Mai caught him, held him while he shook. They watched the river take everything. Their walls, their bed, their first home together. The water carried it all away like time carries memory.

"The strongbox," Tuan said. His voice cracked like broken things. "Your mother's bracelet. All of it gone."

Mai touched his face. Her fingers left mud like tears on his skin. "We're alive," she said. "We have each other."

They stood together in the rain, watched the river eat their dreams.

Granier and Spitting Woman moved through the village shouting in three languages, herding people uphill. The river rose furious, devouring the bank where Spitting Woman had stood minutes before explaining her dreams. Whole trees tumbled past. The water took three buffalo, their terrified bellows cut short.

Through sheets of rain Spitting Woman and Granier watched their own hut splinter. The river chewed the posts first, water black as night rising to the floorboards. "The rifles," Spitting Woman said, but Granier held her back with an iron grip. The floor gave way with a sound like breaking bones. Their home of eight years twisted in the current, the thatched roof peeling back, exposing the inside to rain and fury. The metal box that held their weapons, their papers, their carefully hidden past, disappeared into the churn. The walls folded like wet paper. They watched everything they owned spiral into the flood - Granier's maps, Spitting Woman's medicinal herbs, the small careful life they had built between wars. Their bed turned sideways in the current, floated for a moment like a funeral barge, then vanished. The last wall fell. In seconds there was nothing left to mark the place where they had slept, had healed, had learned to live with peace. Nothing except churning water the color of old blood.

"Higher," Granier shouted above the roar. "Get them higher." They worked against the deluge, dragging children through mud, carrying the old ones who could not climb fast enough.

A child slipped, screamed, disappeared into the churning water. Without hesitation Spitting Woman dove in after him.

"No!" Granier said to the empty air, but he was already running downstream, calculating angles and trajectories and the mathematics of survival. She surfaced with the boy clutched tight, went under again. Her head appeared further out, fighting the current. Granier ran along what remained of the riverbank, then waded in, let the water take him to his waist. He caught her arm as they swept past, his feet finding purchase in mud that wanted to take them all. He pulled them in. The boy coughed river water, lived.

They dragged themselves up the slope to where the village huddled. "Dammit, woman. I almost lost you."

"You would have done the same," she said between heavy breaths. "You know what it means to save a life as well as take one." He said nothing, watching the water continue to rise. It took their homes, their gardens, their simple things that marked the distance between surviving and living.

As the rain eased and the water began its slow retreat, Granier touched her shoulder once. "We rebuild higher," he said. "Away from the river." She nodded, understanding that some arguments needed no words, that some choices nature made for you.

Around them the village began to stir, to count losses, to plan rebuilding. This was not the first flood they had survived. It would not be the last. The water carried their dreams of a new home downstream, mixed with broken trees and dead buffalo and everything else the river had claimed. But they were alive, they were together, they would rebuild. This was what villages did. This was what survivors did. This was what people did who had learned that the river, like war, took what it wanted and left the living to make sense of what remained.

Around them the village gathered. Women brought blankets. Children carried what could be saved to higher ground. The storm rolled overhead like artillery while the river ran black with everything it had stolen.

Later they found pieces. A roof beam. A broken cup. A door that had held so many hopes. They salvaged what they could. Let the river keep the rest. Mai and Tuan worked alongside their neighbors. Cleared debris. Counted costs. Started again.

The rain fell softer then. The river ran on through black stones that had seen other floods other losses other times when water took what people thought they could keep. Mai and Tuan held each other watched the current carry their first home away. They were young. They would build again. The village would help. But something had been lost that day. Something the river would keep.

They started in the mud. Tuan stood with other men hauling broken things from earth gone soft with rain. His hands bled from splintered wood, but he worked without stopping. Mai moved among the women salvaging what could be saved. Her wedding quilt hung heavy with river water while she spread it in morning sun.

The village worked as one body. Old men marked places where new homes would rise. Marked them higher this time away from the river's reach. Children carried stones for foundations while women wove palm thatch into new roofs. The sound of mallets striking wood carried across the valley like heartbeat.

"Here," Granier said. He stood with Tuan on ground that would hold their new house. "Five feet higher than the last. Stone foundation not wood. The river won't take this one." They dug together sweat running black with mud. Made the foundations deep as a man's height. Other men came bringing river stones tumbled smooth by the same water that had taken so many homes.

Mai worked with Tuan's mother weaving walls from

bamboo. The older woman's fingers moved swift and sure showing Mai how to make the weave tight as cloth. "My mother taught me this," Tuan's mother said. "Now I teach you. Some things the river cannot take." They worked in the growing heat while around them the village rose again.

The walls went up first. Men stood bare-chested in the sun fitting posts into holes packed with stone. Mai and Tuan worked side by side. When a post stood true they touched hands quick as birds touching earth. Let the work speak what words could not.

By midday the frame stood complete. Other men came then bringing palm thatch they had cut at dawn. The roof rose like wings against sky. They wove it tight remembering how rain finds weakness. How wind seeks gaps.

Old Binh brought them a cooking pot black with years. "Found it downstream," he said. "The river gives back sometimes. Not everything but enough." Mai took it with hands gone rough from work. Inside she found river mud and small broken things. She cleaned it until the metal shone dull as memory.

They built the bed together. Not ironwood this time but young bamboo that bent without breaking. Mai helped Tuan lash the joints with twine soaked in wax. Made them tight as promise. When they carried it inside the new house smelled of raw wood.

The women came then bringing what makes home from simple things. A new quilt sewn from cloth that had survived. Clay jars for water and rice. A broom of bound grass to sweep dreams back into corners. Mai arranged everything with careful hands. With movements that spoke of starting again.

Tuan worked until dark setting the last roof poles.

Fitting them true and straight against whatever sky might bring. When he came down Mai waited with clean water and rice wine. They sat in their doorway watched evening come to the valley. Around them other homes rose like hope from mud.

"We build stronger this time," Tuan said. His voice carried weight of everything water had taught them.

Mai touched his arm. Her fingers left mud on his skin like promises written in earth. "We build higher," she said. "We build together."

They slept that night on bare bamboo with stars showing through gaps in new thatch. The house creaked and settled around them speaking in wood's own tongue. Outside the river ran quieter now. Ran past homes it could no longer reach. Ran through a village that had learned its lessons in mud and heartwood.

The dust from their labor rolled across the wreckage while the village moved as one organism. They worked as armies worked, coordinated, instinctive, only these hands built instead of destroyed.

Spitting Woman supervised the women weaving palm thatch for roofs while watching Granier direct the men in setting posts. Her dialect flowed among the women like water, their fingers never stopping their work. His French-accented Vietnamese carried across like the mud. It wasn't good. Most just nodded and smiled like they understood his gibberish.

During the midday break Granier found her alone near their ruined hut. "Too many hands rebuilding," he said, watching the children carry water to the workers. "Too many mouths to feed."

She turned to him, her eyes narrowed against what she knew came next.

"The flood took half our stores," he continued. "Rice, dried fish, medicine. Everything you gathered for winter."

"We have survived worse. We rebuild," she said. "We always rebuild."

"Until we can't. Until the food runs out or the next flood takes more than just houses."

"So, we run? Hide in the deep hills like animals?"

"We survive. Like we taught others to survive. Away from roads, away from rivers, away from places armies walk."

She watched a group of children playing in the mud, their laughter carrying across the work site. "Here we have strength," she said. "Numbers. Protection."

"Here we have targets," he said softly. "Here we have graves waiting to be filled."

By dusk seven huts stood again, stronger than before. The village had added reinforcements against future floods, wisdom born of disaster.

As darkness settled, the villagers gathered for rice wine and quiet celebration. In the firelight Granier and Spitting Woman sat slightly apart, their shoulders touching. They had rebuilt after other storms, other wars. But something in the wind, in the jungle's breath, whispered that this peace could not last.

China-Vietnam Border

In the command tent the maps lay spread like prophecies of suffering, candlelight making the terrain lines writhe and shudder against the paper. General Chen stood before his officers, young men with faces hard as river stone and eyes that had learned to see death as mathematics. These were his chosen ones, his select butchers, each handpicked for what lay in their hearts, those darker things that war requires.

"The villages are not military targets," he said, his voice carrying soft as a serpent's belly across sand. "They are the heart of Vietnam. When you break a country's heart you break its will. Each raid must become legend. Each attack must sear itself into generational memory. Let them know first by rumor, let them feel you coming like animals sense earthquakes. Take your time. Let fear do its work. Make mothers wake in the night clutching their children to breasts gone cold with terror."

His finger traced paths through the mountains, paths that would soon run red. "No prisoners. No mercy. The old rules of war do not apply here. You are not soldiers now, you are a natural force like typhoons, like tsunamis, like the earth's own rage given form and purpose."

The officers stood silent, absorbing his words like stones absorb heat, some of them young enough to be his sons, all of them now marked for whatever demons' work would breed in their souls.

"You will strike without pattern, without warning. Today this village, tomorrow one twenty miles distant. Let them think you are everywhere and nowhere. Let them think you are legion."

One officer shifted, touched the pistol at his hip as if seeking comfort in cold steel. "Sir, what about resistance?"

The general's smile came thin as a knife blade. "Resistance is what we want. Resistance justifies escalation. Let them fight back. Let them die like warriors so we can kill them like animals." He moved around the table, stood behind them close enough to smell their sweat, their fear, their hungry anticipation. "You were chosen because you understand that history is written in blood. That peace comes only after terror has done its holy work. That some victories require not just the death of warriors but the death of hope itself. Now go. Make me proud. Make China proud. Make Vietnam remember why empires are feared."

The officers filed out into the night air that smelled of woodsmoke and weapon oil, and somewhere to the south villagers lay sleeping in beds that would soon become pyres. The general watched them go, these sons he was sending forth to birth legends of horror, and somewhere in his chest the heart he'd thought war had burned away stirred like a thing remembering it was once human.

Northern Vietnam

The villagers gathered beneath a sky scrubbed clean by mountain winds, the air carrying autumn's first whispers. The feast smells rose into the twilight, wood smoke and roasted meat and the sweet resin of fresh-cut bamboo that still sweated from the new walls.

Children ran past the long tables where women set out steaming bowls, their feet raising dust from ground that had finally dried after the floods. The lanterns swayed in evening breeze, their light catching the careful joints of the new buildings, the precise angles of freshly thatched roofs.

"See how straight the walls stand now," old Minh said, running his hand along the smooth-planed bamboo that young men had carried from a nearby grove. "My father built crooked, my grandfather built crooked, but we finally learned. The water taught us."

His grandson carted rice wine in clay jugs that had survived the waters, the red earth of their making darker where wet rims had dried, the boy's face proud as he poured for the elders.

Women moved between cooking fires that painted their faces in shades of copper and gold, their hands quick with wooden spoons that had been carved from trees the flood had dropped at their doorstep.

Le and her daughters had strung paper lanterns, their soft glow reflecting off new walls bright as hope. The cook fires made shadows dance against the granary walls where rice lay stored in bins raised high above any water's reach.

Granier watched from the shadow of the new storehouse, its beams still yellow where the adze had cut them, the wood grain catching lantern light like ripples on night water. He counted four new common buildings that hadn't existed before the floods, counted the sharp edges of fresh-cut timber, counted everything new that the village's hands had raised from mud and memory.

A woman he didn't know brought him a bowl of fish soup bright with river herbs, steam rising like river mist at dawn. The scallions floated like small green boats on the surface. "Better than before," she said, nodding at the rebuilt huts with their steep-pitched roofs, the new granary raised half again as high as the old, the deep drainage ditches that would carry the next flood's fury past the village rather than through it.

"We learned from the water's anger. See how the new walls rise from stone now, not earth?" She was right. The foundations stood on river rock hauled up from the valley, stones that had been tumbled smooth by ten thousand years of water's patience. Even the cooking fires now sat in clay rings that would hold them safe when the next rains came. Music started as the evening rolled down from the mountains like silk unfurling. Someone had brought out drums, and their voices carried deep into the valley where the river ran brown and full.

The children danced, their shadows tall against walls that smelled of fresh-cut wood and new beginnings. Even the old women stood straighter, as if the village's new spine had strengthened their own.

Spitting Woman found him as the first stars emerged, her face painted in shades of gold from the lantern light. "They dance because they think they've outsmarted fate," she said, taking the soup bowl from his hands and eating a spoonful. "They think new walls mean new destiny." But she too looked pleased at the straight lines, the careful joints, the work of hands that had finally learned to build for tomorrow instead of just today.

She pointed to where two young men practiced with staves, their movements fluid as water in the deepening dark. "See how they play at war while they can still call it play?" The night deepened around them while the villagers celebrated, their voices carrying up into darkness, their laughter rising against whatever fate scratched at the mountains' far side with iron claws.

The celebration thinned as the moon rose high, its light catching the fresh-cut bamboo walls like silver fingers. Old Minh led his grandchildren home, their feet stumbling with rice wine and contentment. The last drummers packed away their instruments while women banked the cooking fires into red eyes that would wake hungry in the morning.

The new walls caught whispers and laughter as families found their way to bed, the sounds carrying clear in mountain air that had grown teeth with nightfall. Dogs settled into doorways, curling against thresholds that still smelled of new-cut wood.

Granier and Spitting Woman walked the slope to their house that stood separate from the others, a choice that had raised eyebrows but suited them both. The path showed fresh-turned earth where they'd widened it after the floods, the dirt still uncertain under their feet in the dark.

Their house rose against stars, its lines clean as a rifle shot. They'd built it together, every beam and board a compromise between his need for sight lines and her desire to be closer to the water's song.

The door opened soundless on leather hinges he'd cured himself. Inside the house held warmth from a day of sun on new walls. She moved through darkness with the certainty of a woman who'd learned to hunt before she'd learned to love, finding the lamp, bringing fire to wick. Light bloomed between them.

His hand found hers the way it had that first time in war's darkness, when enemies became lovers and bullets became promises. No words passed between them. None were needed. The lamp flame drew their shadows tall against walls that smelled of fresh-cut wood and shared memory. They had grown old together in a land that ate the young, had survived three wars and found peace in a fourth.

Her head rested against his chest where old scars mapped campaigns fought before they met. His arms held her the way they'd held rifles, with the same certainty, the same deadly precision, but gentler now, softer, like the way mountain streams hold moonlight.

They stood together in their new home while outside night birds called and somewhere far to the north an army gathered like storm clouds against mountains.

Southern China

General Chen stood before the map table while Colonel Wang laid out photographs of Vietnamese villages along the border. Black and white images sharp as knife cuts. Rice paddies. Watch towers. Farmers who might be soldiers. Soldiers who looked like farmers. The colonel's fingers traced routes through mountain passes that no army had ever held.

"Sixth Special Operations Group," Chen said. His voice carried flat as stone. "Five hundred men. All veterans. All trained for this work." Through cigarette smoke he studied the villages marked in red. Places where people lived quiet lives. Places that would learn why some wars start with whispers instead of shells.

Captain Luo stepped forward laid more photos across the steel table. "Sir, these villages supply intelligence to Hanoi. Their men serve as militia. Their granaries feed soldiers." His hands sorted images like dealing cards. Each one marking a place that would burn.

"Show me the units," Chen said. Wang opened his folder. Spread sheets marked with names and numbers that measured how many would die. "Teams of forty to fifty men. All experienced in covert work. They cross the border tonight. No uniforms. No insignia. Nothing to mark them as ours."

The general's finger touched village after village. "Here. And here. And here. Kill the leaders first. Then teachers. Then everyone else except a few witnesses." His voice carried precise as artillery coordinates. "Leave bodies where they fall. Let families find them. Let stories spread."

Through smoke thick as battle haze they planned how fear would flow south. How terror would run like water through Vietnam's veins. The colonel made notes in his book. Writing death's schedule with careful strokes.

"Sir what about survivors," Lou asked. Chen's smile came thin as a blade.

"Let them run. Let them carry our message. When the army comes later they'll remember these nights. Remember what happens to those who defy China's will." His hand moved across the map marking places that would become graves. "Five hundred men. Twenty villages. Two week's work to start a war."

Wang gathered his papers. Tucked death's itinerary into his folder. "The men are ready, sir. Have been training for this. Know what's needed."

"Good," Chen said. "Send them tonight. Let Vietnam wake to new wisdom tomorrow." Through windows thick with night he watched his commandos move with enthusiasm. Each man carrying death's own measure. Each step marking time that would paint sky red as prophecy.

Northern Vietnam

First came the sound of breaking branches, clumsy and desperate, wrong for any animal that knew these jungles. Granier rose from his morning rice.

The man staggered from the tree line like something newborn and dying all at once, legs gone wrong beneath him. Blood had made a black apron of his shirt. Granier caught him before he fell. The man's eyes were wide with that look Granier knew from three wars - the look of someone who had seen too much and run too far.

Spitting Woman appeared without sound, her hands already moving across the wound. The bullet had gone through and through, a clean shot delivered by someone who knew their work.

The man spoke in gasps, his Vietnamese becoming a river of terror. "Chinese soldiers in black uniforms. No insignias. They came before dawn. Shot the village headman first. Then the teachers. Then anyone who ran." His voice cracked like dry wood. "My wife pushed me into the jungle's darkness while she ran the other way. The sound of that last shot follows me still."

The man's eyes rolled white as spoiled milk, his hands clawing air that no longer wanted him. He died in Granier's arms, his blood soaking into the same ground where yesterday children had played. Spitting Woman touched the dead man's forehead, whispered words in her dialect that were older than any war. They knew what this meant. They'd seen how violence spread, how it followed old maps and older hatreds.

The jungle had gone quiet, the way it did when killers moved beneath its canopy. Granier lifted the dead man while Spitting Woman gathered the children into the headman's hut. They'd done this dance before, this preparation for war that came disguised as peace. But this time felt different. This time the bullet spoke of purpose, of lists and plans, of an enemy that knew exactly who they sought.

The temple's bamboo walls cast bars of shadow across

the elders' faces while they listened as Granier stepped forward from the shadows. "I know these tactics," he said in French-accented Vietnamese. "This precision. This order of killing." Spitting Woman moved beside him, her bare feet silent on temple stones. "Let us go," she said in the hill dialect that carried more weight with the elders than any modern tongue. "Let us see what story the dead have written."

Elder Tran's face showed the deep lines of a man who had seen three wars bloom in these mountains. "Let us not assume anything. It could be bandits," he said. "or deserters wearing stolen uniforms." But his eyes said he didn't believe it.

"The Chinese would not dare," another elder said, but fear made his voice crack like dry bamboo. Spitting Woman's laugh came sharp as a knife's edge. "They dare because they think we are weak," she said. "Think we are farmers who have forgotten how to kill. Let us show them what these mountains remember."

The elders conferred in whispers while incense smoke wrote prayers in the air between them. Finally Elder Tran spoke. "Go then," he said. "Read what the dead have written. But remember - if these truly are Chinese soldiers, your eyes may be the last to see our village standing."

Granier and Spitting Woman bowed once, precise as ceremony, then turned toward the door where morning sun painted hell's own promises across the temple threshold. "How long?" Elder Tran called after them. "How long before you return?"

"Two to three days," Granier answered.

The elders watched them go, these two hunters who had learned war's wisdom, who moved like smoke through morning light, who carried death's geometry in their hands and revolution's certainty in their hearts.

They ran as they had in old wars, eating ground with the patience of wolves. Spitting Woman carried her bow and a quiver of arrows, while Granier carried a spear with a tip hardened by fire. The jungle passed in green waves, their feet finding paths that existed only in Spitting Woman's memory. During their third hour, they paused where two streams met, their breathing controlled despite the pace. Spitting Woman drank upstream from a fallen log, her movements efficient as a deer's.

"These attacks," she said in her dialect, then switched to French, testing the words like touching old wounds. "They lack... procedure. The Chinese army moves like a river. Wide. Deep. These men moved like snakes."

Granier studied the northern horizon where mountains cut the sky into shards. "Rivers change course," he said. "Beijing hasn't forgotten Cambodia. Hasn't forgotten how Vietnam broke their puppet government. A government the Chinese supported." He took another sip from the stream. "They lost face."

"The Chinese army wouldn't risk war over face," she said, rising, water dripping from her chin like silver. "Not here. Not now. These were probably deserters. Bandits wearing stolen uniforms."

"You didn't see how they killed," Granier's voice carried the weight of experience. "Professional soldiers. Clean. Efficient." He shouldered his pack. "Bandits kill messy. These men killed like they were trained to."

"Then why send so few? Why not come in force?"

"Testing. Probing. Like tigers checking a village's

defenses before the real hunt begins."

She considered this, her eyes reading the jungle's signs while her mind read darker currents. A bird called from deep in the green darkness. Not right for this time of day. "We should move," she said, already flowing into the shadows.

Granier followed, their conversation suspended but not finished. They ran on, two ghosts chasing answers through jungle. The truth, they both knew, waited in the village ahead. Waited in broken bodies and spilled blood. Waited to tell them if this was just another bandit raid, or if the dragon had finally decided to bare its teeth.

They approached like smoke - invisible, testing the air. Spitting Woman read the ground with fingers that knew death's handwriting. She found the first trap near the village well - tripwires strung with professional precision. The second waited by the headman's door, a mine placed exactly where running feet would fall. The third, a punji pit lined with poisoned bamboo, guarded the temple steps. Each device spoke of military supply, of trained hands, of calculated cruelty.

"Not bandits," Granier whispered. The words fell between them like stones in still water. The village opened to them like a wound. Bodies arranged with methodical purpose - the teachers shot first, then the leaders, then anyone who ran. The killing held a grammar Granier recognized from his CIA years. Each corpse positioned to tell a story of power, of consequence, of warning. They found the old headman face-down in his doorway, shot through both knees before the killing round in the back of his head. His wife beside him, executed with a single bullet.

Professional work. Clean. Exact. The kind of killing that requires training.

The bonfire in the village center still held warmth, though the flames had died days ago. Spitting Woman knelt beside it, ran ash through fingers that once taught village children to weave. Rice and dried fish, an entire season's food, reduced to gray snow. Not just killing then. Erasure. "You were right," she said in her dialect, then switched to French as if needing distance from the truth. "Chinese army. Regular soldiers." Her hands closed on the ashes. "They wanted them to starve any survivors."

Granier's eyes never stopped moving, reading the scene like a battlefield report. The precise positioning of sentries during the attack. The clean shell casings, all the same calibers. The boot prints that spoke of military order. His mind mapped it against their own village - approaches, vulnerabilities, choke points. "They'll come for us," he said.

"Yes." She stood, ash falling from her fingers like dark rain. "But now we know them. Know how they think. How they move." Her eyes found his. "How they kill."

They moved through the village with practiced efficiency, gathering intel like collecting spent brass. Each detail became ammunition for what was coming. The height of sniper positions. The placement of boobytraps. The kill zones arranged with geometric precision. Near the village edge, they found a cigarette pack. Chinese military issue. Not dropped by accident - placed where it would be found. A message: We want you to know who we are. What we can do. What's coming.

Granier pocketed the pack. Evidence. Proof.

Promise. They buried who they could before darkness fell, marking graves with stones that would outlast whatever came. The jungle watched with ancient patience, remembering when all wars were fought with bronze and bone instead of bullets and boot prints. "Our village," Spitting Woman said as they prepared to run home through gathering dark. "The children."

"We'll be ready," Granier answered, but his voice carried the weight of knowing what ready meant. Knowing that sometimes being ready just meant choosing how to die. They ran through night like shadows chasing shadows, carrying a truth heavier than weapons: This wasn't just a killing. It was a rehearsal.

Typhoon Rising

Southern China

Through dawn mist General Chen walked the parade ground his boots marking time against wet concrete. Three hundred thousand men stood in formation their rifles black against gray sky. Tank treads ground stone beneath steel weight. Artillery pieces waited patient as mountain cats their barrels covering measured fields of fire. The 54th Army spread before him like an iron river. Twenty thousand men who had trained six months for this morning. Behind them the 55th waited with their tanks. Beyond them stretched more divisions than morning light could touch.

Captain Wu approached staff clipboard tight against his chest. "Sir, final ammunition counts complete. Two hundred rounds per rifle. Two thousand per machine gun. Artillery at full complement." The captain's voice carried mechanical precision. Had learned to speak in numbers that measured how men would die.

Chen nodded kept walking. Past the motor pool where trucks sat in neat rows their beds loaded with supplies, fuel, and ammunition. Past tanks being fueled their crews checking tracks with fingers that knew steel's own language. Past artillery crews adjusting their sights measuring angles of death with practiced grace.

"Show me Third Battalion's readiness," Chen said. Wu led him to where Colonel Zhao's men trained with bayonets. Their boots crushed grass wet with dawn. Steel sang against steel while sergeants shouted cadence. The men moved with dedicated fury. Had spent weeks learning how to kill at arm's length. How to make blade find flesh between ribs and under chins. They were young. Were certain. Were everything soldiers should be before war teaches its own lessons.

Through morning they worked. Weapons cleaned with religious dedication. Ammunition distributed with precise measure. Maps marked with coordinates chosen by men who had never walked the ground they condemned. Chen watched it all. Watched men become machine. Watched peace surrender to protocol.

The radio bunker hummed. Transmission officers coordinated columns that would move like blood through Vietnam's arteries. Lieutenant Chang marked overlays with different colored inks. Red for artillery coverage. Blue for tank movements. Green for infantry advance. The maps spread like prophecy across steel tables. Everything measured. Everything certain.

In the motor pool Major Wong supervised final checks. Fuel trucks topped off. Ammunition loaded. Medical supplies packed with careful attention. The trucks would follow the tanks. Would feed the beast that 300,000 men had become. Wong's clipboard held numbers that assumed victory.

Afternoon brought the final briefing. Officers gathered in the command bunker their collar brass bright as morning sun. Chen stood before maps that divided Vietnam into squares. Into coordinates. Into everything except what it truly was. "Three weeks," he said. His pointer marked phase lines. "Three weeks to break their spirit. To teach them the price of defiance."

Artillery commanders noted firing coordinates with practiced hands. Tank officers memorized routes chosen by men who had never walked mountain paths. Infantry leaders studied objectives marked in red grease pencil. Everything divided into numbers.

Night fell while soldiers wrote letters home. Cleaned rifles one final time. Tried to sleep before dawn would signal their advance to the border. In the command post Chen watched final reports come in. Everything ready. Everything measured. Everything prepared except the things no army can prepare for.

The tanks started rolling before first light. Two hundred machines of steel moving like metal dragons through mountain shadows. Behind them came the trucks. Behind them came the men. Behind them came everything China thought would be enough to break Vietnam's spine. Chen stood on the command ridge and watched his army move. Watched dawn paint tank hulls red. Watched soldiers march. Everything was ready. Everything was wrong.

Through gray dawn the aircraft rose from northern bases like iron birds waking. J-7 fighters slung with missiles screamed south toward the border while the ground still held night's shadows. Behind them came the Q-5 attack aircraft their wings heavy with bombs and rockets. The H-6 bombers followed massive and certain their bomb bays carrying steel seeds that would bloom in fire.

General Chen watched them pass overhead from his command post. Through his binoculars he counted squadrons. Fifty fighters to clear the sky. Thirty attack aircraft to break ground defenses. Twenty bombers to shatter whatever remained. Their engines filled the morning with mechanical thunder while their shadows crawled across tank columns that ground south like steel rivers.

Captain Wu stood beside him marking numbers in his book. "Sir, weather reports show clear skies to the border. Visibility unlimited." His pencil moved across paper with precise strokes. "First strikes begin in forty minutes."

The fighters flew close formation their pilots young and certain. Had trained against targets that never shot back. Had learned war's mathematics in classrooms where death remained theoretical. They crossed the border at 10,000 feet while the sun still hid behind mountains that remembered other armies.

Behind them came the strike aircraft moving lower their pilots searching for targets marked on maps drawn by men who had never walked this ground. The bombers flew higher their crews checking instruments with mechanical precision.

The radio crackled with pilot voices calling positions. Marking targets. Speaking death's coordinates with professional detachment. Chen listened while morning painted sky red as warning. His army moved below while above his air force wrote war's introduction in contrails and trust in machines that had never learned what Vietnam's sky could do.

Northern Vietnam

The temple air hung thick with incense and prophecy. Oil lamps cast trembling shadows across worn planks where elders sat cross-legged, their faces carved deep by years of war and waiting. Outside the wooden walls night gathered while Granier spread his maps.

The maps lay before them like omens. Spitting Woman crouched at his shoulder, her presence sharp as a blade as she turned his French words to hill dialect, transformed his soldier's knowledge to wisdom the elders could grasp.

"The village we found wasn't just destroyed," Granier said, watching comprehension darken their weathered faces. "It was erased. Like a story scraped from stone." He traced the patterns of death they'd found - the precise placement of bodies, the military efficiency of the killing, the calculated geometry of the traps. His hands moved across the maps like reading braille while the elders leaned forward in the wavering light.

Grandfather Vu shifted his ancient bones, lamplight catching the web of scars that marked him from wars fought before Granier drew breath. The old man's walking stick tapped once against temple floor. "You believe we are next?"

Granier reached into his shirt, drew out the Chinese cigarette pack. It passed from hand to hand while the elders read its presence like soothsayers reading entrails. "They left this for us to find. Tigers mark their territory before they hunt." His words fell into silence thick as cemetery dirt.

"They want us to know they're coming," he continued. "Want fear to soften us before their teeth find flesh. But knowing gives us time. Time to make ready."

Spitting Woman's voice carried his meaning across the gulf between worlds, between the soldier's craft and the village's soul. The elders nodded, understanding flowing between them like dark water under ice.

"Do you have any idea when they might attack?" said an elder.

"Hard to say. We could be their next target or it could be weeks before they get to us. But the only question is when not if. They are using the villages to make an example for the rest of Vietnam. We are in the tiger's path."

Grandfather Vu's walking stick struck wood again, sharp as a gunshot. "Then we must become thorns in the beast's foot." The other elders murmured assent, their voices blending like wind through autumn leaves.

Early the next morning just after sunrise, Spitting Woman found Granier in the temple doorway. The morning fog pressed close around them, pregnant with menace.

They watched the village's young men gather, eager and afraid and already changing from farmers to fighters. They saw soldiers waiting to be born in their rough hands, warriors sleeping in their peasant stance.

"First," Granier said, with Spitting Woman translating into the hill tribe's dialect, "Don't overestimate them. Yes, they are soldiers with training and experience, but they bleed like any man. And when they bleed enough they either retreat or die. I will settle for either. The best way to hurt them is to let them come to us. We must be patient as a tiger in the long grass. We wait for our moment, then attack without mercy. Because I guarantee you… they will have none."

As the villagers gathered around him, Granier

crouched in the dirt, drawing with a stick worn smooth from marking too many graves. Rice bowls cooled in villager's hands as they watched him trace lines in the earth, geometric patterns precise as mathematics, certain as death.

"We will build a fortified hamlet like the tribes did in the American war. A palisades of wooden stakes enclosing all the huts, animal pens, warehouses, and lodges. One entrance means one point to defend."

His stick moved in clean strokes, sketching their survival in the soil. "Then a deep ditch around the palisades. The ditch must be deep as a man is tall," he said, his French weaving through Vietnamese like bitter smoke. The old women watched with eyes that had seen too many wars, nodded with the wisdom of those who had built walls before.

"We need every hand," he said. "Even the children must help. The earth we dig becomes our wall, ten feet high with a walkway for defenders." His hands shaped the air, showing them how sharpened bamboo poles would rise like dragon's teeth, thick as a man's arm and angled outward to deny climbing feet.

The younger men shifted their weight, but the elders stood stone-still, remembering how they'd built such things before for armies that flowed through their lives like seasons. Spitting Woman moved among them, her dialect turning Granier's war-craft into words that tasted of mountain streams and forest paths.

"The lookout towers will rise at the corners," she told them, "like the temples our grandfathers built. Twenty feet toward Heaven, with fighting platforms where we will see them coming while we are still dreams in their minds."

"Four towers," Granier continued, marking spots in the dirt. "Two men in each, day and night without cease." His stick moved faster now, laying down killing fields with the same care farmers used to mark rice paddies. "The ditch will grow teeth. The approaches will birth traps. Here," he said, jabbing the earth. "Here. And here."

Once he finished his briefing and the villagers went to work carrying out his instructions, Spitting Woman approached him.

"I must go to Colonel Nguyen," she said. "His garrison has what we need. Troops. Anti-personnel mines. Machine guns. Modern teeth for ancient wolves."

"I should go. How can I lead these people when I don't speak their language?" he said.

"Perhaps it is time that you learned."

"It's a little late for that."

"I must go to the garrison. They will remember me. Remember what I was, what I did in their fathers' wars. We need their men and weapons."

Granier watched the northern horizon where threat gathered like storm clouds. "How long?"

"Two days there. Two back, if the spirits love us." Her hand touched his arm, brief as butterfly, permanent as scar.

"Okay. You go. I'll work on the defenses and get the patrols started," he said. "Show the young men where to dig, where to watch, where to wait." His fingers found hers, callused skin against callused skin. "The old ways and the new. Like always."

Granier watched as Spitting Woman gathered her supplies for the journey. Her only weapons were a bow with a quiver of arrows and a K-Bar knife.

"This is going to be a disaster," said Granier.

"No, it won't," she said. "When we first met neither of us spoke the other's language, yet we found ways to communicate. And that turned out good, didn't it?"

"I guess. But these people… they still don't trust me."

"They fear you. You can be very menacing. Sometimes that's better than trust."

She kissed him on the cheek as if it would somehow soothe him and give him confidence. They moved toward the edge of the village. Before her the jungle opened its ancient arms to welcome back a daughter who had never truly left its embrace. She was gone. Granier turned back to the village and went to work.

The villagers worked through dawn mist their hands raw against wooden poles thick as a man's arm. Old Tran supervised the palisade wall teaching them how deep the posts must go. How earth must be packed tight against wood. How some defenses had protected villages since before gunpowder came to the mountains.

Granier walked the perimeter measuring distances with a soldier's eye. The wall would stand twelve feet high with firing platforms every five yards. The women wove bamboo between posts making a lattice that would turn bullets that thought wood was weak. Children carried water in bamboo tubes while men tamped soil around poles with wooden mallets wrapped in cloth to muffle sound.

"Here," he said marking the ground where the main firing position would go. "Overlapping fields of fire. Anyone who comes through those trees will walk into a crossfire." His hands moved describing killing zones in the air. The villagers nodded drove stakes into earth to mark where death would speak from shadow.

They dug the trench surrounding the village ten feet deep. The sides sloped inward making a trap for men who thought they could cross it. At the bottom they planted sharpened bamboo stakes pointing outward and up. More stakes went into the forward slope so any soldier who fell would land on steel-hard points. The earth they removed became a berm behind the wall. Gave defenders height. Gave their rifles reach.

Young Bao learned to weave tripwires thin as spider silk. His fingers moved with delicate precision while Old Trinh taught him how to string them between trees. How to attach grenades so their pins would pull when wire grew taut. How to hide them so enemy eyes would find them too late. The boy worked through afternoon setting death's own threads through jungle paths.

The old women dug punji pits with practiced hands. Knew how deep they must go. How sides must slope just so. How to weave grass mats across them so they looked like solid ground. At the bottom they planted bamboo spikes smeared with a paste Old Tran's wife made from rotted meat and human waste. Even small wounds would fester. Would kill slow as mercy.

Granier showed them how to build platforms in the tallest trees. How to strap themselves in so they could shoot and reload without falling. How to cover the wood with leaves so enemy eyes would pass over them. The positions gave range. Gave angles no soldier would expect fire to come from. The villagers learned to climb silent as cats. To wait patient as stone.

In the western approaches they buried Claymore mines taken from dead Chinese soldiers. Positioned them to catch troops who would bunch together when the first men fell. Behind these they dug more punji pits. Behind these they strung more wires. Made a maze of traps.

The watchtowers rose twenty feet high gave view of the entire valley. Two men in each tower with captured Chinese rifles. Always watching. Always ready. Below them young runners waited to carry warnings. To spread word when enemy came. The towers were braced against artillery. Had firing slits that let defenders shoot at any angle.

They built bunkers with timber roofs three layers thick. Covered them with earth that would eat shellfire. Inside they stored ammunition, food, water and medicine. Made them strong enough to shelter villagers when mortars came. Connected them with trenches deep enough that men could run between them without showing themselves to enemy eyes.

Through night they worked. Hands bleeding against wood and wire and earth that knew what was coming. Made fighting positions behind the wall. Made spaces between logs just wide enough for rifle barrels. Made platforms that would let defenders fire down into any troops that reached the wall.

The children learned their roles. How to carry ammunition to firing positions. How to run messages between defenders. How to hide when shells came. Which bunkers would shelter them. Which trenches would protect them. The old women taught them songs to sing when fear came. When night brought screaming.

Old men trained young women to shoot. How to brace rifle stocks against shoulders. How to squeeze triggers smooth as breathing. How to reload without taking eyes from targets. They learned to work in pairs. One shooting while the other loaded. Learned to pass rifles between them smooth as a gentle breeze.

The men practiced with spears. With knives. With anything that could kill at arm's length. Learned where soldiers would try climbing the wall. Where they would bunch together. Where they would die if they got too close. Old Tran taught them how his grandfather had killed French troops who thought bayonets made them safe.

They buried drums of fuel in front of positions. Ran tubes underground to firing points. When soldiers came they would spray fuel. Would throw torches. Would teach Chinese troops about other ways that war could burn them. The drums waited patient as grave markers for men who would die in fire.

Through dawn they worked. Through dusk they worked. Through nights lit by stars that had seen other armies try claiming this ground. Made their village into fortress. Into weapon.

The wall rose against morning sky. Fields of fire laid out like maps. Traps set patient as death itself. Everything ready. Everything measured. Everything waiting for the army that thought numbers and technology made victory certain.

"It's good," Granier said. His eyes read killing fields like reading future. Like reading fate. The defenders moved to their positions. Settled into spaces that would become their homes until peace came again or death claimed them all. The village was becoming a war machine.

The days that followed burned like fever in the minds of the villagers. Earth parted beneath their hands, trenches opening like wounds in the soil. Children carried water in bamboo tubes while their fathers dug. Old women sharpened stakes while young ones wove palm leaves to shield the towers from rain. The palisade rose foot by foot, a wall of wooden bones between their homes and whatever hunted them.

Granier worked until his hands bled, but his eyes never stopped reading angles, measuring trajectories, seeing death in the spaces between trees. He taught them to weave paths through their own traps, showed them signs that would guide their feet and betray their enemies.

Beyond the walls they seeded the jungle with death's own harvest. Punji pits lined with sharpened bamboo waited beneath innocent earth. Tripwires ran low through grass like spider's silk. Deadfalls and snares and older things, cruel devices Spitting Woman's grandmother had whispered of.

The villagers worked with the certainty of those who knew that some ground must be held regardless of cost. Their fortress rose from red earth like something born of desperation and determination and the dark knowledge that survival sometimes requires teeth.

Vietnamese Army Base

The army base emerged from morning mist like a fortress of rust. Two days of hard running had turned Spitting Woman's feet to meat, her legs shaking beneath her, but she approached the guards with the rigid spine of one who had carried death through three wars. The young soldiers saw something in her stance that made them step aside, their eyes falling from her gaze like leaves before storm.

Colonel Nguyen's office sat like a tomb of paper and protocol, the overhead fan stirring cigarette smoke into gray wreaths. He kept her standing while he finished reading some document, blood seeping into her foot wrappings while he performed this theater of power.

When he finally looked up his face was carved from stone. The words broke from her like water through a shattered dam. She told him of the neighboring village, of the precision of the killing, of the methodical destruction. She described how the raiders had executed the teachers first, then the village leaders, then anyone who ran. How they had burned the food stores with military efficiency. Her voice caught raw as she described the bodies arranged like messages written in flesh.

"They will come for us next," she said, her hands spreading dirt from two days' journey across his papers. "Without troops, without weapons, they will paint our village in blood."

The colonel's fingers drummed against his desktop, each tap driving nails into hope's coffin. "We have reports of Chinese forces massing at the border. But no confirmation of cross-border operations."

"I just gave you a report that the Chinese are in Vietnam and killing our people," said Spitting Woman.

"We have no official report." His words came wrapped in caution, tied with ribbons of bureaucratic restraint. "Bandits perhaps. Or deserters settling old scores."

The laugh that tore from her throat held no mirth. "Bandits take," she said. "These men only killed. Killed with the precision of soldiers. The dedication of men following orders." When she described how they had arranged the dead in patterns that spoke of military training, his eyes flickered, but his face remained blank as an unwritten page.

"My mandate is clear," he said. "Defend the border. Maintain our position. We cannot disperse forces based on unverified reports."

Each word fell between them like stones into a well. "Then we die," she said, her voice quiet as a blade leaving flesh. "We die and you maintain your position. We die and your mandate stays clear as morning air." Her fingers curled against his desk leaving half-moons in the wood. "The children. The old ones. All dead because your mandate is clear as glass and cold as stone."

He was unmoved. She changed tactics. "Weapons. Give us weapons and we will do your work for you."

"All our weapons are needed for our own forces. They will throw back the Chinese tide should it come."

Her voice dropped low. "We lost our sniper rifles in the flood. Just two rifles, that's all I ask. And ammunition."

The colonel's eyes narrowed. Something shifted in his stance, a soldier's instinct recognizing another predator's need. "Sniper rifles," he said, tasting the words. "Modern ones? With good glass?"

"You know what we can do with them. What we've done before." Her hands spread on his desk. "Two rifles. That's all."

"No." The word fell hard as stone between them. "My men must have the best tools available when that storm breaks."

"And what of us? What of my village caught between?"

The colonel stubbed out his cigarette with precise movements. "You're a ghost from another war, you and your Frenchman both. But this isn't that war. This is something bigger, something that will swallow villages whole if it comes. I need every rifle that can reach out and touch death. For my men. For when the real battle starts."

She felt the truth in his words like a blade between her ribs. The village was nothing to him, just one more piece to be sacrificed in the greater game. Her fingers curled against the wood of his desk. "Then give us what you can spare," she said. "Whatever scraps your modern army doesn't need."

Something moved behind his eyes like fish stirring in deep water. He lit another cigarette, the smoke writhing in the fan's breath. After what felt like years he spoke. "We have weapons. Old ones. French leftovers mostly." His shoulders moved in what might have been shame or merely resignation. "Muskets. Ammunition that's seen better wars than this one."

She thought of Granier waiting in the village. Thought of the children playing in dust that would soon drink their blood. "Old rifles are better than bare hands against modern steel."

The colonel nodded once sharply as if settling accounts with his conscience. He barked orders through the door and soon men were loading crates and small barrels of black powder into two troop trucks. The weapons inside were older than the soldiers carrying them, stocks worn smooth by hands now dust. The ammunition came in wooden boxes stenciled with faded French words that spoke of empires now fallen.

Then he said something that made her blood run cold as mountain streams. "Captain Hoang will accompany you. He's one of our best. Trained in contemporary defensive tactics. He can... advise your people."

She watched as a second truck was loaded though one would have sufficed. Watched as the captain, a man with eyes that had seen too much and told too little, climbed into the lead vehicle. The colonel's sudden generosity settled like poison in her stomach, but she kept her face still as temple stone.

They pulled away from the base, the trucks growling through morning mist. In the rearview mirror she watched Colonel Nguyen shrink to a figure of shadow and smoke. His sudden change of heart turned like a knife in her thoughts. The weapons rattled in their crates behind her like bones in a mass grave. *Not enough*, she thought. *Not nearly enough*. But the captain's presence suggested other currents moving beneath the surface of things.

The jungle swallowed them whole, the base disappearing like a dream of safety while questions multiplied in her mind like flies around corpses. The sun rose higher burning away the mist but not her doubts. She touched the stocks of the old rifles feeling the years in their wood, calculating how many rounds per weapon, how many weapons per defender, how to turn these ancient tools into something that might keep her people breathing. All while watching Captain Hoang from the corner of her eye, wondering if he represented hope or merely a different flavor of doom.

They wound through green shadows carrying answers that felt too much like questions and help that felt too much like hindrance. Behind them the morning sun climbed like a bullet into cloudless sky while ahead the village waited unaware that salvation and suspicion were arriving in the same trucks.

The dust from approaching trucks rolled into the village. Spitting Woman stood in the lead truck's bed gripping the cab roof with one hand, studying the fortifications that circled the village perimeter. A smile touched her weathered face at the sight of the completed trench - Granier and the villagers had accomplished more than she'd dared hope. Along the defensive line women worked with methodical precision, their shoulders gleaming with sweat as they drove sharpened bamboo poles into red earth at killing angles. But much of the palisades remained unfinished leaving a large gap in their defenses.

The trucks ground to a halt and Captain Huang jumped down, straightening his uniform while his men began unloading their cargo. Villagers gathered close, their faces falling as they saw what help had brought them - muskets old as their grandfathers, wooden stocks polished smooth by dead men's hands. Many of the antiquated weapons missing parts that had been scavenged over the years.

Mai touched one of the ancient weapons, her fingers tracing wood worn by years. "These are museum pieces," she whispered. "How can we fight Chinese soldiers with relics?"

"I know," Spitting Woman said, her voice tight. "These were all I could secure. But a musket that fires is better than a modern rifle we don't have." She met Mai's eyes. "We've fought with less."

Young Dang spat in the dust. "French leftovers. They expect us to defend our homes with their garbage?"

Captain Huang cleared his throat. "I must speak

with the village elders immediately. There are new directives from the Politburo that must be addressed." His tone left no room for argument.

The elders assembled in the council house, settling onto woven mats with faces already carved for grief. Elder Binh touched Spitting Woman's arm as he passed. "You did not return alone," he said quietly. "And that worries me more than these old rifles."

The captain waited for proper arrangement before delivering his true purpose. The captain smoothed his uniform and cleared his throat. "I must inform you of new orders from the Political Bureau," he said, his eyes sweeping across the gathered villagers.

Elder Tran leaned forward. "What orders?"

"All villages and cities now fall under universal conscription laws," the captain said, his voice flat and official. "Every able-bodied young man is to be mobilized for immediate military service."

A low murmur of dismay rippled through the crowd.

"You cannot take our sons," Mai's mother cried out. "Not now, not when death walks so close to our walls."

Huang raised his hand. "These orders are non-negotiable. The Politburo's authority is absolute."

What followed moved like a funeral procession. Young men's names called one by one. Small bundles of belongings gathered. Mothers and sisters watching stone-faced while the troops loaded their sons and brothers into trucks that groaned under human cargo.

"Mother, don't cry," Dang said as he climbed into the truck bed. "I will make you proud."

His mother touched his face once. "You already have."

Mai listened to sounds of boots on packed earth of men shouting names of women trying not to weep. Tuan sat on their bed already dressed.

"They have my name," he said. His voice carried weight of knowing some fates come written in iron. Outside the village stirred like a wounded thing. More boots more shouts more sounds of young men being gathered for war's hunger.

Mai helped him pack. Her hands moved through familiar things. His spare shirt. The knife his father had given him. Rice balls wrapped in banana leaves still warm from cooking. Each item went into his pack like memories being buried. The oil lamp cast shadows that moved like memory across bamboo walls. Mai stood before Tuan with the jade pendant caught in her fingers green as river stone bright as morning. "Take it," she said. "It will keep you safe."

"It's your mother's. The only thing you have left of her." His hands stayed at his sides though his eyes followed the stone that caught lamplight turned it to something older than war.

She stepped closer lifted the cord over his head. The jade settled against his chest still warm from her skin. "I have her in my heart. In how my hands remember her teaching me to weave to cook to live. You need this more." Her fingers touched the stone once. "Bring it back to me."

"Mai." Her name came rough in his throat.

"Promise me. Promise you'll bring it home." She pressed her palm flat against the jade against his chest against his heart that beat time like counting days until return. "Promise me, Tuan."

"I promise." His hand covered hers held the jade between them like everything that made promises worth keeping. Outside they could hear soldiers gathering, hear boots in mud, hear all the sounds that meant morning would take him from her.

She kissed him once quick as hunting cats touching earth. "Remember your promise. Remember what waits here." Her hands fell away though the jade stayed warm against his skin. "Go now. Before I make you break your word to the army."

He touched the pendant once then walked into dawn into war into whatever fate wrote its name in jade and the spaces between heartbeats. Mai watched until shadow took him.

The village gathered in the square. Army officers read names from papers that carried authority's seal. Young men stepped forward when called. Some straight and proud some trying not to show fear some already wearing a soldier's mask. Mothers held themselves straight as bamboo while sons stepped away from home.

"Tuan son of Minh," the officer called. His voice carried flat as judgment. Tuan walked straight and sure to where other men waited. Did not look back. Could not look back.

Spitting Woman stood beside Mai. Her hand found the girl's shoulder. Held her steady while the officer read more names. While more sons stepped away. While more women held themselves straight against morning wind that carried diesel smoke and duty's demands.

When the names finished the officer spoke about patriotic duty, about noble sacrifice, about everything war writes in young men's blood. His words fell into silence thick as grave dirt. The women did not weep. Had learned already that some griefs come too deep for tears.

The young men climbed into trucks. Their bare feet left last prints in village earth. Their hands raised in farewell. Their eyes carried weight of knowing some roads lead away from everything that matters. Tuan found place among them. His back straight, his eyes fixed forward, his hands steady on his pack.

Spitting Woman stood rigid and apart. This wasn't the help she'd meant to bring. She'd sought weapons for defense, not this theft of defenders. Through the truck beds young faces peered out, some trying to look brave, others lost as children.

"Good fortune to you," Captain Huang said to the elders, his words hollow as bamboo.

"You brought them here," old Binh said at Spitting Woman's shoulder. "You opened our gate to them."

"I brought what help I could find," she answered, her voice raw. "I didn't know. I swear by my ancestors, I didn't know."

"They would have taken them anyway," said Granier. "It was only a matter of time. It's not her fault."

The dust settled while Spitting Woman remained motionless, her fingers working against each other in helpless rage. Around the village perimeter the sharpened stakes seemed to mock their preparations while the trench gaped like an open wound. She had brought them weapons yes, but in doing so had helped steal away the hands meant to wield them. The weight of unintended consequences pressed down on her like a mountain's own shadow.

Granier found her as night fell. "We adapt," he said simply. "We teach the women to shoot. We remind the old men how to kill. We find strength where we can."

She touched one of the old muskets. "I've brought them death twice over. Once in these ancient guns, and once in taking away those strong enough to use them."

"No," he said. "You've brought us what fate allowed. Now we make fate regret not giving us more."

"Move out," the officer called. The trucks started grinding gears eating distance. Mai watched dust rise around wheels that carried her future away. Watched until the trucks disappeared into morning haze. Watched until nothing remained but tire tracks and memory.

The women stood together while morning wind carried diesel smoke north. While somewhere past sight their men became soldiers. While war's appetite grew deeper. They did not speak. Did not weep. Did not do anything except stand straight as judgment while fate wrote its name in absence.

"I went to them for weapons for protection," Spitting Woman said her eyes fixed on the distant hills where army trucks had disappeared. "I brought them here and they took your man. They took all our men. Some victories taste like ash in the mouth." She touched Mai's arm with fingers gone hard as wood and said "The fault lies with me. Remember that when the nights grow too long without him."

"It's not your fault. Fate touched Tuan, not you," said Mai.

Later Mai sat in their house. Her fingers found things Tuan had touched. The bed they had shared. The cup he drank from at dawn. The shirt he had left hanging like shed skin. Each one carried weight of everything taken. Each one promised things about return.

Spitting Woman came then. Found Mai sitting silent

as stone. "Come," she said. "There is work. There is always work." Her voice carried knowledge of how many men had gone how many had returned how many had left women sitting alone with memory.

Outside the village moved through its day. Women cooked, cleaned, carried water, bore burdens old as army trucks grinding south. Life went on. Had to go on. Would go on until men came home or didn't.

That night Mai slept alone. The bed felt wide as fate. Through dark she listened to village sounds. To women moving through tasks. To children asking questions that had no answers. To all the spaces men had left behind.

Morning came gray as duty. Mai rose. Dressed. Moved through the day's demands. Felt everything war had taken. Everything war might return. Everything war's appetite would demand before peace came walking home again.

In lamplight they worked at the wooden table, the muskets laid out like patients before surgeons. Granier's hands moved across ancient steel with practiced grace while Spitting Woman cleaned decades of grime from wood worn smooth by dead men's grips.

"This one's lock is failing," he said, his fingers probing rusted mechanics. "The spring's nearly gone." He held the mechanism up to the flame squinting at metal that had seen too many wars.

She passed him a replacement part salvaged from another musket too far gone to save. Their hands brushed briefly in the exchange. "We lose two to save three," she said. "Like tending wounded after battle."

"With fewer muskets the riflemen will have more rounds to fire. We will need to select the best shots to receive weapons," said Granier.

"The others can be loaders… or backups if the lead gunner falls."

The lamplight caught the tools spread between them, caught the careful way they touched these relics, caught the worry in their eyes that spoke of time running short as powder and hope. Around them the village slept while they worked to turn museum pieces into weapons that might keep their people alive.

"The stocks are sound at least," he said testing wood with knowing fingers. "French oak remembers its purpose even after all these years."

She nodded working oil into thirsty grain. The wood took the darkness like blood into bandages. "These saved my grandfather's village once," she said. "When the French first came these same guns spoke for our people. Now they'll speak again."

They worked through night's deep hours their hands moving in the ritual of repair crafting hope from rust and remembrance. The muskets slowly came alive beneath their touch, steel remembering its purpose, wood remembering its strength, everything remembering why some weapons outlive the empires that forged them.

Dawn found them still working still hoping still turning relics to weapons one piece at a time. There was still much to be done. The village palisades was still unfinished. The sharpened wooden poles were heavy and hard to fix in position. A large gap still remained. It was their weak link. More villagers were assigned to construction of the perimeter.

In the damp undergrowth Spitting Woman crouched beside Mai's grandmother, guiding ancient fingers across the tripwire's path between saplings. Morning mist clung to the jungle canopy dripping steady rhythm onto the women working below. Around them a dozen villagers moved through shadows like huntresses born to blood and patience.

"Like this," Spitting Woman whispered, demonstrating the special knot that would turn simple wire to a serpent's fang. "Too loose and it fails. Too tight and it breaks." Her hands moved with the practiced grace of one who had set too many of these devices.

The old woman's weathered fingers traced the pattern until muscle knew what bone remembered. Ahead of them three women worked at disguising the pit they'd carved from earth's own flesh the night before. They positioned bamboo spikes with the same care their mothers had used arranging ancestors' altars, each point angled upward like prayers for blood. Leaves and branches spread across the opening transformed killing ground to innocent earth.

Young Lin stripped bamboo for new spears, her infant sleeping quiet against her back. The baby had learned silence as if understanding that some hunts required prayers spoken in whispers. Her knife shaped wood with sure strokes while her child dreamed against her spine.

"Remember," Spitting Woman told them, moving between groups like a priest between altars, "think like water finding lowest ground. They will take the easiest path. That is where we place our secrets."

The women nodded, their eyes already carrying the cold calculation of hunters. They had learned to read ground like reading fate, to see where prey would step before prey knew its own path. When Grandmother

Thi found the natural depression in earth that channeled movement like a funnel, Spitting Woman smiled. Together they began crafting something that would teach soldiers why some ground hungers for blood. "When the first soldier falls into one of our traps, the soldiers around him will spread out and avoid the path he was on. That is a good spot to place traps in the surrounding foliage that will catch them like a spider's web."

The sun climbed while they worked, while hesitation became hatred, while soft hands learned lethal arts. These women who had once flinched at sharpening bamboo now set deadly triggers with fingers steady as mountain stone. With their young men stolen away they had found harder truths within themselves. They needed to be tough if the village was to survive.

When morning mist burned away they gathered their tools. The jungle looked peaceful, looked innocent, looked exactly as it had before they seeded it with death's own geometry. Spitting Woman caught Mai's grandmother's eyes and saw there something new, something forged in the fire of loss.

The old woman nodded once, fierce as fate. They would make their enemies count distance in blood drops, would make them measure ground in dead men, would make them learn why some paths remember how to kill those who dare claim them.

At jungle's edge Granier crouched and pointed toward the natural lanes where enemies would flow like water seeking lowest ground. The villagers gathered close clutching their spears watching how he moved through green shadows without sound without hurry without breaking the forest's ancient rhythms.

"Never straight lines," he said soft as morning mist. "Move like snakes. Keep to darkness. Let your eyes hunt always." He led them through the undergrowth teaching them to read earth's stories in broken twigs in disturbed leaves in the soft messages feet left behind.

They reached the great banyan its roots writing ancient letters in red soil. "Here," he said touching the massive trunk. "This is where you fall back if they come. Your task is warning not dying. The village must know what comes hunting."

At the watchtowers he climbed weathered wood positioned observers at different heights taught them how to read the horizon's stories. "They'll try to hide," he said pointing toward treeline. "But wind betrays them. Birds speak their presence. Nature breaks its patterns when strangers walk."

He showed them hollow bamboo turned to simple telescopes showed them how to quarter their sectors with methodical patience. "Watch for dust clouds," he said. "Listen when dogs speak to darkness. Count their cigarettes at night. Every light is a man every man is a target every target must be known."

From the village square Spitting Woman's voice carried sharp and clear while she laid out the muskets on woven mats. Granier descended, joined her, faced the villagers who had never held such weapons, never dealt death from farther than a spear's reach, never learned war's modern grammar.

"These are old," she said lifting one of the ancient guns. "But they remember how to kill." Her hands moved through the ritual of loading powder and ball while aged eyes watched and learned.

Granier adjusted grips showed them how to brace

against recoil's anger showed them how these tools that once served empire could now serve village. "Aim low," he said. "The gun rises like startled bird. Shoot fast, shoot sure, shoot before they know where death speaks from."

They worked in careful tandem he and Spitting Woman their words weaving together French and Vietnamese and the older language of survival. The villagers learned slowly their hands remembering new patterns their bodies accepting new wisdom their souls preparing for what must come. They gained confidence in their art of war.

As shadows lengthened they ran final patrol watchtowers calling darkness's first messages patrols moving like smoke through assigned sectors musket teams finding their places along wooden walls. Spitting Woman watched from high tower called corrections called encouragement called everything needed to turn farmers into fighters.

Granier met her eyes in gathering dark. They had done what they could with time fate allowed. Now only question remained whether these people could learn war's grammar fast enough before war came to test their lessons with steel and fire and death's final examination.

The evening fell like a shroud over the village as Granier found Spitting Woman perched on the watchtower platform, her form carved black against the bleeding sky. He settled beside her without words, their legs swaying above empty air while cooking fires bloomed beneath them like earthbound stars.

"My daughter would have been their age," she said, watching young women ferry water from the well, their vessels balanced like birds on their shoulders. Her voice had shed its warrior's edge, turned soft as temple ash. "She loved it here. That summer I brought her, she wouldn't leave. Said these mountains had voices only she could hear."

A mother's call drifted up from below, gathering children like scattered leaves before nightfall. "We stayed three months," Spitting Woman continued. "She learned the weaving, wore her hair in valley braids. Found belonging here she never knew in Hanoi's streets."

"What took her?" Granier asked cautiously.

"Fever," she said. "Simple as sunrise, fierce as flood. Two days of burning and she slipped away quiet as morning mist. The village women washed her body, wept over her like their own blood." Her hand lifted, gesturing toward the cemetery where plum trees kept their silent watch. "Twenty years they've tended her rest."

"They're your family," Granier said.

"All I have." Her fingers twisted together like living rope. "When war came growling at our gates, I could have led them to city walls. But they chose to stand, to hold their ground, to guard their dead." The old steel crept back into her voice. "I won't lose them too."

Children's laughter rose up like prayer smoke, mingling with the steady heartbeat of rice poles striking. Life's rhythm carried on beneath war's gathering shadow.

"They're stronger than you know," Granier said.

"They have to be," she answered. "War won't pass us by just because we wish it. Strength isn't choice now, it's survival."

Darkness claimed the sky while stars pierced

through like distant rifle fire. A gecko's call echoed across the valley, sharp as broken faith. Granier thought of all the causes he'd bled for, all the ground he'd claimed and lost. None had mattered like this village, this woman, this last stand against empire's hunger.

"We'll hold," he said, forcing certainty into words that felt hollow as spent shells.

"Yes," she whispered, eyes fixed on the mountain's black spine. "We'll hold." But they both knew she meant more than mere survival. She meant memory, family, belonging - the things worth dying for when all other reasons had bled away into night.

Spitting Woman found Granier crouched by the northern wall, his hands moving across the sharpened stakes like a blind man reading prophecy. She waited for his inspection to end before breaking the silence. "The other villages," she said, "they'll have lost their young men too."

Granier stood and wiped his palms against his pants. "The politburo would have taken them all," he said, seeing the thought uncoil in her mind like a serpent waking. "Scattered, we're weak. Easy targets."

She swept her hand toward their defenses, the gesture taking in walls and trenches that rose like mountain bones through earth. "But here we have walls, weapons, you," she said, her eyes marking each fortification like counting ammunition. "We have room inside the palisades. The other villages could bring their food, their weapons, their families."

"That would help. That could make the difference," said Granier.

"First we speak with Grandfather Vu," she added.

"His word carries weight with the village elders. They'll heed him where they'd dismiss a woman, no matter my standing." Her mouth twisted with old knowledge of men's ways.

They found Grandfather Vu in the council house, deep in talk with the elders about their thinned ranks. The old man listened to Spitting Woman's words with fingers laced like prayer beads in his lap. When she finished, he nodded with the slowness of mountains considering change.

"The old alliances," he said. "In my grandfather's time, villages joined as one when threats came prowling. It's good to remember." His eyes found Granier. "You believe our walls can shield so many?"

"More people means more defenders," Granier said. "River village has hunters for scouting, northern village has a blacksmith. Together we stand stronger."

Grandfather Vu rose like an ancient tree straightening. "I'll go tonight. The paths still live in my bones, though many seasons have passed since I walked them." He looked to Spitting Woman. "You know these villages. Guide me. And you two," he said to the young girls assigned to be runners, "will carry our words once the first agrees."

Granier's mind was already moving through the village like water seeking its level. "We'll need to reorganize storage, make sleeping space. We can begin while you negotiate."

"Speak of old alliances," Grandfather Vu told Spitting Woman as they readied for night travel. "Remind them of debts between villages, marriages binding families. Sometimes ancient bonds cut deeper than fear."

Spitting Woman checked her weapons with hands that knew battle better than sentiment. "They'll come. They know what waits for villages standing alone."

"Go then," Granier said. "We'll be ready." He watched them fade into dusk like smoke into sky - the elder straight-backed as youth, Spitting Woman moving like a hunting cat, the runners silent as shadows. They carried four villages' worth of hope in their steps.

He turned back to what would become a fortress, not just village. The enemy thought they'd weakened these people with fear. Instead, they'd woken alliances old as the mountains themselves, sleeping like tigers in the valleys' bones.

The first village council opened at moonrise, with oil lamp smoke writhing against the bamboo walls like restless spirits. Grandfather Vu sat in honor's place, his face carved by lamplight into something ancient as the mountains themselves while Spitting Woman knelt silent as stone behind his right shoulder.

"Our grandfathers' grandfathers knew unity's strength," Vu said, his voice heavy as river stones. "When tigers prowled in hungry times, we stood as one. When floods took the rice, we shared what remained."

Chief Ban leaned forward, his shadow dancing against the wall. "Those were nature's threats, brother. The Chinese bring artillery, planes. Together we make easier targets - one shell can kill dozens where before it killed few."

"And this Frenchman," another elder cut in, suspicion etched deep in his face, "how can he know our ways? French build with stone and concrete. They don't speak the tongue of bamboo and vine, don't know the hills' wisdom."

Spitting Woman felt their hopes slipping like water through cupped hands. She touched Vu's shoulder, light as morning mist. At his slight nod, she spoke, her voice measured as rifle shots. "Granier isn't like other French. Thirty years he's fought in these hills, respects our ways. More important - he knows our enemy's mind, their movements, their attacks. This knowledge, joined with our understanding of the land, that's what keeps us breathing."

They argued through the night like wolves circling prey. When dawn broke, the village had split - half choosing to come, half to stay. As families gathered their lives into bundles, Ban came to her. "I pray you're right," he whispered. "Those who stay choose slow death."

The second village yielded easier, news of lowland atrocities having reached them. Their headman remembered Spitting Woman's help during cholera times, those she healed, and his trust swayed the others.

But the third village fought them hardest. "You speak of ancient bonds," their elder spat, "while bringing us under a foreigner's command. Making us abandon ancestor graves for borrowed walls."

Vu remained calm as temple stone. "The graves wait for our return. Stay, and you join our ancestors sooner than the spirits wish."

A young elder spoke then, fear threading his words like steel wire. "Three days past, word came. The river village resisted alone. Chinese left nothing breathing, not even children."

By morning, most had chosen to come, though some fled deeper into the hills and let the jungle be their shield. The column that wound back to the village stretched longer than hope had dared suggest - families with bundled lives, cattle walking slow as time, pack carts heavy with possessions. The blacksmith brought his tools like sacred things, hunters carried their weapons, old women clutched seedlings in damp cloth like holding future's own heart.

At the final ridge, Spitting Woman and Vu watched people flow through the jungle below like a river finding new course. "Not all came," she said, "but enough to fight."

"They come not just from fear," Vu said, leaning on his stick like time itself needed support. "They come because you and the Frenchman offer chance to strike back. Fear sends people running. Hope makes them stand."

Spitting Woman watched a mother balance her baby and belongings like carrying past and future together. Fear marked her face, but determination lived in her spine. "Hope," Spitting Woman echoed. "Let it be enough."

The sun bled its last light when they reached the village. Granier stood at the gate watching them file past - two hundred souls carrying more than possessions. They brought skills, strength, and that fierce thing that makes people choose to die standing instead of living on their knees. Terror and resolution warred in their faces. The choice was made. Together they would write victory's signature, or together they would feed the earth.

In the morning, Spitting Woman found Granier by the storage huts counting their supplies. "Two weeks," he said, eyes fixed on his calculations. "Maybe three if we stretch the rice thin. After that..." His words dissolved in morning air.

"We knew this would come," she said, watching women sort dried mushrooms like counting copper coins. "The jungle still runs rich, the river deep. We'll find what we need."

"If we are not under siege. Then all bets are off."

The village broke apart like scattered seeds, each group to its own task. River village hunters led teams into the jungle, teaching others to track pig and deer. Women who spoke the forest's secrets gathered those who would learn where medicine grew wild. The oldest ones drew maps in dirt, marking spots where mushrooms rose like ghosts, where fruit bats hung, where roots waited patient as stones.

By the river, children's laughter turned to shrieks as their fishing boat capsized, sending game crashing through brush while hunters' faces darkened like storm clouds. "No more helping," an elder commanded, and they trudged back to the village, dripping and ashamed.

Days fell into rhythm like water wearing stone. Dawn hunters passed dusk gatherers on narrow trails. Women taught each other death's alphabet in mushrooms. Fishermen shared secrets of river giants that could feed many mouths.

But it was Spitting Woman who found salvation, following a path old as memory to a hidden valley where wild rice waved green as hope. That night she and Granier marked maps like plotting stars, measuring how many could harvest without leaving their walls naked to steel.

Not all went smooth as polished rice. Children, stung by the fishing shame, snuck out for berries and came back painted red with juice and poison oak's cruel blessing. The healer cursed softly over wasted medicine. Yet fortune smiled sometimes - old women gathering wood found honey's gold, paying in stings for sweetness that would keep meat from rotting. The blacksmith turned scrap to hooks that pulled silver from the river.

Each evening, they counted their harvest like misers counting coins that kept starvation from their door. Spitting Woman watched women smoke meat under leaves thick enough to strangle its betraying scent. Granier's eyes never stopped reading the jungle's edges like searching for words in a dark book.

A week passed and four villages became one, sharing secrets old as the hills themselves. Even the children found purpose, watching birds that knew where fruit hung ripe as summer's promise.

But in night's quiet, Spitting Woman and Granier shared the same fear, unspoken as a hunter's footfall. They could strip the land like locusts, but unlike their wandering ancestors, they were chained to these walls, these defenses. The jungle's bounty was vast but not endless, and their enemy's patience might outlast its gifts.

Still, watching the villages merge like rivers finding sea, teaching forgotten wisdom, learning lost ways, Spitting Woman felt pride fierce as mother's love.

Mai found Spitting Woman in the herb garden at dawn. The woman's hands moved through plants like reading prayers written in leaves. Without looking up she said "Your husband carried a knife, but you do not."

"I never needed one," Mai said. The morning air carried dew thick as blessing.

"You need one now." Spitting Woman's fingers found fresh ginger pulled it clean from earth. "The world has changed. The blade I will give you belonged to my grandmother. She used it to heal. Used it to kill. Used it to defend what mattered." She stood wiped earth from her hands. "Come."

They walked to the practice ground behind the temple. The space lay flat as fate worn smooth by feet that had learned war's wisdom here. Spitting Woman drew the knife. The blade caught morning sun like captured lightning. "Hold it," she said.

Mai took it. The handle felt wrong in her fingers. The weight sat strange against her palm.

"No." Spitting Woman moved behind her. Adjusted her grip with fingers gone hard as wood. "Like this. Feel how it balances. Feel how it wants to move." She guided Mai's hand through forms old as memory. "The knife remembers even when you forget."

They worked through morning heat. Mai's hands grew blisters, learned to ignore them. Her arms burned, learned to move through fire. Spitting Woman taught her where men go soft where they break where they learn why some women carry steel beneath silk.

"Here." Spitting Woman touched her own throat. "When they come close, when they think you're weak, when they forget why grandmothers teach granddaughters to kill." Her hands moved Mai's knife through patterns that spoke death's own tongue. "Remember how the blade goes. Remember why it goes there."

When sun stood high they gathered herbs. Spitting Woman's fingers moved swift and sure through green things. "This one stops bleeding. This one fights infection. This one kills if you use enough." She taught

Mai how to find them how to dry them how to make them serve needs gentle or harsh.

They worked in the garden while afternoon heat pressed down. Mai's hands learned new patterns. Learned how to take life how to save it how to balance scales that war had broken. Spitting Woman spoke soft and sure about things that women had known since before men made steel into law.

"The knife does not make you strong," she said crushing herbs with hands gone dark with juice. "The herbs do not make you wise. They are only tools. Like any tools they wait for hands to give them purpose."

When evening came they sat in temple shade. Mai's arms ached from forms her fingers stained green from medicine. Spitting Woman passed her tea bitter as truth sweet as mercy. "You learn quick," she said. "Your hands remember things your mind does not. Things written in bone and blood. Things women have always known."

"I never wanted to learn killing," Mai said. The knife lay across her lap. The blade had gone warm as skin.

"None of us did. But the world does not ask what we want. It asks what we will do to keep what matters." Spitting Woman touched the knife with fingers that had killed, had healed, had done everything fate demanded. "Your husband learns war's ways. You must learn yours."

They worked each dawn after. Mai's hands grew calluses grew skill grew everything needed to survive what came. Spitting Woman taught her how death moves through flesh, how life flows back, how both require knowledge old as broken bones.

Some days they ground herbs, made poultices, made things that save. Other days they practiced with blades made bodies remember why women learned steel's wisdom. Through it all Mai felt herself changing. Felt silk becoming iron, felt peace becoming purpose, felt everything soft growing edges.

"You are ready," Spitting Woman said one morning. Mai's knife moved clean as thought through forms. Her hands knew herbs by touch alone. Knew how to heal, how to harm, how to hold both kinds of knowledge in balance.

"Ready for what?"

"For what comes. For what always comes. For everything your grandmother's grandmother knew would need defending." Spitting Woman gathered herbs with hands that had taught many, had buried some, had watched all learn why women carry knives beneath their grace.

Mai worked beside her. Her fingers moved sure through plants through patterns through everything fate had decided she must learn. The knife rode warm against her hip. The herbs waited in garden rows. Both promised things. Both demanded things. Both spoke in tongues old as women defending home.

Big Brother

Near Chinese-Vietnam Border

Through the gray dawn Tuan moved with the other recruits along the muddy trench their boots heavy with clay. Sandbags rose head high on either side and water stood six inches deep in the low spots. The sound of Chinese artillery came distant as thunder.

Sergeant Bao walked behind them barking corrections. "Keep your rifle up. Yes, like that. No, not like that." He slapped the back of Tuan's helmet. "You want to die with mud in your barrel."

They practiced changing positions in the narrow trench. High port to firing stance. Back to ready. Again and again until their arms burned. Brass casings from earlier fighting lay scattered in the mud. Some of the men collected them like talismans.

"Incoming!" someone shouted. The recruits dropped into the firing steps pressed against the forward wall. Shells screamed overhead exploded somewhere behind the lines. Dirt rained down on their helmets. "Just ranging fire," Bao said. "The real stuff sounds different. You'll learn."

They moved to the bunker for weapons training. Inside smelled of damp earth and cigarettes. Bao demonstrated how to break down their rifles showed them the weak points. "These parts break first. These you can fix in the field. These you pray hold together." His hands moved swift and sure across the metal.

A Chinese machine gun opened up somewhere north. The bullets passed high with a sound like angry wasps. None of the recruits ducked. They had learned that much already. Bao nodded approval continued his instruction. "Strip them clean. Again. Again. The mud gets everywhere here. A dirty rifle makes you dead."

Through morning they worked with the weapons. Learning by touch and repetition. The artillery continued sporadic ranging shots that rattled the bunker walls. Tuan's hands moved mechanical and precise across his rifle. He had killed two men in the last probe. The rifle had worked clean then. He would make sure it worked clean next time.

At noon they ate cold rice from metal cups while Bao taught them to read maps. The network of trenches spread across the paper like black veins. "These routes you memorize. These you avoid. These you use only if dying where you stand is worse than dying running." He tapped key points with a dirty finger. No one wrote anything down. Such knowledge lived in memory or not at all.

The day went on like that. Learning the tools of killing learning to live in mud and noise. Sometimes the Chinese guns spoke harder and they practiced moving under fire. Sometimes scouts reported movement in the wire and they manned fighting positions. Through it all Bao watched them with eyes that had seen three armies try to take this ground. He said nothing, but his silence carried judgment enough.

Northern Vietnam

Morning mist clung to the valley when Bien saw the first sign - broken branches head-high, too tall for pig. He raised his hand and the scouts behind him dissolved into shadow, becoming part of the jungle's flesh like the river hunters had taught them. Then came the sounds - metal clicking soft as snake scales, a man's stifled cough, canvas and leather whispering against leaves.

Through green gauze they watched the Chinese patrol emerge from the trees like ghosts made solid. Two men probed ahead while the platoon spread behind them like deadly fingers. Bien's throat went sandpaper dry as he counted. Ten, twenty, thirty... fifty troops moving with the clean grace of men who knew their trade. Light packs marked them as hunters, not carriers. Their weapons gleamed with oil and care in the filtered light.

Bien caught Minh's eye, gestured stay-watch-count, then turned to Chi, a young woman that had learned the art of scouting from Spitting Woman. His hands shaped Granier's signals in the air. Go. Warning. Numbers. Direction. Chi melted backward, fluid as water finding its level, silent as starlight. Bien and Minh sank deeper into the earth's embrace, becoming stone and shadow.

The platoon's point man paused, reading two-day-old tracks from the hunters' passage. He was good -

noted direction, murmured to his officer in words soft as falling leaves.

Meanwhile Chi ran through the jungle, her feet finding paths Spitting Woman had shown in the spaces between root and vine. Her chest burned, but she kept her silence sharp as a blade. Four hours' walk to the village. She'd make it in two.

Bien marked everything - weapons' makes, officers' badges, grenade counts. But most telling was their movement, how they read the ground like hunters seeking spoor. This wasn't chance patrol but purposeful search, looking for villages gone to ground like animals in winter.

The platoon stopped at a stream, their lieutenant consulting maps while men filled canteens. They moved careful but carried confidence like a second weapon, too sure to think they were watched by eyes that knew the jungle's every mood.

Chi burst through the village gates trailing breath like smoke. "Chinese patrol," she gasped. "Fifty men. Heavy weapons. Northeast." The warning raced through the village quick as flame in drought grass. Granier and Spitting Woman appeared like summoned spirits, pulling details from her.

In the jungle, Bien and Minh watched the patrol's dance, noting each pause and turn. Their zigzag advance spoke of uncertainty - they hadn't found the village yet, but they were hunting with purpose, searching for communities that had become invisible as morning mist.

When the patrol finally passed, they waited the thirty minutes Spitting Woman had carved into their minds, then took the long way home, watching their back trail like men expecting ghosts. The Chinese might have missed them, but the jungle had whispered its warning clear as temple bells - the enemy was coming closer, and they hunted with hunger in their hearts.

Granier stood at the gap in the palisade wall, watching morning mist curl around the sharpened logs that lay on the ground like abandoned prayers, never raised, never secured. Time had finally claimed its victory here, thirty feet of naked vulnerability no amount of fog could hide.

"We should have finished this section first," Spitting Woman said beside him, her voice carrying the weight of contained fury, "The rest of the wall, the trenches, the stakes - none of it matters if they find this gap."

"They'll find it," Granier said, "They're too good not to." Behind them the village's evacuation unfolded like a dark tide.

Grandmother Dao led her line of women through predawn shadows, each guiding children whose faces carried adult determination. The oldest ones bore the youngest on their backs, thin arms wrapped tight around thinner necks. "Remember," Grandmother Dao whispered fierce as a blade, "like the jungle deer - silent, swift, invisible."

Through the gap came the bird calls that spoke of Chinese advance, and Granier gestured their people to prepared positions. The river village hunters dissolved into foliage with their crossbows while musket teams took their places along the wall's completed sections.

Spitting Woman moved among the women who would reload, their practiced motions with powder horn and ramrod smooth as water over stone. Behind them the others clutched their final hopes - bamboo spears, machetes, farming tools with edges hungry for blood. "We'll funnel them toward the eastern approach," Granier said, pointing where they'd spent weeks shaping the earth to their purpose, "Make them think it's their idea to attack there."

The blacksmith and his apprentices, their faces streaked black with labor's soot, distributed their night's work - arrows barbed to tear flesh and hundreds of iron caltrops, four-sided spikes that could punch through sandals or even boots.

Led by Spitting Woman a group of women took the caltrops and hid them in the grass to funnel the Chinese into the killing zones the villagers had created.

Grandfather Vu walked the lines burning herbs against enemy dogs, his prayers carried soft as smoke - not for victory but for steady hands and steel hearts.

The last children vanished into jungle mist, guided by women who knew every shadow's path, carrying with them their people's tomorrow.

Granier made his final rounds, measuring with his eyes the fierce light of those who fight for home and blood and right to exist. "The wall gap," Spitting Woman said when he returned, "We should put our best fighters there." Granier nodded, " Our poorest shots, our weakest spearmen on the strong sections. Keep our best close to the gap. When they find it..."

The changed bird call cut his words like a blade through silk. The enemy had been spotted in the jungle just outside the village. Morning mist began its retreat while Granier surveyed his forces - old men with ancient muskets, women with spears, hunters with crossbows. Not soldiers but something perhaps more deadly: people with no choice but victory or death. The gap stood like judgment against them, mocking their efforts, reminding them that no defense holds perfect. Spitting Woman climbed a watchtower with three muskets on her back. With her was her loader, Grandmother Giang that was still strong and agile. She carried powder horns and leather bags of lead shot as she climbed. Once Spitting Woman placed her muskets where she wanted them, she climbed back down and joined Granier.

The village held its breath, waiting for war's tide to break against its shores.

Captain Wei raised his fist and the Chinese company halted behind him, over 160 men strong, all armed with China's latest weaponry. Through his binoculars he studied the village walls rising from morning mist, something in their construction troubling his soldier's instincts. These weren't farmer's fortifications but military engineering - the stakes placed with professional precision, the trench cut to exact depth, the killing zones cleared and arranged like a geometric proof.

"Lieutenant Doan," he called soft as falling leaves, and his second appeared beside him, face weathered by combat like stone shaped by hard years. "Take the men to assault positions, standard encirclement, but hold them in the tree line until my signal. Have the mortar units set up in front of the treeline so they're visible. I want these farmers to understand what they are facing." Wei lowered his binoculars. "And Doan - someone with training built those defenses. Watch for prepared fields of fire."

Doan shifted his rifle. "Sir, regulations require immediate assault on suspected rebel positions."

Wei's smile came thin as morning frost. "Regulations were written by men who never lost half their platoon taking a fortified village." He checked his pistol with practiced hands, adjusted his uniform with precise movements. "Position the men. I'm going to talk with these villagers," he said handing Doan his pistol.

"Alone, sir?"

"They'll be less threatened by one man. And I'll see more. You know the protocols if anything happens." Wei walked the trail open-handed, counting firing positions, noting how the ground had been shaped to channel any attack, seeing in every detail the work of someone who understood modern warfare's geometry. He saw a caltrop in the grass and slowed his step, watching the ground in front of him carefully as he advanced. Two armed men emerged from the gate, their weapons, muskets, held ready but not aimed - trained soldiers' response, not village militia panic.

Wei stopped, bowed slight as courtesy required. "I request to speak with your village leaders," he called in Vietnamese, then added in French, "Or perhaps with the person who designed your defenses."

The guards exchanged glances, and moments later an old Vietnamese man emerged with a weathered Frenchman and hard-faced woman whose eyes missed nothing. The Frenchman's stance spoke of combat years, the woman moved like command was her native tongue, the elder's calm suggested they had expected this visit.

"Your fortifications are impressive," Wei said

pleasant as market talk. "The use of terrain to create killing zones. I studied similar principles at Nanjing."

The elder's face stayed blank as new paper. "You honor our humble village. We are simple people who wish only to farm in peace."

Wei's eyes caught movement in the towers – crossbows and muskets well-positioned for interlocking fields of fire.

"Peace is all reasonable men desire. Which is why my superiors worry about villages with military defenses. About multiple villages gathering. About weapons being stockpiled."

"Troubled times make farmers cautious," the woman said, her northern accent cultured as jade. "Bandits roam. Who would not take precautions?"

"Indeed," Wei said, "though I wonder what troubles simple farmers fear that require such elaborate precautions." His gaze found the Frenchman's eyes and held them, two warriors recognizing their own kind across the divide. "My superiors would be reassured if I inspected your village. To confirm that only agricultural activities are being pursued here."

The elder's voice carried the weight of mountains. "Our customs forbid armed outsiders within our walls. Surely an educated officer understands the importance of respecting local traditions?"

Wei held up his arms revealing his empty holster. "I have no weapon. I pose no threat.

Vu considered for a long moment, then, "Very well. You may pass."

Granier and Spitting Woman exchanged a look – this was not a good idea. But they said nothing. The village leader had spoken and was not to be questioned.

Vu turned, and Wei followed. Granier and Spitting

Woman took up the rear as they walked toward the village gates.

Captain Wei moved through the village like a serpent testing air, his military eyes consuming every detail of their defenses while morning shadows stretched long across the packed earth. The height of walls, the placement of stakes, the geometry of trenches - all of it filtered through his consciousness with mechanical precision.

From darkened doorways and behind stacked baskets of rice, villagers watched his progress with faces carved from stone though their muscles coiled tight as springs, ready to respond with violence when trouble arose.

Wei's mind had cataloged everything. The gap in the western wall stood too obvious, like bait in a snare. The number of defenders exceeded what any single village could field. And their movements carried the discipline of men who had learned war's own dance. But young men were noticeably missing from the village ranks. Wei wondered if they might be hidden in the jungle as a flanking force or maybe they had been conscripted by the Vietnamese Army to strengthen its ranks along the border.

Granier watched Wei's gaze linger on their defensive positions, marking their strengths and probing for weakness with the practiced eye of a professional soldier. Wei had all he needed when his mood suddenly changed.

"You stand on Chinese territory now," Wei announced when he reached the village center, his boots planted firm as pylons in the dirt while Grandfather Vu faced him. "These lands fall under the protection and administration of the People's Republic of China," he said, his Vietnamese precise as a scalpel's edge.

Only the scratching of chickens broke the silence that followed. "These lands have belonged to our people since before your grandfather's grandfather drew breath," Grandfather Vu said, his voice mild as morning mist.

"The situation has changed," Wei replied, "but the Chinese army is generous. Surrender now, submit to proper authority, and no one need be harmed. Your villages can continue as they were under Chinese protection."

Spitting Woman stepped forward then, and Wei's hand twitched toward his empty holster as if the pistol were still there. "Remove your troops from our lands," she said, her voice carrying like thunder across the village square. "Once they are gone, we will consider your proposal."

Wei's composure cracked. "Who is this woman to make demands of the Chinese army?"

"I am the woman who will take your head when you least expect it," she said, and her smile gleamed like the edge of a freshly-whetted blade.

Wei's face flushed crimson before hardening to stone. "If you want war with China, then war you shall have," he said, each word falling cold as winter rain. He turned on his heel and strode toward the gate, his spine rigid with military bearing.

Granier whispered to Spitting Woman, "Remind me never to get you mad."

"You'll know if you do," she said with a slight smile.

Granier watched the Chinese commander go, noting how the officer's eyes still gathered intelligence even in his rage - counting defenders, measuring distances, marking targets for his artillery. Here was a professional who would remember everything. Granier was impressed with the man.

The village listened as Wei's footsteps faded, knowing the next sounds from that direction would be war's own drums.

"He'll be back with more men," Granier said, stepping from shadow into harsh morning light.

"Yes," Spitting Woman replied, her gaze fixed on the gate, "but now he'll be angry. Angry men make mistakes."

Grandfather Vu shook his head. "And what of our mistake? Provoking the dragon?"

"The dragon was always going to try to burn us no matter what we did," she said. "At least now he'll come at us in anger rather than careful strategy." She turned to Granier. "How long?"

"Minutes, hours, maybe days. I can't tell. But the one thing we can count on is that they're coming. We should be ready for the worst."

The village stirred around them with new urgency, the confrontation making real what before had only been preparation. Battle was coming, wearing Wei's face and carrying China's rage in its teeth.

Spitting Woman touched the knife at her belt, her promise to Wei still hanging in the air like the smoke from the morning cooking fires. "Then we have work to do," she said, and moved off to join Grandmother Giang on the watchtower and fight against the storm she had just guaranteed would come.

The fury tightened Wei's jaw like a vise as he reached his men at the treeline. "Prepare the mortars," he snapped at Doan. "Target their center. When the first shells land, we advance. You may open fire as soon as they are ready."

The mortar teams bent to their work while morning mist clung low around their boots. The tubes made soft thumps, like a giant's cough, and the first shells vanished into pearl-gray sky. Three heartbeats passed before the explosions tore through dawn's quiet. The blasts painted clouds orange and black while screams rose from the village like startled birds. More shells followed, their explosions walking a line through the village center. The villagers fought panic as they had been taught, but it wasn't easy. Artillery was effective at demoralizing the enemy.

"All units forward, fire at will," Wei commanded, and his men flowed from the trees in practiced formation, rifles held high against their shoulders, firing at the villagers on the walls and watchtowers. They had done this before, dozens of times in dozens of villages - mortars to crack the shell, infantry to spill the meat. Simple. Effective. "Keep tight spacing," he called. "Watch your sectors."

As several villagers were hit, the defenders on the wall and watchtowers quickly hid behind cover.

The first screams that reached them didn't come from the village. "Sir! The ground—" A squad moving through what looked like open ground vanished into earth's own throat. Three men fell into a pit where sharpened bamboo waited like tiger's teeth. Their howls of agony froze the advancing line. Blood ran black in the haze.

"Keep moving," Doan shouted, but his words died as the ground betrayed another soldier. Private Ming stepped forward, then the earth gave way beneath him. A counterweight dropped and a spiked log swept through the air like death's own scythe, catching him and two others, throwing them back boneless as rag dolls. "Medic!" someone screamed, but there was nothing to be done for men cut nearly in half.

The traps woke hungry. "Wire! Watch for wire!" But the warning came too late. Trip wires sang and bamboo whips slashed through undergrowth. "My leg!" Corporal Wu went down, a noose snatching his ankle, dragging him screaming into darkness. The simple devices, born from desperation and jungle wisdom, turned their advance into a butcher's yard.

Wei saw it then, his trained eye catching the pattern. "They're herding us," he said to Doan. "See how the traps channel us toward that open ground?" But pride had him by the throat now. To hesitate was weakness. To retreat was death. Eleven men dead already, their blood soaking into soil that had tasted Chinese blood before.

"Second squad, clear the traps," he screamed. "Third squad, covering fire. The rest of you - forward!" He raised his pistol high. "For China!"

His men surged ahead, grenades blooming in suspect ground to set off the traps. The killing field consumed them like a beast that had waited centuries to feed. Another soldier fell, his chest pierced by a spring-loaded spear that rose from innocent-looking grass.

"Sir," Doan's voice cracked. "Twelve dead. The approaches are death—"

"Irrelevant! I want that village! Redirect the mortars to tear down the palisades. Machine guns on the watchtowers! Everyone else - forward!" Spittle flew from his lips. "Show these peasants what real soldiers can do!"

Mortar shells walked closer to the village palisades now, but the walls stood mostly untouched through drifting smoke. No defenders showed themselves, but Wei felt them waiting, patient as spiders. Let them wait. He would feed this ground every man he had, but he would not give that woman the satisfaction of seeing him break.

On the watchtower Spitting Woman and Grandmother Giang kept their heads down. Through the gaps in the floor of the wooden platform, they watched the Chinese advance, but still out of range for the ancient muskets.

"Push through," Wei screamed as battle's chaos swallowed his words. His men pressed forward over their dead, fighting through the maze of killing grounds. The real fight hadn't started, but there was no turning back.

They would take this village or feed its soil. Defeat at the hands of peasants and a woman who dared threaten him wasn't just unthinkable - it was impossible as tomorrow's sunrise coming from the west.

The Chinese soldiers moved with cautious steps through what seemed safe ground, picking their way between obvious traps like men walking through a snake pit. Not one of them saw the slight rises in the earth, the living moss that breathed with the jungle's breath, the hatches that waited patient as graves beneath their feet.

The first attack came silent as prayer. Earth thrust upward and a spear punched through young Private

Lu's chest, lifting him onto his toes. The weapon withdrew like lightning and the hatch dropped back, leaving nothing but a dying man and ground that looked innocent as morning. The soldiers' rifles cracked in panic, bullets churning soil that had already swallowed their killer.

"There! Another—" but Sergeant Wu's warning died in his throat as a hunter rose from earth ten feet away, his spear finding flesh beneath ribs. The ghost was gone before rifles turned, the hatch closing without sound. In darkness below, calloused hands found guide ropes that led to safety through tunnels old as war itself.

The hatches opened like hell's own maws. Each strike came precise as surgeon's cuts - thrust, withdraw, vanish. Chinese soldiers broke formation, fired at shadows, tried guarding against earth that had turned against them. But the villagers were already gone, crawling through their secret paths.

Old Thua's spear struck clean between a soldier's ribs, but fate had grown tired of his killing. As he dropped back into his hole, a shadow darkened the opening above. A soldier, quicker than most, had seen where death lived. Thua's hands reached for his hatch but time had run out. Something small and dark tumbled down after him.

The grenade rolled to rest at the tunnel's bottom. Thua lunged for it, his fingers that had killed so many now stretching for salvation in the dim light. Metal brushed skin, but the explosion came first. The blast filled the narrow space like a demon's breath, the earthen walls turning force back on itself.

Above, the Chinese heard the muffled boom, saw smoke puff from hastily sealed earth. But their victory was ash in their mouths as more hatches opened, more spears rose from below, more defenders vanished into ground.

In the tunnels, survivors pulled their ropes as Granier had taught them. Support poles snapped like brittle bones, bringing down sections of tunnel in controlled collapse. The earth that had sheltered them now sealed the enemy's pursuit, leaving their hunters nothing but dead ends and darkness.

The jungle floor grew still again, innocent as a killer's smile. Only fallen soldiers and the dark stain spreading from Thua's tomb marked the truth of what lay below. The earth had taken back its secrets, and with them, one of its most faithful sons.

Granier let the musket settle against his shoulder like easing into an old lover's embrace. The weapon that had waited years for this moment pressed familiar iron to his flesh while below, Chinese soldiers pushed through ground already drinking their dead companions' blood.

The musket's roar shattered dawn's peace. Through drifting smoke Granier watched his target fold, clutching chest turned suddenly red, mouth open in a scream lost to battle's growing thunder.

In the next tower Spitting Woman's shot punched through a Chinese officer's throat, opening him like a butchered pig. "Thank your captain for that," she snarled through powder smoke that bit at her nose like an angry snake. Her hands moved in the dance she'd practiced ten thousand times - aim, fire, switch. Another soldier fell screaming, his leg shattered by her third round.

"Your men fall like all the others," she called into

the smoke-thick air.

"Save your breath," Granier shouted across the gap. "They're about to—"

The Chinese answer came in sheets of automatic fire. Bullets chewed through bamboo like iron teeth through flesh. Granier's loader, young Truc screamed as splinters raked her face, blood painting her cheeks in red streaks.

"Down!" Granier yanked the girl to the platform's rough boards as death sang inches above. Granier could see she was severely wounded as blood dripped down to the platform floor. He feared she might go into shock. To get her mind off her wounds he kept her busy. "Stay there, Truc. Load like we practiced." Even though wounded, her fingers moved through the familiar ritual - powder, ball, prime. "Steady hands make steady hearts," he told the trembling girl. "Every shot must sing true."

Spitting Woman's curse cut through gunfire as lead kissed her arm. Blood ran hot down her sleeve while she ducked behind the tower wall, hands working the reload by memory alone. Sweat stung her eyes as she measured powder. Beside her, Grandmother Giang's weathered hands danced between two muskets.

"Careful with that powder, Giang," Spitting Woman warned. "Better slow than—"

"I loaded for your grandfather, girl," Giang snapped, her fingers precise as fate itself. "Save your worry for our enemies."

Through the waist-high grass the Chinese squad moved in a standard assault formation, their boots finding earth soft from the morning's dew. Li kept his eyes on the trees ahead where village walls rose through dawn mist. His training told him to look up, watch the walls, but something made his neck prickle, made instinct whisper warnings about the ground beneath the grass.

The first scream came from Chang, to Li's left. "My foot," he shrieked, his leg jerking up like a puppet's. Blood ran black down his boot where a cruel metal point had punched through leather, through flesh, chipping bone. Before Li could shout warning, Zhu toppled forward, his own cry strangled as he tried to maintain tactical silence even with a steel spike driven through his foot.

"Caltrops," the sergeant hissed. "Don't move." But panic had already broken their formation. Duy stumbled backward, trying to escape, and fell hard. His hands flew to his feet where metal barbs had pierced straight through, pinning him to bleeding earth. The morning filled with the wet sounds of men trying not to scream.

Li watched his squad dissolve into chaos, six men down, their feet shredded by ancient weapons. The sergeant knelt beside one of the fallen, tried to pull the caltrop free, but its barbs had done their work. The metal would need to be cut out, and the nearest medic was half a kilometer back.

Granier watched the Chinese soldiers learn why it was unwise to underestimate the farmers. The caltrops had done their work. Now lead balls would do theirs.

Through gunsmoke thick as river fog the Chinese came at the walls like starved wolves, their officers' screams carrying shrill above the battle din. "Forward! For the People's Republic!" Their boots crushed fallen comrades as they pushed through the killing ground. The lieutenant's whistle cut air gone thick with cordite and they dropped to firing positions with mechanical grace.

"Here it comes," Granier whispered. The words had barely left his lips when Chinese guns erupted.

The first burst reaped through the defenders with terrible precision. Old Tai shot still trying to reload, his ancient musket clattering down the tower steps. Young couple Lan and Duan fell together, their wedding not three weeks past. Hong took the burst through her chest, her crossbow falling unfired from lifeless fingers. Her sister's scream cut through gunfire. "Hong!" She broke cover, running to where her sister lay. The next burst caught her halfway there. They died reaching for each other's hands.

Old Le, who had fought three wars in these mountains, managed one final shot with his bow before being shot. "I go to my fathers," he whispered as his lifeblood soaked the earth that had birthed him. His eyes stayed open, staring at the sky that had watched him kill Japanese and French and American soldiers on this same ground.

The mortars came then, their shells floating lazy as dragonflies before bursting against the walls. The first round landed in the pig pen, turning flesh to red mist. Animals screamed with almost human voices as shrapnel scythed through wood and meat alike. Another explosion caught three men reloading, their bodies thrown against the palisade like children's broken dolls.

"They're walking the mortars into the palisades!" Granier's voice barely carried above the thunder. "Spread out! Don't bunch up!" The air grew thick with cordite stink and the copper-sweet smell of fresh blood. Young Tu ran below with water for the defenders, her feet leaving red prints in the dust. "Use the trenches, girl!"

"Others fight standing," she called back, defiant to the last. The sniper's bullet took her through the throat, her water jug shattering as she fell.

"Keep firing!" Granier worked his reloaded muskets like a man possessed. "Make the bastards pay in blood!" Beside him, young Truc took a round through her shoulder. She dropped the musket she was reloading.

"I failed you," the girl whispered through bloodied lips, her eyes already growing distant.

"You fought well," Granier pressed cloth to the wound though he knew it was too late. "Save your strength, brave one."

Through drifting smoke dark figures appeared, running crouched toward the walls. "Sappers!" The cry went up from a dozen throats. The Chinese engineers sprinted forward with deadly purpose, their satchel charges bouncing against their backs. Defenders' fire dropped two, but three made it to the palisade. They worked with terrible efficiency, setting their charges against the wood poles.

"Get back!" Granier screamed, but his warning drowned in thunder as the charges detonated. The explosions came like angry gods speaking all at once. Wood turned to deadly splinters. When the smoke cleared, three ragged holes gaped in their walls like mortal wounds.

"Form up!" Spitting Woman's voice cut through the chaos like a knife through silk. "To the breaches!" Defenders rushed to the gaps carrying whatever would kill at close range - spears, machetes, farming tools turned to weapons. The Chinese would have to pay dearly for every foot they took. A young mother picked up a bag of caltrops and flung the metal spikes through the hole in the palisades. The Chinese soldiers would have to choose between watching their enemy or watching the ground covered with caltrops.

Through the breaches they could see the enemy gathering, bayonets gleaming dull in the smoke-filtered sun. The villagers gripped their weapons and waited, knowing that what had come before was merely prelude. The real killing was about to begin. It would be hand-to-hand like the days of their grandfathers.

The battle consumed them like some ancient god devouring its children. Spitting Woman's musket cracked and she watched the Chinese machine gunner setting up in front of the palisades topple, his blood black against the morning sky. But where one fell another rose in his place, their weapons hammering against the walls like iron rain. The mortar shell screamed down and burst the storage hut apart, flames leaping into the dawn.

"My daughter's rice," the old man wailed, "our winter stores." His voice was lost in the thunder of combat.

The orange morning light painted them all in shades of hell, defenders firing and dying, Chinese officers pushing their men forward through mud gone slick with blood. The burning huts cast wild shadows across faces twisted in desperation.

Mai knelt in the firing pit her hands steady on the rubber hose. Three days they had worked in darkness. Had buried the fuel drums deep had run the lines through earth had waited patient as death for soldiers who thought villages easy prey. Gia lay beside her torch already lit. They did not speak. Had said everything needed when darkness came.

Through morning mist the Chinese troops came in formation. Their rifles caught dawn light while they advanced with pride that knew nothing about what waited beneath their feet. The first ranks passed the outer markers. Mai felt Gia's hand squeeze her arm once. Not yet. Let them come deeper.

The Chinese commander stood in his truck watching through field glasses. His voice carried sharp and clean across morning air. "Forward. Take the village. No prisoners." More troops came then. Filled the killing ground like water filling bowl.

When they crossed the second markers Granier's voice came soft as falling leaves. "Now."

Mai opened the valve. The fuel came thick as blood through the hose. She directed the stream high let it arc through morning air let it paint Chinese soldiers with their own death. Other streams rose from other pits. The soldiers stopped confused by rain that carried scent of fuel. That painted their uniforms dark that ran into their boots.

"Hold" Spitting Woman called. Her voice carried calm as temple bells.

The Chinese troops stood in spreading fuel. Their boots made dark prints in mud gone black. Their commander shouted orders that meant nothing now. That carried no weight against what came next.

"Now!" Granier said and the torches flew. Mai watched Gia's torch arc high and true. Watched it fall among soldiers who had no time to understand. The fire came like God's own judgment. Like everything Hell had ever promised. Like death wearing flames instead of hood and scythe.

The soldiers died screaming. Fire ran swift as sin through their ranks. Those who tried running fell in mud gone slick with fuel. Those who stood died where they were. Those who shot blind through flames hit nothing but morning air.

Mai watched it all through smoke thick enough to cut. Watched men become torches. Watched steel become furnace. Watched everything war thought it knew about killing become child's play against village wisdom. The sounds they made would walk her dreams forever.

When it finished the ground had become a crematorium. The air ran thick with meat smoke and victory's cost. Mai felt Gia's hand on her shoulder. Felt her shaking felt herself shaking felt everything that makes people human trying to crawl away from what they had done.

"We had no choice" Gia said. But her voice carried weight of knowing some choices mark souls deeper than others.

The villagers fought with everything God and ancestors had given them. Muskets boomed from the walls, arrows hissed through gunsmoke thick enough to chew. Mai's mother grabbed her dead husband's musket, squeezed off one shot before the Chinese guns found her. "Tell my children," she whispered to her neighbor, blood bubbling at her lips, "I died for their future."

In her tower, Spitting Woman worked with mechanical precision - aim, fire, pass the smoking musket, take a loaded one. "Your soldiers die as easily as village pigs," she screamed across the killing ground. Her shot caught a man setting up a heavy weapon.

"You send boys to do a warrior's job," she taunted. When a soldier rose to fire at her, she put a ball through his throat.

Old Ngo dropped two soldiers with his crossbow, clean kills both, before the sniper's round took him in the throat. His son's scream cut through the battle. "My father."

Granier watched it all unfolding, the tide of battle turning against them like a river changing course. The Chinese paid in blood for every step, but they had blood to spare. His people fell one by one, their muskets deadly but too slow against the storm of automatic fire.

"We need more ammunition," someone shouted from the killing ground below.

"Save your shots," Granier called back, "make each one count, no wasted rounds."

Another mortar crashed down, blasting a home to splinters and screams. "My house," a woman cried, "everything we own."

"Houses can be rebuilt," Spitting Woman shouted from her watchtower, "the dead cannot, keep firing."

They fought on with whatever came to hand. Empty muskets became clubs, bows gave way to spears, spears to rocks. Old Cuong took three rounds charging a Chinese soldier with just his hoe, but he split the man's skull before darkness took him.

The Chinese advance slowed but would not stop. Their officers drove them forward over their own dead, determined to take the village or die in the attempt.

"For the glory of China," an officer shouted.

"For our homes," Spitting Woman answered, and her last musket ball sent him to whatever gods waited for men who died far from their own soil.

Granier watched the next wave of Chinese soldiers surge forward like dark water against stone. "Here they come again," he called down to Spitting Woman, her muskets out of ammunition, on the ground using one of the rifles as a club.

She turned to him, her face streaked with the blood of friend and enemy alike, eyes burning with a fury old as the mountains themselves. "Let them come."

The battle consumed them all now, neither side able to retreat, neither willing to yield. Their village would live or die, each bullet writing another word of their fate, each fallen body marking another step toward victory or annihilation. The clouds above turned black with gunsmoke while below them men killed and died.

The village defenders rose like ancient spirits to meet the Chinese advance, each warrior knowing the ground they must hold or die trying. When the enemy closed to fifty meters, their ancestral weapons began to speak.

Tam stood from behind the barricade, his spearman's arms hardened by years of river fishing. "For my father's father," he whispered. The spear flew straight and true, punching through a soldier's chest and pinning him to earth. Before the body stopped its death dance, Tam had launched two more. "For my brothers, taken by your army."

He ducked as bullets splintered wood above his head.

"They're in range of the blowguns," old Nam shouted from the gate, his weapon raised after fifty years of hunting birds. A dozen bamboo tubes lifted in unison, their darts glistening with ancestral poisons.

"What is this," a Chinese soldier screamed, clawing

at his neck where the dart struck and the poison tip dove deep. "What have they done to me?" He fell writhing, his death a warning to those who followed.

Granier's musket thundered from the watchtower and a machine gunner's head vanished in red mist. "Watch their officers, take their leaders." His next shot dropped a lieutenant organizing an assault.

"How many musket balls left?" he called to his new loader, Grandmother Giang.

"Fourteen and three powder horns," the grandmother answered, working the smoking weapons with desperate speed. "Make them count."

Granier grabbed a reloaded musket and sighted on another officer. The musket roared and the officer crumbled to the ground dead.

The Chinese answer came in sheets of automatic fire. Young Dui fell back from the wall near the main gate, chest torn open. His sister Lin screamed and rose to help.

"Lin, stay down," voices cried in unison, but she was already moving.

"Brother, hold on." She reached him just as the bullets found her too. She fell across him, their blood mixing in ancestral soil.

Elder Y Nhien took three rounds but loosed a final arrow before falling. "I die free," he gasped. "Remember that. We die free men."

The battle continued like this, in blood and fire and screams, until the very air tasted of gunpowder and death. But the villagers fought on with weapons old and new, with desperate courage and deadly precision, making the Chinese pay for every step toward their walls. Even when mortars rained down, even when children died carrying water, even when winter stores burned - they fought on. Because this was their ground, their home, their way of life. And they would defend it to the last arrow, the last bullet, the last breath.

Through the breach the Chinese soldier came screaming empire's fury, his submachine gun stitching death through village air. The weapon's muzzle flash painted his face in devil light while villagers dove for cover. But Spitting Woman moved toward the flame, her empty musket gripped like ancient club. Her strike came fast and precise, the wooden stock smashing the submachine gun's barrel earthward where it chewed dirt and roots and everything except what its owner intended.

His hand dropped his submachine gun and flew to the bayonet on his belt, but Spitting Woman's musket butt caught his jaw, turned teeth to blood, turned bone to broken things. He staggered backward, feet finding empty air where earth fell away to trench's hungry mouth. Down the embankment he tumbled, a broken doll in uniform, until sharpened bamboo welcomed him with points honed by women who remembered how wood should taste flesh. The sound he made when the spikes took him carried something older than screaming.

The Chinese lines began to waver, their dead littering the ground like fallen leaves after storm. The advancing soldiers picked their way through corpses of fallen comrades, each step bringing them closer to the defenders' killing ground.

"Sir," Sergeant Zhang shouted to his commander, Lieutenant Liu, pressing against a fallen log while arrows sang overhead, "we've lost too many. Third squad is down to four men. Second squad isn't responding."

The lieutenant felt a musket ball tear his collar. He surveyed his broken ranks - more than half his force lay dead or dying, yet still the village weapons spoke with deadly precision. His men's courage crumbled beneath the relentless fire.

"How can farmers fight like this," he muttered, watching another soldier fall to an arrow's kiss. A spear buried itself in the earth beside him, its shaft humming with deadly promise.

"Sir," Zhang pressed, "we must decide. The men won't take more."

Liu knew Wei's fury would be terrible, but watching his command die for nothing was worse. "Pull back," he ordered, the words bitter as grave dirt. "Fall back to the tree line. Carry our wounded."

The Chinese retreat started slow then quickened as more officers took up the cry. "Fall back, fall back." Some dragged wounded comrades while others simply ran, their spirits broken by the village's fierce defense.

"They're running," young Loan screamed from the wall, putting an arrow into a fleeing soldier's back. "Run faster, invaders."

"Save your ammunition," Spitting Woman commanded. "They'll return with more men, more guns." Her arrow spoke one final time, dropping an officer trying to organize covering fire. "Sorry. Habit," said Loan with a shrug.

Granier watched them withdraw through gun smoke thick as morning fog. The killing ground before the walls lay carpeted with Chinese dead and dying. Wounded men crawled away leaving crimson trails in the churned earth while others lay still, their bodies already stiffening in the humid air like creatures carved from stone.

Victory had cost them dearly. Their dead lay scattered like broken dolls across the churned earth, and the wounded moaned in voices that would haunt dreams. Houses burned against the morning sky, their walls now orange skeletons that cast twisted shadows. Dead animals dotted the ground like dark islands in a sea of trampled mud, and the precious winter stores smoldered in the ruined granary.

"How many?" Granier called to Spitting Woman, his voice raw from shouting commands.

"Too many," she answered, her eyes moving across their fallen. "Sixty-eight dead that I can see. Hundreds wounded. But we held." Pride blazed in her face like the burning buildings behind her.

"You're damned right we held," said Granier almost unbelieving the miracle.

The Chinese mortars fell silent one by one until only the cries of wounded men broke the sudden stillness. They had survived their first true test, but Granier knew in his bones the enemy would return stronger, harder, more determined to break them.

Young Lian appeared at his side, her face a mask of soot and blood, offering water from a clay jar. Though she'd seen Hell itself this day, her eyes still burned with fierce resolve. "Will they come back?" she whispered.

"Probably," he drank deep from the jar. "But now they know the price of taking this village." He nodded toward their walls where defenders still stood ready. "Next time we'll make them pay even more."

"Good." She clutched her dead brother's crossbow like a talisman. "I have more arrows to give them."

Spitting Woman approached, face black as midnight with powder smoke. "Check the wounded," she commanded. "Gather our dead. We honor them tonight, but first we rebuild. We reload. We prepare." Her eyes found the burning storage huts. "And we pray the rains come soon. We'll need food more than ammunition in the days ahead."

The village moved with grim purpose - tending wounds, salvaging what fire hadn't claimed, mending broken walls. Their first victory was won, but in the distance Chinese bugles called their soldiers home like wolves gathering for another hunt.

"They thought we would break," Granier said softly as they watched their people work. "They thought we would run."

Spitting Woman smiled like a blade in darkness. "They thought we were just farmers and fishermen."

"We are farmers and fishermen," old Minh said, plucking his poison darts from Chinese corpses. "But this is our land. Our homes. And we will teach them what that means. One arrow, one spear, one dart at a time."

Through her smoke Spitting Woman watched the Chinese soldiers retreat into morning shadow. Her lips curled like a wolf's before the kill. She moved toward an opening in the palisades.

"Where are you going?" Granier called after her.

"Keeping my promise," she said, snatching a fallen defender's machete. The weight settled in her palm like greeting an old friend. Without another word she slipped through the hidden gap in the palisade wall.

The jungle welcomed her as it had always welcomed her, like a mother embracing her most dangerous child. She flowed through shadows that remembered her, feet finding ancient paths while lesser warriors would have stumbled and fallen. The thick vegetation swallowed her whole as she paralleled the battlefield, moving faster than the retreating soldiers who struggled with their wounded.

Her breathing came slow and measured as a hunting cat's while sweat ran unchecked down her face. The machete caught filtered sunlight as she ran. She knew every root, every shadow, every tree that had stood sentinel since before gunpowder came to these mountains. The Chinese soldiers followed the obvious route back to their lines, exactly as she'd known they would.

Through gaps in the leaves she glimpsed them stumbling along - dragging wounded, limping, helping broken comrades. Their formation had dissolved into chaos, their discipline shattered by retreat. Perfect.

"You threatened my village," she whispered into the green darkness. "Big mistake."

She moved through her kingdom like death's own shadow, closing the distance with each silent step, the machete growing hungry in her hand.

Captain Wei stood raging before his shamed officers in the hastily made command post. His men stood rigid at attention while his fury washed over them.

"Farmers!" He spat the word like venom. "You retreated from farmers and old women. The People's Liberation Army running from peasants with spears." His boots cut sharp tracks in the mud as he paced. "Your cowardice shames your uniforms, shames China herself."

His men remained silent with eyes fixed forward, but something in their expressions shifted. A widening of eyes, a subtle change of focus. Wei felt the charge in the air behind him like lightning about to strike.

Twenty yards away in the dense foliage, Spitting

Woman coiled tight as a cobra before the strike. Her breath slowed to nothing, muscles tensed like steel springs. The machete came alive in her grip, hungry for what waited. Time crystallized around her into one perfect moment of purpose.

She exploded from the jungle like vengeance made flesh, her feet barely kissing earth as she reached full sprint, the machete held low behind her like death's own scythe. The space between her and Wei vanished with each powerful stride.

Wei began to turn, soldier's instincts finally screaming danger into his blood. He caught one glimpse of her face - fierce and focused as a tiger's - and in that fraction of time saw his death approaching and knew he could do nothing to stop it.

Spitting Woman's voice cut through morning air like the steel she carried: "I told you I would take your head!"

The machete swept up and across in one perfect arc as she passed him. The sound came wet and final - sharp metal parting flesh and bone like a butcher's knife through market meat. Wei's face froze in horror as his head left his shoulders, a fine red mist following the blade's path through morning light.

His body stood for one impossible moment before dropping to earth. The head rolled to rest at his officers' feet, the eyes still holding that last terrible moment of recognition.

Without breaking stride she whipped the machete back for a second cut, taking the long-range radio antenna in one clean stroke and silencing any chance of calling reinforcements.

The Chinese soldiers stood frozen as statues while their minds struggled to understand what their eyes had witnessed. By the time the first man thought to raise his weapon, by the time the first cry of alarm tore free from a throat, Spitting Woman had melted back into her jungle sanctuary. She was gone.

Wei's blood soaked into foreign soil while his men finally broke from their paralysis, firing wild into the green wall of vegetation. But they knew in their bones, knew with a certainty that would haunt their dreams forever, that she had already vanished - a deadly shadow returned to the darkness that had birthed it.

One officer found his voice at last: "The woman... the one he mocked... she..."

"She kept her promise," another whispered, staring down at their commander's empty eyes.

Through the jungle Spitting Woman ran with the sure grace of someone born to these shadows, someone who knew every root and branch as intimately as a lover. The machete in her hand left a trail of Wei's blood to mark her passing - a trail the jungle would soon erase, leaving no trace of her visit, no evidence of her killing.

Her promise had been kept. Her message delivered in blood and steel. Let them come again with their mortars and guns. The jungle held darker lessons yet for those who would threaten her people.

In gray dawn Spitting Woman slipped through the village gate like rising smoke, her clothes dark with other men's blood, a captured Chinese rifle riding her shoulder. She found Granier checking bodies with mechanical precision, sorting weapons into piles as if harvesting war's crop. His eyes asked the question and she answered, "It's done. The radio will never speak again, and their commander," she touched the blade at her hip, "has no more orders to give."

Granier nodded, pulling a magazine from a dead soldier's vest. "They'll run north, try to make the front lines, tell their commanders what happened here. We can't let them reach the border."

Spitting Woman's smile came thin as a sword's edge. "Then we hunt."

They moved through the village gathering weapons like grim harvesters, collecting Chinese rifles still warm from their last fire, bandoliers heavy with ammunition, grenades that promised swift arguments. "These weapons have already learned to kill our people," she said in her dialect, then switched to French, "let them learn to kill their masters."

They took only what they could carry, what would serve them in the hunt, moving fast and silent past the temple where morning sun caught brass shells scattered like fallen coins. The trail lay clear to those who knew how to read such signs - broken branches, blood on leaves, the marks of men moving fast without woodcraft.

Granier touched a smeared boot print. "One, maybe two hours ahead, moving north but staying off the main trails. They know we have teeth."

Spitting Woman checked her captured rifle, tested its action like a musician tuning an instrument. "They'll be tired now, scared, running with their dead commander's eyes still haunting them."

Granier shouldered his weapon and they moved into the jungle's green shadows, becoming part of its ancient hunger. They ran as they had in old wars, eating ground with the patience of wolves, the Chinese rifles bobbing across their backs like modern totems. The jungle accepted them as it always had, opening paths that others would miss.

Somewhere ahead their quarry fled carrying stories that must never reach the northern camps - tales of a village that fought back, of a woman who kept her promises, of death that came silent as a lover's touch in darkness. Granier and Spitting Woman ran easy and smooth as water over stones, their feet finding purchase where others would slip, their breath measured, their purpose absolute.

"Let them run," Spitting Woman said in her dialect as they paused to read the signs of passage. "The running makes them blind, makes them clumsy, makes them forget to listen for death's quiet feet."

Granier checked his captured weapon again, numbered its remaining rounds like counting prayers. In the shadows ahead somewhere their quarry fled carrying tales that would die with them. The hunters moved on, filtered sunlight dappling their faces like war paint. They had become something ancient, something that stalked the edges of nightmares.

Granier and Spitting Woman moved through morning mist like spirits of vengeance, their captured Chinese rifles held close as lovers. Three sets of tracks lay ahead - desperate men running blind.

The first soldier died by a stream where he'd stopped to drink, Spitting Woman's round taking him through the throat, his blood mixing with water like wine at communion. The other two heard death speak but ran wrong, climbing uphill where tired men make mistakes, where gravity betrays those who don't know mountain wisdom.

"We have them now," Granier whispered, touching marks in mud where exhausted feet had slipped. "These boys learned war in classrooms, never learned how earth speaks to those who know its tongue."

They found the second soldier collapsed against a tree, chest heaving, lungs raw from running. His eyes went wide seeing death come wearing human skin, wearing faces that had learned killing through experience. "Please," he said in schoolbook Vietnamese, "I have a son." Granier's shot answered in a language older than words.

The last one ran until his legs betrayed him, sprawling in grass wet with dew and fear and knowing some stories never reach their endings. He tried raising his rifle but muscles that had run too far, too long, failed him. Spitting Woman emerged from green shadows like something birthed from jungle's heart. "You ran well," she said in her dialect then switched to Chinese so he'd understand his dying. "But this is our ground, our air, our death you carry in your lungs." His eyes held questions that would never find voice as Granier's bullet opened his future to morning air.

They searched the bodies, taking ammunition, maps, last letters home. The earth would claim what remained, would add their bones to its collection of war's leavings.

"Three less stories for their commanders," Granier said, checking rounds in his rifle.

Spitting Woman nodded, touched earth made wet with strangers' blood, spoke words older than any war that would speed these dead boys to whatever gods waited. The jungle wrapped them in green silence, accepted their offering of ended lives.

They moved on like shadows through shadow, leaving cooling meat for earth's other children, leaving brass shells like copper coins to pay death's ferryman, leaving history written in blood on mountain stone.

Through gray dawn mist Granier and Spitting

Woman read earth's warnings - broken twigs, torn leaves, signs that spoke of men moving north. But the signs changed, grew too numerous, became a language of thousands of feet moving over ground.

They belly-crawled through wet grass to a ridgeline overlooking the northern valley and there all words died in their throats. Tanks stretched horizon to horizon like iron beetles, their guns long as prophecy. Artillery pieces waited with mouths pointed south, hungry for range coordinates. Soldiers moved between vehicles by the thousands, checking weapons, adjusting packs, their faces young as morning.

"Christ," Granier whispered, his soldier's mind already counting numbers, calculating odds, measuring the mathematics of nightmare. Spitting Woman touched his arm, pointed east where more armor, more men, more instruments of war's hunger emerged from morning haze like dragons waking from ancient sleep.

"This is madness," she said in her dialect then French as if searching for words that could contain such insanity. "They would invade us like this? Now?"

Radio traffic crackled below, sharp commands in Chinese that spoke of preparation, of imminence, of empire's will made manifest in steel and flesh and fire. A helicopter passed beneath them, rotors cutting clouds too close, and they pressed into mud holding breath that seemed too loud in a world suddenly gone mad with war's promise. More trucks, more tanks, more soldiers endless as stars.

"They're going to roll south," Granier said, "going to try to break Vietnam's spine in one strike." His hands checked his rifle from habit though such weapons meant nothing now against what waited below. *Like a child's toys*, he thought, *against such numbers, such steel, such destiny made real in morning light.*

"We have to warn them," Spitting Woman's voice carried urgent as bleeding. "The village, the other villages, Hanoi, everyone."

They broke contact, crawled back into jungle shadow, became part of earth's green memory. Then they ran. Ran as they had in old wars eating ground with the patience of wolves, but now that patience carried fear's edge, carried knowledge that behind them a dragon gathered its strength, prepared to unleash fire across their homeland. They ran through streams leaving no trace, ran through shadows leaving no mark, ran as they had taught others to run but now running felt like retreat, felt like surrender, felt like history's hot breath on their necks.

The morning sun rose behind them like judgment as they raced south carrying warning in their bones, hoping they would reach the village before steel dragons rolled across border stones, hoping Vietnam would have time to gather its strength, its wisdom, its endless patience before China's fury found its full voice. They ran and behind them an army waited, armored and endless and hungry for glory, never knowing that two ghosts had seen their gathering, never knowing that Vietnam would be ready, never knowing that empires always look strongest just before they learn why these mountains have teeth, these jungles have memory, these people have forever.

Invasion

The bunker air hung thick with cigarette smoke and the weight of coming violence. Maps sprawled across steel tables, marked and annotated like a butcher's diagram before the slaughter. General Chen stood before his commanders, their faces sharp and predatory under the harsh fluorescent light, insignias glinting dull as dried blood on their collars.

"Three weeks," he said, "three weeks to break their spirit, to teach them what it means to defy China." His pointer moved across the map like a prophet's staff marking the paths of devastation.

"The artillery batteries will advance here and here, creating corridors of destruction five kilometers wide. Nothing left standing, nothing left alive. Your guns will speak without pause, without mercy." The artillery commander nodded, making notes in a leather book that would soon hold Hell's coordinates.

The Air Force colonel stood beside his own maps where red strikes bloomed like wounds across the countryside. "Your bombers will strike these population centers at dawn," Chen continued, "No warning. Maximum civilian casualties. The shock must ripple through their society. These people must learn that defiance has a price their children will pay in screams. Turn their streets to slaughterhouses." His pointer glided across the map. "The antiaircraft units create a shield here, protecting our advance. The Vietnamese pilots are skilled, but they'll die in their own sky."

The assault commanders stood silent, memorizing their roles in this orchestration of death. "If their soldiers surrender, take them. We need witnesses to carry our message south. But civilians..." he paused, "civilians are not to be burdened with survival. Let them feed the earth, let them become statistics, let them haunt their government's dreams."

His voice dropped soft as a confessional whisper. "It's unfortunate that Vietnam has chosen this path, but empires cannot allow rebellion. Our task is simple - maximum damage, maximum death, maximum terror. In three weeks we withdraw, leaving behind lessons written in blood and bone."

The field commanders saluted and filed out while tanks waited in the predawn dark, their engines thrumming low and hungry. General Chen watched them go, these architects of death, while somewhere south, families sat down to breakfasts that would be their last moments of peace. History's wheels had begun to turn, and they would grind exceedingly fine.

The dawn came red while General Chen watched the first wave of aircraft lift into the bruised sky. Through the command post window he counted the bombers black against the sunrise, their wings heavy, their bellies swollen with bombs.

The radio chirped and crackled, spitting coordinates and confirmations in sharp military bursts.

High above the border, Lieutenant Quang tasted copper in his mouth as he yanked the MiG into a vertical climb, his teeth clenched against G-forces that threatened to drag him into darkness.

Beside him, Bac's fingers danced across the radar screen, leaving smears of sweat on the glass. "Three more coming in fast from the north," Bac said, his words barely audible over the scream of their engines.

"They're trying to get above us." Quang eased the stick right, watching his airspeed bleed away as the fighter clawed for altitude. Warning lights flashed red across his instrument panel. The MiG wasn't meant to fly like this, wasn't meant to stand on its tail and challenge gravity, but Quang had learned things about aircraft during the American war that weren't written in any manual.

A missile streaked past their canopy, close enough that Quang could see its guidance fins catching the dawn light. He rolled the aircraft hard left, trading height for speed, watching his radar as two Chinese fighters followed him down. "Let them come," he whispered, waiting until the enemy pilots committed to their dive.

The third Chinese fighter appeared suddenly above them, cannon fire walking across the sky where they had been half a second before. Quang's hand was already moving, decades of combat carved into muscle memory. The MiG pivoted impossibly in the air, bleeding speed but bringing its nose to bear.

Bac swore softly as the G-forces peaked, but his fingers never stopped moving across the weapons panel. "Fox Two, Fox Two," he called as their missiles launched.

The Chinese pilot tried to break right, tried to run, tried to remember everything his instructors had taught him about dogfighting. But no instructor could teach what three generations of war had written into Vietnamese pilots' brain. The missiles struck home, turning metal to fire, turning pride to ash, turning empire's arrogance into flames that painted the morning clouds red.

Around them, the sky erupted in brief, deadly flowers as more aircraft died. A voice cut through their radio, young and fierce and already dying: "For my brother who fell to American bombs," and then static as another MiG became fire.

Quang felt something tear loose in his chest, something older than rage, something that remembered when these mountains had seen French planes fall, had seen American planes fall, had seen everything that dared claim Vietnamese sky learn why air belongs to those who have bled most defending it.

Two more Chinese fighters appeared on their radar, their pilots still believing altitude alone made them safe. "Let's teach them differently," Bac said, his voice carrying the weight of knowing the air battle would be fought in Heaven's own vault. Quang pushed the throttle forward, feeling the MiG's frame shudder as they rose to meet empire's newest sons, their weapons ready to write revolution's next chapter in fire and steel and falling stars.

They sat cleaning their weapons in the forward bunker while rain fell steady as grief. Tuan worked his rifle's bolt feeling how metal remembered mud and blood and everything that made soldiers count days by kills.

The radio crackled once then spoke in a voice he knew carried news from home.

Minh got to it first held the handset like it might turn to smoke. His face went still as temple stone while he listened. When he turned to them his eyes held something Tuan had not seen since rice fields and simple days. "The village," Minh said. "They held. Drove the Chinese out. Killed them to the last man."

The words fell between them while rifles lay forgotten while rain drummed against earth that had seen three armies try to claim it. Loc touched the stock of his captured Chinese gun. "How many? How many did we lose?"

"Some," Minh said. "But the Chinese lost more. Granier and Spitting Woman led the defense. The women fought too. Your Mai she killed three with that knife you gave her." He looked at Tuan. "The Chinese commander tried using hostages. The village rose up killed their guards took their weapons. Killed everything that wore their uniform."

Tuan felt the jade pendant warm against his chest, felt how it carried Mai's promise, felt how some things lived deeper than mere survival. The other men from their village gathered close while Minh told how home had learned to bare teeth against invaders. About the women who had turned farming tools to weapons. About old men who remembered how their grandfathers had killed French soldiers with simple steel.

They cleaned their weapons after while outside rain turned to mist, turned to something that belonged to mountains more than men. Each motion carried weight of knowing why they fought why they killed why some ground could not be surrendered. Tuan worked his rifle's action smooth and clean and precise while in his chest his heartbeat time against jade that remembered Mai's hands. Some victories came measured not in ground taken but in ground held. In that they were rich as emperors. Rich as gods. Rich as men who had learned why villages survived when armies fell.

Through the false dawn the Chinese artillery crews moved with mechanical precision, their hands performing tasks drilled into muscle memory. Behind the Type 66 152mm howitzers, ammunition carriers stripped shells from their wooden crates while gun captains checked firing tables against pre-registered coordinates.

"Gun One, ready," a sergeant called, his voice carrying across the battery position where twelve heavy guns waited like steel beasts in the morning mist. "Gun Two, ready," came another voice, then another, rippling down the line while crews made final adjustments to their sights. The battery commander stood with his radio handset pressed to his ear, listening to final corrections from forward observers. "Battery, adjust fire," he commanded. "Grid reference four-six-three-eight-nine-one. Elevation three-zero degrees. High explosive." The gun captains repeated the coordinates while crews swung their massive barrels upward, hydraulics whining in the pre-dawn stillness. "Battery, fire when ready."

The first gun spoke with a flash like lightning, its shell screaming skyward while the barrel recoiled almost two meters. Before it had settled back, the second gun fired, then the third, rippling down the line in a thunder that shook earth and air. Loaders moved like automatons, ramming fresh shells home while gun layers adjusted their sights micrometers at a time.

The battery found its rhythm then - load, fire, adjust, reload - each crew performing their lethal ballet while forward observers called corrections.

"Battery, fire for effect," the commander ordered, and all twelve guns spoke at once, their shells writing death's own arithmetic across morning sky.

Behind them, trucks moved constantly, bringing more ammunition forward while empty crates accumulated like wooden tombstones.

Through the rain Tuan checked his ammunition while beside him Duc whispered, "You think they reached the mountains by now." His voice barely carried over the sound of distant artillery.

"The village will make it," Tuan said. "Granier knows the passes. And Mai she's strong. Stronger than both of us." He worked his rifle's bolt, tried to focus on the immediate ground the wire the markers, but his mind kept seeing Mai leading the children up mountain trails.

"Should have gone with them," Duc said. "Should have—"

Sergeant Bao's voice cut between them sharp as a blade. "You're here now. Both of you. The village has its warriors. We have our place." He moved closer spoke lower. "The Chinese come with everything they have. You start thinking about mountain trails you'll die in this mud. Then who defends your people."

They nodded, kept their eyes forward. Through the rain they could hear tank treads grinding closer like metal being torn. The sound filled the air; made speech impossible. Made thought impossible. Bao touched both their shoulders once; moved on down the line.

More runners came with ammunition boxes. They stacked them in the firing steps divided the grenades. Each man checked his neighbor's load. Through the rain they could hear tank treads clearer now. The sound carried like something vast and metal being born.

Lieutenant Quan came through the trench spoke quiet words to Bao. They saw him mark something on his map. The rain ran off his helmet like tears. When he moved on Bao turned to the men. "They come in force," he said. "But this is our ground. Make them count the cost in blood."

The shells were falling closer. Through the wire they could see the first Chinese scouts moving like shadows through the rain. Bao gave the order and they mounted their weapons on the firing step. The sound of bolts being worked ran down the line like a steel wave.

More shells fell behind their position. The explosions came steady as a drumbeat now. Tuan pressed against the firing step felt the wet earth against his chest. Duc worked his weapon's action one final time. Neither spoke again. The rain fell colder and through the wire they could see the first Chinese scouts moving like ghosts through the growing smoke. They waited while the morning gathered darkness and everything they loved lay balanced on the edge of whatever came next.

General Chen watched through his binoculars. A slight smile creeping across his lips. Things were going well.

The howitzers fired until their barrels glowed dull red in the gathering light, until shell casings lay scattered like copper coins, until the morning air ran thick with cordite and the mathematics of modern artillery turned ancient wisdom about how some battles are fought with steel and smoke and precise calculations of how to turn coordinates into casualties.

The Vietnamese artillery used their radar to sight the Chinese battery positions and returned fire. The counter-batteries were effective but outnumbered by the Chinese guns. The Chinese batteries adjusted their own counter-batteries to take out the Vietnamese artillery.

General Ma stood in the forward observation post, his hands steady on his binoculars while the world erupted around him. "Ranging shots," he said to his radio operator. "They're walking them in." The Chinese batteries opened up in full then, dozens of guns speaking at once, their shells turning morning air to steel rain.

Private Duong's voice crackled through the radio, coordinates coming fast and precise from his position on the ridgeline. "Battery Three is taking direct hits," he reported, his words nearly lost in the thunder of explosions. "They're using counter-battery radar, targeting our gun positions."

Ma watched through smoke as Vietnamese artillery crews worked their weapons with desperate speed, men who had learned their trade in the American war now teaching Chinese gunners why some battles must be fought shell for shell.

The ground buckled as Chinese rounds found their mark, turning Vietnamese Gun Four into screaming metal and dying men.

"Adjust fire," Ma commanded into his radio, reading coordinates off his map while around him the observation post's walls shook with each impact. "All batteries concentrate on their radar positions." The Vietnamese guns answered then, their shells rising into morning sky like prayers made of steel and smokeless powder. Through his binoculars Ma watched the rounds land, turning Chinese artillery positions into fountains of earth and flame. His forward observers called corrections, each man's voice carrying the cold precision that came from knowing their own gun's survival depended on silencing the enemy's artillery.

"Battery Six is gone," someone shouted through the radio static. "Direct hit on their ammunition." The explosion lit up the valley like false dawn, cooking off hundreds of shells that arced into the sky like dying stars. Ma felt the heat on his face even from two kilometers away.

More Chinese shells came in, their gunners having found the range now, turning the ridge line into crater-pocked hell. The surviving Vietnamese batteries kept firing, their crews working with mechanical precision while around them the earth itself seemed to tear apart.

"Counter-battery fire is slacking off," Duong reported, his voice steady despite the chaos. "It appears their western radar array is down." Ma watched another Vietnamese gun position disappear in flame and steel, its crew having paid blood price to keep firing until the last. But their shells had found their marks. Through drifting smoke he could see the Chinese guns falling silent one by one as their targeting radar died, their crews learning why the Vietnamese fought with skill and experience, not merely shells.

The mountains shook with each impact, three generations of war having taught them how artillery duels ended - not with victory but with counting who survived to fire again. "Eight guns left," his battery commander reported, voice carrying weight of knowing how many friends had died in the barrage. "But their radar is finished. They're firing blind now."

Ma watched the last Chinese shells arc overhead, their gunners reduced to area fire without the precision their modern equipment had provided. His surviving batteries turned their attention to the Chinese armor now, their reduced numbers still enough to turn valleys into killing grounds while around them the morning air ran thick with cordite and radio calls and the mathematics of modern war turned to ancient wisdom about why some battles are won by those who know the ground.

The artillery duel died slowly, guns falling silent one by one until only the wounded cried and the dead lay silent and the mountains themselves seemed to hold their breath, waiting to see what new violence the day would bring.

Through it all Ma stood watching, counting surviving guns, measuring victory not in ground taken but in how many crews would live to fight again, how many guns would speak revolution's tongue when next the Chinese batteries dared to claim Vietnamese sky with their steel rain.

General Chen raised his binoculars again and watched his infantry advance in endless waves, tanks crawling among them like iron beetles. Through morning mist the tanks advanced grinding steel against mountain roads T-59s and T-60s their hulls painted forest green their treads leaving deep scars in earth wet with dawn. Behind them the Type 63 armored cars followed their wheels churning mud their mounted guns traversing back and forth like the heads of hunting beasts.

The Vietnamese soldiers lay in their bunkers and trenches hands steady on weapons breathing slow and measured while their officers whispered coordinates into field telephones.

"Five hundred meters," Lieutenant Tran said into his handset. The words passed down the line quiet as prayer.

General Chen stood on the command ridge his eyes peering through his Russian field glasses. The horizon had become a river of green uniforms and steel armor flowing south with mechanical precision. A dragon made of men and metal going to teach Vietnam about empire's reach.

"Beautiful" he said. "Like watching history write itself in iron."

The observer beside him shifted uncomfortable with such poetry from a man known for tactical mathematics. "Sir, the first wave approaches their forward positions."

Through his glasses Chen watched the tanks lead the advance their main guns elevated slightly as if sniffing the air. Behind them 10,000 infantry moved in perfect formation their rifles catching morning sun like scales on some great serpent.

The first shot came from a hidden Vietnamese position. A single heavy round that found a tank commander who had risen too high in his cupola. The man's body folded backward disappeared into his iron tomb.

Then the hills erupted. Every Vietnamese bunker spoke at once machine guns and mortars creating walls of metal that turned the advancing infantry into broken dolls. The tanks answered their main guns thundering while their coaxial machine guns stitched the defenders' positions.

"They're not running," the observer said his voice tight with something between admiration and fear. "Sir, they're standing and fighting."

"Of course they're standing," Chen said. "This is their ground. Has been since before our grandfathers drew breath." He watched another tank die from a hidden AT gun its turret thrown skyward like a toy in a giant's hand. "The question is how many will we spend to take it from them."

A Vietnamese 12.7mm heavy machine gun opened up from a hidden bunker its huge rounds punching through the side armor of a Type 63 turning the crew compartment into a butcher's shop. The vehicle slewed sideways blocked the advance of three others.

The morning turned into a ceremony of fire and steel. The Vietnamese held their ground while Chen fed more men, more tanks, more pieces of empire's pride into their killing zones. The sun rose higher painting the battlefield in colors that had no names in any language of war.

"Send in the second wave" Chen said. He lowered his glasses wiped condensation that might have been tears if generals were allowed such things. "And tell the field hospital we'll need more body bags. Many more."

Through his glasses he watched the next wave of tanks advance their engines roaring like dragons waking from ancient sleep. The Vietnamese guns spoke again like thunder chewing up the Chinese infantry with high explosive rounds.

"We will see how they fare against iron rain," Chen

said, then had his observer radio the battery commander. "Change to Beehive rounds and target the Vietnamese trenches."

The remaining Chinese guns spoke with a new voice that morning, a deeper throat-rending roar that made even veteran soldiers pause in their trenches. The rounds arced high against the gray dawn sky, their paths traced by Vietnamese spotters who had seen too many artillery shells to count. But these were different. When they burst, they didn't tear the earth with simple high explosive force. Instead, they split open like deadly seed pods, releasing thousands of iron darts that filled the air with a sound like angry wasps.

The first Vietnamese soldiers died before they could understand what was happening, their bodies pierced by dozens of needle-sharp flechettes that turned flesh to ruins.

"Get down, get down," Lieutenant Minh screamed, but his words were lost in the whistle of iron rain. The darts found soldiers in their foxholes, found them behind trees, found them in places normal shrapnel could never reach. A young private tried to run, his body jerking like a puppet as multiple flechettes struck him. He fell still clutching his rifle, blood seeping into earth.

The Chinese gunners had found their range now, walking their fire across Vietnamese positions with mechanical precision. Each burst sent another cloud of darts searching for flesh, turning the morning air into a killing field that reached into every crack and crevice.

Medics couldn't reach the wounded without becoming targets themselves. The lucky ones died quickly. The others lay crying for mothers who couldn't hear them while more rounds came, more darts fell, more soldiers learned why some weapons earned special fear.

When the barrage finally lifted, the survivors emerged to find their positions littered with small metal darts, each one perfectly machined, each one designed to do exactly what it had done. They collected them like grim souvenirs, these new messengers of death that had turned their trenches into abattoirs.

Lieutenant Minh stood among his dead, face carved from stone, knowing the next dawn would bring more of the same, knowing some weapons changed not just bodies but souls.

South of the border more Vietnamese planes took off from forward airfields and climbed like circling vultures.

Through thickening smoke Chen watched his men fall in neat rows but more came, always more, crashing against the Vietnamese positions in human waves.

A fuel depot died in a mushroom cloud that shook the earth. Mortar and artillery rounds cooked off in a random series of explosions each lighting up the sky.

The border had become a wall of smoke threaded with tracers and shrapnel. "Sir," his radioman's voice tightened with awe, "it's like this everywhere. They're fighting and dying, but they won't run." Another wave of his men moved forward into the maelstrom.

The Vietnamese had learned from their American war how to dig deep, how to survive beneath the earth. Helicopters burst like paper lanterns, their crews tumbling into the inferno below.

Chen lit a cigarette and watched his plan unfold. Let

them die bravely in their trenches. Dead men couldn't hold Cambodia. His army flowed forward in endless waves while the Vietnamese extracted payment for every foot of ground. The morning turned black with smoke and burning fuel and the ash of men. Through smeared lenses Chen watched the battle devour flesh and steel, knowing somewhere a Vietnamese commander was counting the same costs. Soon Hanoi would understand the price of defiance, would learn the cost of forgetting China's strength. This dawn would live in nightmares, but Chen knew empire wrote history in blood and fire, and this was merely the opening line.

Above the mountains steel dragons twisted through clouds thick as history, MiGs wheeling and diving while their Vietnamese pilots carried generations of war in their blood.

Lieutenant Minh watched the Chinese fighters come in high and arrogant, like young hawks who'd never tasted another predator's claws. Banking his aircraft through killing space, he spoke soft to his weapons officer Tran, whose hands moved over switches with a surgeon's grace. "These boys think war is simple," he said, "think the sky belongs to them. Let's teach them what Vietnamese airspace costs."

The first Chinese fighter died screaming metal and flame, its pilot's last words cut short by fire. More came, always more, China's endless abundance made solid in aircraft and missiles.

In the lead Chinese fighter Captain Nong watched his wingman die and spoke sharp into his radio. "Maintain formation, maintain discipline," he barked, "these Vietnamese are not farmers with rifles, they are

sky-killers, old wolves who've hunted for decades."
Anti-aircraft fire stitched black patterns through the clouds over Vietnam. Another Chinese fighter spiraled down trailing smoke like a comet's tail, its crew cursing their ancestors for birthing them to such a death.

Minh's fighter slipped through clouds and found angles that existed between moments. "There, Tran, look there." The missiles leaped away like angry ghosts and two more Chinese fighters died, their pilots having just enough time to understand that experience outweighs numbers.

A Vietnamese MiG exploded high and bright, its pilot's last words coming calm across the radio: "Brothers, I go to our fathers but I take three of them with me."

In his cockpit Chinese pilot Nong watched fire blossom where men died, watched these Vietnamese move their aircraft like they were born in sky's womb. "Command this is Thunder Six, we're losing angels, losing birds. These bastards know things about air war we've never dreamed."

Through clouds thick with burning fuel Minh found gaps between death's fingers that led to Chinese throats. "They come too direct, too obvious," he told Tran. "They haven't learned that the sky has curves, has shadows, has places to hide death in its beauty." More missiles birthed brief suns where men died.

Over the radio a Vietnamese pilot's voice came tight with fury: "For every ancestor who bled defending our sky." His fighter cut through a Chinese formation and left burning metal in his wake.

Nong watched another wing dissolve into flame and smoke. "Command requesting permission to withdraw," he called, "We're dying up here."

Minh allowed himself a small smile as the Chinese fighters turned north, streaming survivors like blood drops in their wake. The clouds swallowed burning metal and dying screams. Somewhere north Chinese generals counted losses and wondered how farmers had learned to kill their golden sons so easily in the high blue spaces above revolution's bones.

"Sir, they'll send more tomorrow," Tran said softly, touching panels that had delivered death. "Always more." Minh banked his fighter toward home through air still sharp with burning fuel. "Then tomorrow we teach more of them how Vietnamese metal tastes," he said, "how our sky has teeth."

The mountains watched metal dragons wheel above their peaks while fire blossomed in cloud banks. The sky told its stories in falling fire and broken wings and the long slow spiral of burning metal seeking earth's embrace.

Through smoke and rain Tuan saw the RPG team die. The Chinese mortar rounds bracketed their position five rounds walking in precise as math. The fire team never had a chance to run. When the smoke cleared Nguyen and Phuc lay scattered across their fighting hole. The RPG tube lay intact between them still loaded. Tuan watched the blood mix with rainwater and run in red streams toward the low ground.

The tank came through drifting smoke forty meters north its treads churning mud black as oil. The steel beast ground forward like something ancient and blind. More tanks followed, but this one led the column; its commander upright in the hatch sweeping the ground with binoculars. Behind them Chinese infantry advanced in squads their weapons at high port.

Tuan looked back at his own trench saw Sergeant Bao motioning him forward. The RPG position had to be manned. Had to be. He went flat crawled through the mud while bullets cracked overhead. The wet earth felt cold against his chest. He kept his rifle close tried not to think about the remains of his friends as he crawled through their position.

The RPG tube felt heavy against his shoulder, unfamiliar. One rocket left. The sights were wet with rain and something else. He wiped them clean checked the back blast area while the tank ground closer. His hands shook but steadied when he pressed them hard against the metal. Nguyen had spent three hours teaching him how to use the weapon but seeing was different from doing.

Chinese infantry advanced behind their steel shield moving in broken rushes through the rain. A machine gun opened up from their lines bullets kicking dirt around him snapping past close enough to feel the displacement of air. Tuan forced his breath steady remembered Nguyen's training. Wait for the side armor, wait for the treads. No room for error no second chance. The tank filled his world now massive and metal and moving with mechanical precision.

The tank commander stayed upright in his hatch confident in his armor. Tuan could see the man's throat where the collar gaped, see him speaking into his radio, see the curve of his helmet against the gray sky. Could have killed him with a rifle shot, but the tank would still live. He waited– let them come. Twenty meters now. Fifteen. The treads threw mud in wet arcs each revolution bringing death closer.

Chinese infantry reached the first trench line found it empty. Their shouts carried sharp through the rain sound of men who thought they had won something. The tank turned to cover their advance steel treads grinding earth. Perfect. The side armor lay flat to Tuan's position. He raised the RPG tucked it tight against his shoulder just as Nguyen had taught him. The sights settled on a spot just above the road wheels where the armor ran thinnest.

He breathed out squeezed the trigger. The back blast kicked dirt loose around him burned hot against his neck. The rocket left a smoke trail through the rain. Time slowed. He watched the round track straight and true strike exactly where he aimed. The explosion came white and hot metal screaming against metal. The tank shuddered threw a tread. Black smoke poured from the engine compartment thick and oily.

The crew bailed fast through the hatches like rats abandoning a ship. Tuan's rifle came up smooth as silk. The first round took the commander in the chest. The driver caught one in the throat as he emerged. The gunner made it three steps before Tuan's bullet found him. They fell like broken dolls their blood black against the mud. The tank burned beside them storm wind driving the smoke north. Chinese infantry pulled back from the flames their confidence broken by burning steel.

Tuan reloaded his rifle settled deeper in the fighting hole. Through the rain he heard Sergeant Bao's voice calling targets. Other tanks ground forward through the smoke, but they came slower now more cautious. The morning gathered darkness while he lay in the mud among his dead friends and killed whoever came too close. Each shot he took each man he killed was for Nguyen and Phuc who had died teaching him how to destroy steel monsters. He worked his rifle's action smooth and clean and waited for whatever came next.

Through the wet morning air Lieutenant Dao watched Chinese soldiers come in waves across the hills, their tanks moving among them like metal islands. He spoke quietly to his men who huddled in their bunkers, hands steady on weapons that had known other wars. "Today we teach them what Vietnamese earth costs," he said, "how their numbers mean nothing against our experience."

The advancing Chinese platoon died in sheets of machine gun fire, their young faces surprised at how death felt as their bodies folded like empty clothes. More came, China's endless sons fed into war's hunger.

Captain Wu watched his men fall and shouted into his radio, throat raw with fury. "They're dug in deep," he screamed, "got positions we can't see, killing zones that overlap like spiderwebs." His radioman took a round through the throat, blood spraying across Wu's face like warm rain.

Vietnamese artillery opened then, precise as butcher's knives, finding paths between Chinese guns, finding soldiers who thought steel helmets could stop mountain rage.

Dao touched his sergeant's shoulder and pointed to where Chinese troops bunched too tight. "There old friend," he said, "there's your father's revenge." The mortar rounds fell and shredded young men who'd never learned that courage alone means nothing against experience.

A Chinese soldier no older than Dao's son cried for his mother as he tried holding his insides in place. His lieutenant lasted longer, enough to see three more waves of his men die before a sniper's round opened his thoughts to morning air.

Still they came, the sons of China, the boys who thought war was numbers and youth and destiny. Dao's men killed with the precision of craftsmen who'd learned their trade in American fire. "See how they bunch," he said, "see how they move without reading the land, see how they die like wheat before scythes."

A Chinese tank died screaming metal, its crew cooked inside by RPG rounds, its death drawing more soldiers into killing spaces. Wu watched his platoon dissolve into red mist. "Command," he gasped, "they kill from angles that don't exist."

More artillery, more tanks, more men came as Chinese reinforcements arrived. The hills dissolved into smoke and flame and flying meat. Private Huynh, nineteen years old last week, watched his friends die and screamed into radio static. "How can farmers fight like this? How can peasants kill us so easy? We are China's mighty army, we are—" The bullet took his words, his life, his future all at once.

Dao moved through trenches touching shoulders, offering calm words to men who dealt death like merchants selling old wares. "They'll keep coming," he said, "but each wave gets smaller, each attack costs them more, each death teaches lessons their generals need to learn."

Wu felt his arm go numb and looked surprised at the sleeve turned red. "Command," he whispered, "we're not fighting farmers. We're fighting ghosts who've burned their humanity away in American napalm, who've—" The bullet finished his thoughts, sprayed them across dirt that had seen three armies die.

Through smoke and flame Dao counted ammunition, checked weapons, spoke soft to men who'd learned war from fathers who'd learned it from grandfathers who'd carved resistance into mountain stone. The hills watched and told their stories in spent brass and broken iron and the long slow seeping of young blood into old soil.

Through smoke thick as history Colonel Hien watched his lines crumble, men dying in waves as ammunition ran low against China's endless army. "Sir, we're down to our last belts," his radioman whispered, voice raw from twelve hours of screaming coordinates.

In the forward trenches young Giang fed his last rounds into his machine gun, its barrel smoking from a day's worth of killing. "They die and die but still they come," he said, "like ants crossing water on their own dead."

Through mud and cordite smoke Liu moved behind the advancing line his medical bag slapping against his hip. The canvas had gone dark with blood where others had grabbed it with desperate hands. Two men down fifty meters ahead. The call had come urgent across the radio spitting static and fear. Shrapnel or punji stakes they weren't sure. He ran in short bursts between shell holes while bullets cracked overhead.

"Doc here. Coming up" he shouted. A machine gun opened up somewhere north. The rounds passed high with that angry wasp sound. The radio squawked again. More casualties third platoon. He kept moving.

The first casualty lay curled around his gut blood pumping between his fingers. Private Chen new to the unit still had peach fuzz on his cheeks. The boy's eyes went wide when he saw Liu. "Bad?" he asked. Liu didn't answer just worked fast cutting away the uniform. The shrapnel had opened him low and deep. No exit wound. Bad. He pushed morphine into the boy's thigh packed the wound tight with gauze.

"Hold here," he told the squad leader showing him where to press. "Keep pressure. When the bleeding slows get him back to the aid station." He checked Chen's eyes. "Stay awake, Private. That's an order." The boy nodded, but his skin had gone gray as the sky.

The second man had caught it in the legs. Punji stakes driven up through his boots into the muscle. The wooden shafts still protruded dark with blood and something else. Poison. Liu had seen what these wounds did if not treated fast. He started cutting away the boots while the man screamed.

"Hold him," Liu told the others. They pressed the soldier down into the mud. The first stake came out with a wet sound. Liu poured antiseptic into the wound but knew it wouldn't be enough. These people had learned about poison from their grandmothers had learned how to make even small wounds speak with death's tongue.

"How bad, Doc?" the squad leader asked. His voice carried the fear they all felt. These weren't wounds they'd trained for weren't injuries that made sense.

"Get him back fast. Tell Lieutenant Wu what happened. He'll know what to do." Liu didn't mention the discoloration already spreading up the man's calf. Some truths were better left unspoken.

More calls came across the radio. More men down. The Vietnamese had salted the ground with these traps; laid them precise as a doctor's incisions. Liu found himself running again through smoke and mud while the battle moved forward without him. Each position he reached held broken men. Some screamed. Some didn't. He worked methodical as he could. Cut. Clean. Bandage. Morphine when he had it. The wounds kept coming. Shrapnel. Bullets. Spears from the earth itself.

"We're running low" his assistant Zhang said holding up their last bag of plasma. "Aid station says they're getting overrun with casualties." They knelt beside a soldier whose chest rose and fell in a way that meant death was already walking beside him.

The medevac chopper couldn't land too much incoming fire. Liu got the men on stretchers marked their foreheads with morphine doses in his own blood. His hands had stopped shaking hours ago. Thunder walked across the sky as artillery opened up. He kept working. Some he could save. Some he couldn't. A bullet cracked past close enough to feel. He didn't flinch. Just reached for another pressure bandage.

"Doc" Chen called weak from his stretcher. "Tell my mother—"

"Tell her yourself, Private. That's why I used all my good thread on you." Liu checked the dressing. The bleeding had slowed. Maybe this one would live. Maybe.

Through mud and rain and growing darkness Liu moved among the wounded. The blood soaked black into the earth. More calls came. More men fell. The day gathered shadows while he knelt in the muck and tried to hold steel-torn bodies together with thread and gauze and whatever faith he had left.

The Chinese tanks rolled forward now, crushing their own fallen, using dead men to fill trenches Vietnamese guns had turned to graves.

Major Wong stood in his command vehicle and watched his men finally break through. "Forward, forward sons of China," he shouted, "show them what empire means, show them the price of defiance."

The Vietnamese lines fractured then broke, soldiers falling back in twos and threes, carrying their wounded when they could, leaving their dead to become part of earth's own hunger.

"We can't hold," Colonel Hien's sergeant major reported, blood sheeting down his face. "These old eyes have never seen such numbers." A Chinese shell found their command bunker and blew the old soldier into red mist and burning memory.

Through black mud the Chinese tank sat canted; starboard track sunk deep past the road wheels. Inside the steel hull Tang wiped sweat from his eyes checked the engine gauges again. Red across the board. Bad. The number two fuel pump had seized throwing the drive shaft out of true. Metal and hydraulics screamed warnings at him. In the gunner's seat Manh ran diagnostics on the main gun its servo motors whining as he worked the controls.

"Try it again," Tang called down to Chen in the driver's compartment. "One more time, easy on the clutch." The starter ground three times then died with a sound like metal drowning. The batteries were going. They'd been stuck six hours now while artillery walked across the hills north where the rest of the battalion pushed toward Hanoi. Through the vision blocks Tang watched tree lines for movement. Vietnamese infantry had been probing their lines all day hitting then falling back into jungle shadows.

Manh slapped the gun breech in frustration.

"Stabilizer's shot completely fucked. Can't traverse more than twenty degrees." He grabbed the manual crank tried to force it. Metal screamed against metal. "We're a bunker now. A stuck bunker full of men waiting to die."

"Shut up about dying," Tang said. The inside of the tank stank of fear and sweat and hydraulic fluid.

Chen climbed up from the driver's hole leaving muddy handprints on the steel. "Track's wrapped around the road wheel bad. Need to break it loose get a jack under there." None of them wanted to go outside. They'd seen what happened to exposed crews. Had watched Vietnamese snipers work from the trees. Had counted the bodies.

The radio crackled. Third platoon had run into heavy resistance two kilometers ahead. The sound of combat carried clear through morning air. Tank guns and heavy machine guns. Their friends dying while they sat useless in the mud. "Taking casualties need support," the radio spat. Tang wanted to smash it.

"No choice," Tang said. "We go out, we fix it, we get back in. Fast and clean." They gathered tools grabbed their rifles checked their loads. Tang went first scanning the trees while Manh and Chen attacked the thrown track with steel bars. The mud came up past their boots thick as clay stuck to everything. They worked fast as they could, but the track had bound tight required muscle and curse words to break loose.

"Almost got it," Chen said. Then a bullet cracked past, sparked off the turret inches from his head. They dove for cover, pressed themselves against the tank's hull. More shots came precise and ranging walking closer. Tang saw the sniper's position a glint of scope glass in the treeline. He put three rounds into the shadows. The firing stopped but that meant nothing. They kept working. What else could they do.

"Jack's slipping," Manh shouted. His hands shook as he tried to steady it. "Need more foundation." Chen grabbed steel plates from their kit started laying them under the jack's base. Each movement exposed him to fire. Tang gave him cover, watched the trees. The radio kept spitting reports of combat moving further north. Their company hitting serious resistance.

"Got it," Chen called. The jack bit steel teeth into the plates started lifting. The tank rose slow and indifferent to their fear. Manh muscled the track links with a pry bar while sweat ran down his back soaked his uniform. A mortar round burst fifty meters out showered them with dirt. They didn't stop working. Through the mud they worked while death watched from the trees and their friends fought without them.

"Almost there," Manh said. His arms trembled with effort. "Another meter of track." The sun climbed higher, burned away the morning mist. Made them better targets. Tang heard movement in the brush, couldn't tell where. They were exposed vulnerable. Prey. But the tank was everything. Without it they were just three men with rifles in enemy territory. With it they were steel and fire and something the Vietnamese had to fear.

The track came free suddenly almost knocked Manh down. They muscled it back onto the road wheels. Chen started tightening the links while Tang gave him cover. More shots came from a new position. They worked faster. The radio kept calling for support they couldn't give. Through morning heat they fought mud and metal and fear while somewhere in the trees death waited patient as stone.

Through his scope Lieutenant Wang watched the Vietnamese retreat, his young face split with fierce joy. "Look how they run," he laughed, " these legends, these teachers of war's wisdom. Now they learn what it means to face China's strength." His men cheered and fired victory shots into the smoke-dark sky even as their dead lay cooling in mud turned iron-hard with blood.

Colonel Hien moved among his retreating men, touching shoulders, offering what courage retreat allows. "We fall back, brothers," he said quietly, "we regroup, we remember this day, we teach our sons what it means to face dragons." The Chinese advance rolled on unstoppable now, young soldiers racing forward through fields their brothers had died taking hours before. "For China, for glory, for empire," they shouted, their voices high with victory's wine. "On to Hanoi!"

A Vietnamese machine gunner waited till they came close, spent his last belt and cut down sixteen before a tank round ended his argument. "See you in Hell," he whispered as flames took him.

Major Wong watched his men secure ground that had cost 10,000 lives to take. "Tell command the Vietnamese are falling back," he ordered, "breaking, running like water from a broken jar. Victory is ours."

In the rear the Vietnamese column moved south through jungle shadows, their faces set hard as stone, their weapons held ready. An old sergeant spat and spoke quiet to men who'd survived by learning war's deepest truths. "They think this is victory, think numbers alone make empire, think we're beaten because we retreat." His laugh came bitter as venom. "Let them learn what Vietnamese earth costs, how retreat doesn't mean defeat."

Colonel Hien listened to Chinese victory cries fade behind them and spoke soft to troops who carried generations' worth of war in their bones. "Today they win, tomorrow they count their dead, next week they learn why no army holds Vietnam's ground for long. We carry something they've never learned, something Americans, French, Japanese all learned too late."

The jungle wrapped them in green shadow while behind them Chinese troops planted flags in foreign soil and sang victory songs.

Major Wong stood on captured ground and watched night come on like judgment. "Sir," an aide reported, voice trembling, "10,000 dead to take five miles." The major nodded and lit a cigarette against darkness rising like ghosts from Vietnamese earth. "Send word to command," he said. "Vietnam bleeds, but China bleeds more. History remembers only victory, not its cost."

Through night thick with burning fuel and black smoke Colonel Hien led his men south, speaking calm words to warriors who knew retreat was not surrender. The jungle told its stories in spent brass and cooling flesh and the long slow whisper of Vietnam's endless patience.

Raiders

Through twilight thick with woodsmoke Granier and Spitting Woman approached their village. The bodies of the dead Chinese soldiers were gone, burned in a bonfire that turn flesh and uniform to ash. A clear path was marked through the boobytraps. Torchlight painted the village walls amber flickering across sharpened wooden stakes that crowned the palisades. From the nearest watchtower firelight caught the steel of a captured Chinese rifle.

"Stand where you are!" an old man's voice called from above. "Let the torch show you."

They stopped. The evening wind carried cook-fire smoke from the village, carried children's voices, carried the sound of women singing old songs while they worked. Granier kept his hands away from his weapon. Spitting Woman stood beside him straight as mountain stone.

"Who comes to our gates with night falling?" Another voice older female harder. Through torch glow they could see her leveling a Chinese rifle.

"Your hands taught me to weave palm leaves, Grandmother," Spitting Woman called. "You said my fingers were too impatient. Said I would never learn the patience baskets need."

A pause. Torch flame danced catching gray hair above. "And did you learn patience, daughter?"

"I learned. But it took time," said Spitting Woman.

"Good things usually do."

Movement along the palisades. More torches showed faces lined with age, showed women who had learned to carry rifles instead of water jugs, showed what village became when war took its young men.

"The man beside you stands quiet," the old woman said. "In times like these quiet men make us nervous."

"I cleaned your grandson's cuts when he fell from the jackfruit tree," Granier said. "Three stitches in his arm. He didn't cry."

"He cries now," she answered. "Somewhere north wearing army green. If he still lives." She turned called down to the gate guards. "Let them in. These two are ours."

The gates opened slow still swollen from recent repair. Two old men stood guard with captured rifles. Behind them teenage girls carried torches their free hands holding sharpened bamboo spears. They had tied their hair back like warriors.

"Teacher," one girl said. Her voice caught broke steadied. "We heard stories. They said you hunted the Chinese who escaped. Said you followed them three days through the mountains."

"Stories matter less than standing guard," Spitting Woman answered. "Your eyes should be on the dark not on us."

The girl straightened. Pride came into her stance.

The spear in her hand looked less like borrowed weight more like something she had earned the right to carry.

Above the watchtower guards resumed their vigil while behind the walls village life moved with the strange rhythms war had taught it. No young men's laughter came through torchlight. No sons called to fathers through the gathering dark. But the village endured. The village had learned to bare different teeth against the night.

Once inside the gates, Granier and Spitting Woman found the village transformed, swollen with newcomers - refugees, warriors, families who'd heard how Chinese soldiers learned to die in these hills. Grandfather Vu met them near the gate, his face carved deep with knowing. "They come from three valleys away," he said, "come to learn your wisdom, come to fight beneath your flag, Frenchman."

The village square had become an arsenal, captured Chinese weapons stacked like firewood, ammunition sorted by caliber by girls who last week had only sorted rice. Through firelight Spitting Woman counted faces, counted weapons, counted hope rising into the darkening sky. "Too many mouths to feed," she whispered in French, "these walls cannot hold so many souls."

But Granier watched old men training with spears and teaching young women to load rifles and shoot. "These are our strength now," he said, "these determined desperate people."

A village headman approached and spoke softly about numbers, about fighting age men, about ancient alliances renewed in modern blood. "We have four hundred who can hold weapons," he said, "who can die standing and make Chinese soldiers count their victories in corpses."

Spitting Woman touched the rifle at her shoulder, remembering the army they'd seen gathering north like storm clouds, like destiny itself given flesh. *Even 1,000 men*, she thought, *even ten thousand would break like waves against such steel, such numbers, such terrible purpose.*

They met in the temple while night gathered thick as regret. Granier spread his maps and spoke truth hard as bullets. "They come in force," he said, "come with armor, with artillery, with numbers beyond counting." The village leaders listened, faces gone sharp with understanding that some fights cannot be won, only survived.

"We fight anyway," said an old man who'd fought French, Japanese, and American armies in these hills. "We fight because running means forgetting who we are."

"Our first priority should be to repair and finish the palisades," said Granier.

They planned through darkness, positioned defenses, arranged fallback points, knowing all such planning was smoke, all such preparation ash against what gathered north like judgment. But they planned anyway because planning is what men do when facing death, because preparation is how warriors greet their ending.

Dawn found them still planning, still counting ammunition, still measuring ground that would soon drink deep. Spitting Woman watched their faces lit by lamplight, watched hope wrestle fear, watched determination burn bright as morning. "They will come," she said in her dialect, then French, then Vietnamese so all would understand. "They will come with fire, with steel, with empire's endless hunger. But we will show them these hills have teeth."

The village stirred around them like a beast waking. They would fight because fighting was memory, was wisdom, was the price of being Vietnamese. They would fight knowing victory was impossible, knowing survival was unlikely, knowing only that some battles must be fought so future generations would remember how to stand, how to die, how to make invaders count their victories in blood and bone and burning hope. Dawn came red as prophecy, and they prepared for war, prepared for death, prepared for whatever history had written in its book of fire and steel and endless human courage.

They counted captured weapons like misers counting gold, spreading them across temple floors. Chinese rifles lay still warm from their last owners' hands, ammunition pulled from cold fingers, grenades that promised swift answers to empire's questions. "Not enough," Granier whispered, watching militia men handle modern steel with reverence and hunger, understanding that weapons meant survival.

As the sun rose, the villagers worked the wooden poles rising like spears against grey sky their hands moving with the surety of those who had built such walls before. The sun caught sweat on bare backs turned it to copper while men fitted posts into holes deep as a man's height tamped earth around them with wooden mallets wrapped tight with cloth to muffle sound.

Old Hai directed the work his voice carrying quiet as moving water. "Deeper here," he said touching earth. "The Chinese found weakness where we struck stone. This time we dig until we find soil that will hold."

The women moved in lines passing up fresh-cut wood their feet silent in mud their arms straining against the weight of poles thick as a man's thigh.

Xinh worked beside her husband her child sleeping against her back while she tamped earth around the posts. "They will come again," she said. Not a question but a truth.

"Let them come," her husband answered. His hands bled from stripping bark, but he worked without pause. "These walls will stand and our people will hold the Chinese back like we did the first time."

The poles rose higher three men's height now with sharpened ends that would teach soldiers about gravity's cruel hands. They wove smaller poles between the uprights creating lattice strong enough to turn bullets meant to break weaker things.

Granier moved among them checking angles checking strength checking everything that made walls more than mere wood. "The weave must be tight," he said. "Bullets find small gaps like water finds a stone's weakness."

Spitting Woman worked beside him her hands teaching younger ones how to tie knots that would hold against more than simple wind. "Like this," she said. "The bark strips must bite deep into wood. Must become one thing not two."

The wall grew higher while the sun overhead watched while they rebuilt what war had broken what pride had shattered what necessity demanded be stronger than before. When evening came the new wall stood straight as judgment.

"It will hold," old Hai said touching poles that had become more than simple wood. The others nodded their faces streaked with mud and pride.

The wall stood patient as mountain stone its shadow reaching toward whatever waited beyond horizon where empire gathered its strength for next testing of what village folk could build in one night's desperate labor.

Standing in her rice paddy, the mud ran cold between Mai's toes while mountain wind pressed her shirt against her back. She worked the rows alone checking each rice shoot with fingers that remembered his touch. She pulled weeds that would steal water from their crop dropped them in her basket moved to the next plant with the patience of women who had learned to wait for men to come home.

The sun rose higher turned her shadow short against water gone mirror bright. Their footprints from that last morning had faded, but she could still feel where they had walked together still see where he had lifted her still know every place that held memory like earth holds rain. She worked steady and sure letting her hands speak love's language to each green shoot.

A bird called from the mountains. She remembered how Tuan could name them all, could tell by their sound what weather came, what season turned, what promises the sky held. Now she listened with ears that had learned deeper things. Listened for boots on paths for gunfire for everything that marked how war wrote its name across quiet days.

The weeds came loose in her hands their roots pale as bone. She worked them free gentle as pulling threads from silk. Each plant needed the right touch. Too rough and the rice would tear loose too gentle and the weeds would stay. She had learned this from his mother had learned how rice grew stronger from proper tending.

When the basket grew heavy she carried it to the paddy's edge emptied it began again. The sun marked time across sky while she moved through water that knew her feet that held sky's reflection that carried everything worth keeping. Sometimes her fingers found the empty space at her throat where the jade pendant had hung. Sometimes they found tears on her cheeks. She wiped them away kept working kept tending kept faith with earth and man and whatever gods watched women wait.

Through afternoon she worked through heat through wind through everything that tried to take their crop. Each shoot held promise each root held memory each row held straight as the path he would walk home. The mountains watched while Mai kept their rice alive while war wrote its name in mud and blood and the spaces between heartbeats.

Through twilight the engine noise came wrong. Foreign sounds that didn't belong to these hills where even birds spoke careful. The old woman's captured Chinese rifle sighted down toward road curve.

"Trucks coming. North road." Her voice carried tight. Below women grabbed children pulled them inside while teenage girls took positions with their spears behind the sharpened stakes. "Three trucks maybe four."

The sound echoed off valley walls engine noise grinding against mountain roads. More torches bloomed along the walls steel winking in firelight.

"Could be traders bringing food to market," an old man said, but his rifle stayed ready where the road emerged from shadow.

"Could be Chinese," another answered. "Could be they've learned our weakness. Lost our young men to army draft. Left us with old ones, women, and children."

The engines grew louder. Through evening haze shapes resolved. Green trucks moving slow on broken road their headlights cut against growing dark.

"Vietnamese army markings," the old woman called. "But Chinese could have captured their trucks. Could have learned our paint. Hold your fire but keep them in your sights."

The lead truck stopped thirty yards from gate. A soldier stood in back uniform crisp voice carrying sharp across twilight. "Open in the name of the People's Army."

"Show us your papers," the old woman called. "Show us slow and clear in torch light. War has taught us to trust nothing that comes after dark."

Papers passed forward caught fire glow. More trucks appeared behind the first their engines grumbling like restless beasts. The guards kept their rifles ready kept everything war had taught them about why some welcomes must come slow as mountains trusting spring rain.

The gates opened, but the captured rifles stayed leveled, stayed ready, stayed remembering why even army trucks might carry death's own shadow until the last doubt burns away.

Colonel Nguyen himself stepped down, his boots touching earth like a priest entering sacred ground. "News travels fast in these mountains," he said, watching his men unload crates heavy with war's promise. "Even Hanoi's generals speak of the village that broke Chinese teeth." His smile came sharp as shattered bone. "We bring gifts - iron rice, steel fortune, bullets blessed by bureaucrats who understand that some victories must be fed."

The crates yielded their secrets - AK-47s cleaned and oiled, hungry for purpose, RPGs that promised arguments with armor, ammunition that spoke of Hanoi's deep understanding. "This is not charity," the colonel said, watching villagers handle weapons with careful reverence. "This is investment. This is wisdom. This is knowing that some ground must hold, some lines must not break."

Granier and Spitting Woman helped distribute steel fortune, watching farmers become soldiers, old men remember skills learned in American war, women handle deadly gifts with mothers' care. "More than weapons," the colonel said quietly, for their ears alone. "We bring warning. China gathers and moves its forces eastward."

Spitting Woman touched new rifles, watched men learn their voices. "We know," she said. "We've seen, we've counted, we've measured empire's hunger with our own eyes."

The colonel nodded and lit a cigarette against morning cold. "Then you understand that these gifts, these tools, these promises written in gunmetal and brass may mean nothing against what comes. May buy only time, only blood, only expensive dying."

"Yes," Granier said, "but dying expensive is all we have left, all we can offer, all history asks of us now."

The village stirred around them like a beast waking. The weapons found hands, found purpose, found their place in a story old as invasion. They counted their new strength, measured it against what gathered north, knew it was not enough, knew it could never be enough.

"Frenchman," said the colonel. "If I may have a word in private?"

Granier nodded and moved off toward a storage hut, Spitting Woman and the colonel following him.

Through candlelight that made shadows dance like dying things Colonel Nguyen laid the maps across the temple floor. His fingers traced lines where Chinese armor had broken through where Vietnamese forces bled into earth.

"Le Duan sends his respect," he said in French then switched to English. "And his gratitude for what you did here. For holding the village." His eyes swept the room found captured Chinese weapons stacked like firewood. "But gratitude won't stop what comes next. Their armor moves south. Three hundred thousand men. Two hundred tanks. They mean to take Hanoi."

"We can't let that happen," said Spitting Woman.

"If they overrun Hanoi, it'll be close to impossible to eject them from the North, even after reinforcements arrive," said Granier.

Colonel Nguyen spoke words heavy as artillery shells. "Le Duan remembers your work with CIA," he said, watching Granier's face for echoes of old wars. "Remembers how you turned the Ho Chi Minh Trail against itself, how you wrote strategy in fire and hunger. Sherman broke the Confederacy's spine by cutting its supply lines, by making Georgia howl. Now we need such songs written behind the Chinese frontlines."

Granier's hands moved across the maps reading terrain like reading fortune. "These valleys. These passes. Their supply lines will stretch thin as patience."

Spitting Woman watched the colonel's hands spread more maps showing supply routes showing ammunition dumps showing everything empire needed to feed its war machine.

"Choose your men," Nguyen said. "Anyone you want. Le Duan gives you full authority. Choose your weapons too." He touched a crate they hadn't noticed before. Inside two American sniper rifles lay in green cloth. "M40A1s. For those shots that must not miss."

"The village," Spitting Woman said. Not a question but a demand hard as mountain stone.

"One thousand land mines." The colonel's voice carried certainty. "Enough to make Chinese commanders think twice about the value of such a village and the sacrifice needed to take it."

Granier touched the rifles checked their actions found them clean as sin, fresh as judgment. "When?"

"Tomorrow night. The trucks will be waiting along with the men you select. Everything waits except time." Nguyen's eyes caught candlelight. "Le Duan offers Vietnamese citizenship when this ends. Legal status. A future without shadows."

"If we live," Spitting Woman said.

"If any of us live," the colonel answered.

They stood in temple dark, while candles burned, while maps showed China's iron rivers flowing south, while somewhere Chinese commanders counted tanks instead of counting cost. The choice lay between them like a blade wanting blood.

Granier's hands moved against each other like fighting snakes, his mind already reading maps, already seeing paths, already measuring distances between victory and annihilation. "Let us speak alone," Granier said to Spitting Woman in her dialect, so Nguyen wouldn't understand completely.

They found privacy behind the temple where incense still burned, where their feet had worn paths deep checking defenses. "If we go they die," she said, simple as blade against throat.

"If we stay they die anyway," he answered, watching smoke rise like souls seeking Heaven. "The colonel speaks truth. Cut their supplies, make them hungry, make them spread thin searching for new routes."

"Our people," she whispered, "the children, the old ones - who will protect them, who will teach them how to die standing?"

"Better they live because China's army withers than die because we stayed to hold their hands through dying."

Her laugh came bitter as snake venom. "You think like tactician, like strategist, like a man who has learned war's deepest truth. Sometimes dying beside your people is not the best way to save them."

They found Nguyen waiting patient as mountain stone, smoking cigarettes that burned like tiny signals in growing dark. "We accept," Granier said, "but we choose my team, choose our paths, choose our targets."

"Agreed," said the colonel.

Through night thick with portent they chose their team. Not the young proud ones eager for glory, but the quiet ones, the scarred ones, men with eyes that had seen too much and hands that never shook. The ones who moved like smoke, who killed like thinking about killing, who understood that some victories come silent and wrapped in shadows.

By dawn they had thirty ghosts assembled in temple

square, their weapons clean, their eyes calm, their souls already measured against whatever waited in northern shadows. "Le Duan says if you succeed," Nguyen said, watching them form like mist into deadly purpose, "he offers citizenship, legal status, future without shadows."

Granier smiled thin as knife edge. "If we don't succeed there may be no Vietnam left to offer citizenship. But they'll remember why empires fear these mountains."

The dossiers lay spread across the wooden table like tarot cards promising death. Granier moved each photograph with precise fingers, studying faces that had seen too much war. Afternoon light filtered through bamboo walls, casting bars of shadow across intelligence reports and combat histories. Spitting Woman stood behind his shoulder, her breath making the papers shift when she leaned closer.

They worked in silence, the way they had done in three wars, sorting the living from the soon dead. The first candidate's file showed a man with winter in his eyes - former Viet Minh sniper, eight confirmed kills against Chinese patrols along the northern border. Spitting Woman tapped the photograph. "His hands are good. No tremors," she spoke in French, testing the words. "But he drinks. The signs are there in his face."

"Next." Second file - young face, old eyes. Scout from the mountain tribes, specialized in long range reconnaissance. French learned in Catholic school. "Too young to be so quiet," Spitting Woman shook her head. "Fear makes him careful. Fear will get others killed."

The afternoon wore on. They sorted men's lives into yes, no, maybe, creating piles of fate with bureaucratic precision. This one too eager, that one too hesitant, a third too much like soldiers they'd seen die in forgotten jungles. Some they rejected for physical reasons - hands too unsteady, eyes too worn. Others for deeper flaws that only those who had hunted men would recognize.

Combat records meant less than the way they held their rifles in photographs, the set of their shoulders, the shadows in their eyes. A file showed a soldier who had survived three ambushes - good numbers, well-documented kills, medals for valor. "Non," Granier said, "his French is academic, book-learned. Combat French is different. He'll miss the quick words when they matter."

The maybes became nos. The nos became kindling. The few chosen files they set aside had a weight beyond paper. These men had something in their faces that spoke of patience, of silence, of the ability to wait three days in mud to make one shot count. By sunset they had selected thirty from several hundred - thirty who spoke French with the fluency of survival, thirty who had proven they could kill with professional precision, thirty who might live long enough to make their deaths count.

The Vietnamese commander returned as the light failed, studied their selections, nodded once. "Ces hommes mourront bien," he said. These men will die well.

Spitting Woman gathered the chosen files, her fingers lingering on each face. "Some of them will live," she said in French. "The others will make good ghosts."

In the growing dark, Granier and Spitting Woman sat silent among the discarded files, the rejected lives, the men who would live because they had not been chosen. Tomorrow they would meet their thirty, begin to shape them into something beyond soldiers. Tonight they sat with the weight of selection, with the knowledge that they had become death's recruiters, with the certainty that some of the faces spread before them would soon join the legion of ghosts that haunted their dreams.

The trucks sat black against the treeline their canvas covers snapping in the mountain wind. Granier checked his new sniper rifle one final time the metal cold beneath his fingers. Behind him thirty Vietnamese commandos stood silent as stones their weapons clean their eyes fixed on nothing.

Spitting Woman moved among them inspecting each man and his weapon. The air carried wood smoke from the village and something else. Something like iron, like fate.

"We go north to break their spine," Granier spoke in French, his voice carrying the weight of commands that had sent other men to other deaths. "The Chinese army moves like a snake through our mountains, but a snake must eat. We will starve it. We will kill its hunters. We will burn what feeds it."

The men stood immobile, their eyes fixed on middle distance the way soldiers stand when death has become a business transaction. "Make no mistake," Granier continued, his voice cold as mountain streams. "We are not soldiers here. We are saboteurs. The Chinese will give no quarter and we will ask for none. If any man thinks his stomach too weak for this work, step away now. No shame will follow you."

The silence stretched like a knife against throat. No one moved. No one spoke. These were men who had already died in their minds and were now merely waiting to see if their bodies would follow.

Spitting Woman stepped forward, her movements liquid. She spoke in combat French, the dialect of killers and heroes. "Squad leaders to me now," she said. "We need lists. Explosives. Detonators. What you carry is what keeps you alive. Food we find. Water we find. Ammunition we take from the dead."

The squad leaders produced notebooks, wrote with swift precision. She continued, her voice carrying ancient echoes of hill tribes who had fought invaders before gunpowder came. "We destroy everything that feeds their war. Bridges fall. Trains die. Radio towers burn. Supplies become ash."

The men nodded, understanding the mathematics of devastation. These were hunters who had learned to kill from their fathers who had learned from their fathers before guns came to the mountains. A bird called from the jungle's edge as morning mist began to burn away.

Granier watched his killers, his hunters, his chosen thirty, and saw in their eyes the same cold calculation he had seen in mirrors during midnight operations in forgotten wars. They would go north like smoke through forests. They would kill with professional precision. They would become the demons that haunted Chinese dreams.

The squad leaders finished their lists, handed them to Spitting Woman who read each one with eyes that had watched too many men die. She nodded once. "We move at dusk," she said. "When we return these mountains will have new ghosts."

The men stood silent in the growing light, already becoming the shadows they would need to be, already becoming death's quiet servants, already becoming the nightmares that would make Chinese soldiers wake screaming in the dark.

The warriors climbed into the trucks with fluid grace their boots finding purchase on worn metal their bodies arranging themselves with the precision of men who had killed together before. Granier watched them settle, watched them check weapons, watched them become something more than simple fighters. In the driver's seat old Minh who had driven trucks in three wars turned the key and the engine coughed alive. Spitting Woman sat beside Granier their shoulders touching through worn fabric. The convoy moved west through valleys. The warriors swayed with the truck's motion their faces blank. The moon rose huge and white above peaks that had seen armies come and go like seasons. In the truck bed warriors cleaned weapons by touch alone their hands moving with ceremony's own precision. They had become something older than mere soldiers. The trucks ground west through dark that held no mercy.

The trucks crawled through mountain darkness, their muffled engines and slotted headlights barely illuminating the treacherous road ahead.

Granier sat rigid in the lead vehicle, reading every betrayal in the worn pavement, while beside him Spitting Woman's fingers never strayed far from her rifle. The convoy followed in strict blackout discipline, their Vietnamese drivers muttering curses as wheels found holes in the ancient road.

When they crossed the old bridge it groaned beneath them like a dying beast. The third truck's wheels punched through rotted planking and the vehicle tilted toward the waiting void, but the men inside moved as one, throwing their weight against gravity's pull.

Granier was already moving across the darkness, his boots finding purchase where others would slip, while Spitting Woman materialized on the far side with ropes appearing in her hands like conjured snakes.

They worked the problem with a hunter's patience, testing boards and finding what strength remained in the rotted wood. The team emptied the wounded truck by hand while its driver eased it backward, guided by whispered commands that mixed French and Vietnamese. Metal screamed against splintering wood until finally the truck found solid ground again. The men reloaded in silence, already moving like a single organism. The bridge vanished behind them into darkness.

Granier watched his chosen ones draw closer together, strangers becoming brothers in the shared shadow of death. The mountain road unwound before them black as spilled ink while the trucks ground forward in low gear, their engines protesting every foot gained. Dawn waited hours away, by which time they would be ghosts in the jungle. By then they would know if these men were truly worthy of the task ahead or if they would join the legions of dead already haunting Granier's dreams.

The mountain peaks loomed around them like ancient judges while the roads sought to destroy them with every turn. Somewhere ahead Chinese supply columns wound through valleys that would soon become their graves, while the trucks drove on through darkness.

The trucks sat silent as panthers at the edge of the ruined earth. Even from a kilometer back, the stench reached them - that copper-sweet reek of death mixed with scorched metal and the deep rot that follows when armies tear the world apart. Granier lifted his hand in the pre-dawn gloom and the convoy went dead quiet. They slipped from their vehicles like smoke, boots settling on earth with the practiced silence.

No one spoke. They had rehearsed this dance in darkness until they knew each other's shadows, until they had become something more than mere soldiers. The supplies came off with fluid grace, ammunition distributed according to each man's burden and skill. Ahead lay the battlefield like a mouthful of broken teeth, its edges still flickering with fires that refused to die three days after the last shells fell. That ground belonged to the dead now.

Spitting Woman moved through their ranks, her hands speaking an ancient language as she adjusted their gear. She shifted a low-riding pack with fingers that had prepared for war before its bearer was born, adjusted a rifle sling with a mother's careful touch where a weapon was held too tight against its owner's chest.

Qi materialized from the darkness, speaking in clipped combat French, "Chinese patrol, two kilometers east. Regular pattern. No dogs." Granier nodded. Even the enemy avoided the killing fields. The dead taught lessons that all soldiers learned eventually.

The team flowed into formation like quicksilver

finding its shape. Point men glided forward reading the treacherous ground, while security teams drifted to the flanks. The main body settled into position without a whisper, transformed into the war machine they had trained to become. They would move north through valleys the Chinese overlooked, through shadows no army could hold.

Above them, the battlefield's dying fires painted the clouds the color of old wounds. The team moved out in combat spacing, each step placed with deadly precision. Behind them, the trucks dissolved into the mountain shadows, their drivers wise enough not to linger. Ahead lay the border and beyond it a hundred valleys where Chinese supply columns wound their way through hostile ground.

They had become something ancient, neither army nor guerrilla but hunters. The battlefield smoldered at their backs while the mountains loomed ahead, and somewhere in those peaks Chinese soldiers who didn't yet know they were prey studied their maps and counted their supplies, trying to ignore the whispered rumors in the dark.

The Hunt

The tanks came in false dawn, their steel tracks leaving crescents in the wet earth while behind them mechanized infantry moved like black waves through morning mist. Peasants stood in their doorways clutching whatever possessions they could carry, watching dark shapes approach through the rice fields.

The sound came first, a low mechanical growl that sent chickens scattering and dogs howling, then the shapes themselves emerged from fog, vast and terrible. Children stood transfixed until their mothers grabbed them and ran. Old men who had survived three wars knew better than to wait and see. They took only what they could carry in one trip, leaving behind the work of generations.

The evacuation held a terrible geometry, as if choreographed by some ancient hand. Whole villages emptied like water from broken jars, people flowing south in long ragged columns. The tanks kept coming.

Their commanders had studied maps and calculated fuel consumption and plotted artillery coordinates, but they had not accounted for the chaos of civilian flight. Families with small children moved slower than military calculations allowed. The elderly refused to be left behind, clutching their grandchildren's hands as they stumbled through muddy fields. Water buffalo lowed in confusion as their owners drove them south ahead of the advancing armor.

The Vietnamese army units along the border could do nothing but watch. Their positions had been carefully chosen to defend against infantry assault, but they had few weapons that could stop main battle tanks. They radioed reports south in clipped professional tones that did not convey the helplessness in their eyes. "We are overrun. We are falling back. The civilians are on the move."

Morning mist began to burn away, revealing the full scope of the invasion. More tanks, more troops, more vehicles stretched back beyond sight like a river of steel flowing south. The peasants kept moving, carrying their lives in bundles, their children on their backs, their future uncertain as morning fog. Some sang old songs as they walked, songs that remembered when other armies had come and gone.

The Chinese tanks crushed empty homes beneath steel tracks, leaving only splinters and memories.

Vietnamese soldiers withdrew in good order, firing only when they had clear shots, preserving ammunition for battles yet to come. They knew reinforcements would arrive eventually. They also knew that eventually might be too late.

The refugees continued south, their feet marking ancient paths their ancestors had walked in other wars. The tanks followed, pushing through the morning, carrying their own memories of other invasions, other victories, other defeats. The sun climbed higher, burning away the last of the mist, revealing a land in transit, a people in flight, an army in retreat. The morning was very still except for the sound of tank tracks and children crying and old women that remembered when all of this had happened before.

The mountains breathed mist that morning. Now a corporal from a field promotion, Tuan held his rifle across his chest and moved through shadows while beside him Minh and Loc picked their way between stones. They had grown up racing each other through village streets but here they walked with the careful movements of men who knew bullets found the clumsy first.

The pass rose ahead narrow and treacherous. No vehicle could fit but men could and Chinese commanders had learned to think like mountain people. Tuan touched the jade pendant at his neck once then led them up. Their boots made no sound on wet stone.

"Water," Minh whispered pointing to a stream that crossed their path. Tuan knelt and touched the mud at its edge. Fresh tracks. Maybe six hours old. He held up three fingers then pointed north.

They moved faster now following the sign. The mist clung to them thick as smoke while overhead clouds threatened rain. Loc who had learned tracking from his grandfather read the ground like a blind man reading prayers. He touched a broken twig showed how it had snapped downward. "They went up" he said. "Trying for the high route."

The climb turned steep. Their breath came hard in the thin air, but they kept moving, kept watching, kept counting the distance between themselves and whatever hunted these peaks. Tuan thought of Mai and their rice field but pushed the memory away. Here only the next step mattered.

They found the first body where the pass narrowed to a knife edge. A Chinese scout sprawled against stone his throat opened by something with claws. "Tiger," Minh said.

A sound came soft as falling leaves. Metal touching stone. They went still as death while above them voices murmured in Mandarin. Tuan pressed against rock felt its cold through his shirt. Hand signals passed between them swift and sure. More voices now. Many more.

They belly crawled to the edge looked down into a bowl of stone where mist turned men to shadows. Chinese soldiers moved in formation their weapons held ready. Tuan counted them as his father had taught him to count ducks on the wing. Forty maybe fifty. Too many for this to be simple scouting.

Loc's hand found his arm squeezed once. Through gaps in the mist they saw others moving up the far side. Heavy weapons teams with mortars. They meant to take the high ground then rain death on the Vietnamese positions below. Tuan felt Minh trembling against him knew it was rage not fear.

They watched while Chinese soldiers established positions while more men moved through the pass while the noose drew tight. No chance of attacking. No chance of stopping them. They had come to count and count they would.

The rain started then soft as mercy. Tuan touched his friends once then they crawled backward silent as smoke. The mountain would remember these invaders. Would remember and teach them why some paths led only to graves. But now they had to run had to carry warning had to tell their commanders that death came walking through morning mist.

They moved down the mountain fast as they dared. The rain fell harder covered their sounds. Behind them Chinese soldiers prepared their positions never knowing they had been seen never knowing that mountains had eyes. Tuan led them home through water and shadow while in his chest his heart beat time against the jade pendant Mai had given him. Some promises could survive even this.

The command bunker smelled of wet earth and cigarette smoke. Major Nguyen stood at the map table while Tuan marked positions with a grease pencil. His fingers trembled from the run but his voice stayed steady. "Here, sir. The Chinese have three mortar teams setting up on the ridgeline. About fifty infantry dug in to protect them."

The major studied the marks. Rain drummed against the tin roof while outside men moved through trenches checking weapons. "How long before they start dropping rounds on us."

"Two hours maybe less. They're moving fast but careful. They know the ground."

Nguyen's finger traced contours on the map found the angle of attack the Chinese had chosen. Simple. Effective. From there they could shell his whole position force his men down while their infantry advanced. He had seen such tactics before. Had used them himself. "We can't withdraw. If we lose this position they'll push straight through to Hanoi."

Tuan touched another spot on the map. A line so thin it almost vanished between the elevation marks. "There's an old trail here, sir. From when my grandfather hunted these mountains. It splits from the main pass about half a kilometer back. Runs higher than where they've set up."

"You're sure about this trail."

"Yes, sir. Steep but solid. Twenty good men could make it up there before the Chinese are ready. Get above them. They won't be watching their backs."

The major lit a cigarette let smoke curl between them while he measured angles and options and the weight of necessary choices. "You'd have to move now. In this rain. In the dark."

"Better in the dark sir. We know the way. They don't."

Thunder broke overhead like artillery. The major crushed out his cigarette. "Pick your men. Good climbers. Men who can move silent. You'll need to be in position before first light."

"Sir, we'll need Bangalore torpedoes. The Chinese have razor wire surrounding their position."

"Already thinking like a proper soldier." The major wrote out the order for the explosives. "Take what you need from the armory. But Tuan if you're wrong about this trail."

"I'm not wrong, sir. The mountain is ours. Has been since before empires came looking for glory."

The major watched him go watched how he moved with the careful grace of a man who had learned to hunt before he learned to kill. The rain fell harder pressed against the bunker roof like bullets like judgment like everything that makes men trust other men with death. Through the door he could see his soldiers checking weapons cleaning guns making ready. The major touched the map once more then went to prepare his men for whatever word came down from the mountain's high place.

Tuan led them through rain thick as grief. Twenty men moved behind him their weapons wrapped in cloth their feet finding purchase on stone gone slick as glass. The Bangalore torpedoes weighed heavy across their backs like iron serpents waiting to speak their own kind of truth.

He found the trail by feel alone remembering how his grandfather's hands had guided him here teaching him to read stone with his feet to trust the mountain's own memory. Lightning cracked overhead painted the peaks in colors that belonged to older gods than any that wore uniforms or carried rifles. Thunder followed loud enough to cover their sounds.

"Careful here," he whispered touching Minh's shoulder. "Drop's about twenty meters." They moved sideways across the face while below them clouds turned the valley into a river of shadow. Another flash of lightning showed Chinese positions below. The mortar teams had their weapons set were ranging them now. Soon they would begin turning the Vietnamese trenches into graves.

The trail narrowed until they had to go single file. Tuan felt the mountain breathing against him felt how it waited patient as stone while above them the storm spoke in tongues of fire and fury. They climbed through water and wind and the kind of darkness that turns minutes to hours.

Loc slipped once caught himself against rock. They all went still as death while below a Chinese sentry called something to his companions. Rain dragged at their weapons at their clothes at everything that marked them as soldiers instead of simple men trying to survive mountain weather. But they kept climbing kept following Tuan's feet that remembered what his grandfather's hands had taught.

The Chinese razor wire gleamed dull as old silver in the storm light. They belly crawled the last fifty meters while lightning turned the peaks white as bone. Through the rain Tuan counted enemy positions. The mortars sat in sandbagged holes with machine guns placed just so. Simple. Professional. Clean as a knife against throat.

He passed the word back. The Bangalore torpedoes came forward passed from hand to hand silent as prayer. They assembled the charges while thunder shook stone. Below them Chinese soldiers huddled under tarps against the rain never looking up never thinking death could come from such heights.

Tuan checked his watch. Almost time. The major would be moving his men into position would be counting minutes would be trusting that twenty men could do what armies could not. Lightning flashed again showed his companions faces gone sharp with knowing what came next. He touched the jade pendant once then gave the signal.

Tuan held up his bayonet for the others to see, then attached it to the end of his rifle's barrel. The others followed attaching their bayonets. Next, Tuan pulled out a grenade and showed it to his men without a word. Each man grasped their own grenade and slipped their fingers through the safety ring waiting for Tuan's signal. Tuan waited until all his men were ready, then turned to the engineer holding the Bangalore torpedo detonator. The engineer nodded that he was ready. Tuan pulled the pin on his grenade. The others followed. Twenty grenades arced across the night sky and through the pouring rain.

The explosions ripped into the Chinese soldiers killing more than a dozen. The remaining soldiers were confused, not knowing the assault was coming from above their position. They fired their weapons aimlessly into the darkness below.

Tuan gave a nod to the engineer. He plunged the handle into the detonator.

The Bangalore torpedoes wrote their names in fire and thunder. Chinese wire turned to smoke turned to memory turned to nothing that could stop twenty men who had learned to kill before they learned to trust mountains. They came down the slope like water like stone like everything that makes soldiers wake screaming. Their rifles spoke in voices older than empire clean as morning precise as fate final as whatever gods handle prayers of those who die far from home.

The Chinese soldiers stumbled in confusion firing down the mountain while death came from above. Tuan led the charge his rifle tight against his shoulder the bayonet catching lightning like stolen silver. He took the first soldier through the back the blade punching between ribs. The man made a sound like a sleeping child then fell.

More Vietnamese came down the slope their bayonets finding flesh in the dark. A Chinese machine gunner tried to turn his weapon tried to understand why death spoke from the wrong direction. Minh's blade opened his throat. The gun fell silent.

The mortars sat useless now their crews caught between steel and stone. A Chinese officer screamed commands, but his words drowned in thunder and the wet sounds men make when bayonets find them. Loc moved through the chaos like his grandfather had moved through jungle hunting tigers. His blade came red from each kill.

Some Chinese tried to stand tried to fight. The rest broke ran scattered into rain and darkness. Their training meant nothing against men who had been born on these slopes who had learned to kill from fathers who had killed French and American soldiers on this same ground. Lightning turned the killing ground white showed the dead scattered like fallen leaves.

Tuan reached the first mortar found its sights still set, found its shells still stacked neat as ceremony. He touched the weapon's steel felt how it waited patient as stone. More Vietnamese appeared through the rain gathering weapons gathering ammunition gathering everything that could make Chinese soldiers count cost in blood.

When the killing finished they counted. Thirty-two Chinese dead. The rest vanished into storm into shadow into whatever darkness waited to accept them. The Vietnamese had lost two. The mountain would remember them would keep their bones would add their names to its long memory of men who died defending stone against empire.

Tuan ordered his men to pack up the captured mortars and shells. The Vietnamese needed all the weapons they could find, especially mortars with ammunition. They would do little against the Chinese tanks, but the Chinese infantry was another matter.

The rain fell softer now while men who had been farmers three months ago prepared to speak iron languages with stolen tongues. Tuan felt the jade pendant warm against his chest while behind him the dead lay cooling in mountain water that ran red then clear then red again.

The Chinese supply depot sprawled beneath them in the valley, its floodlights slicing through the mountain darkness like white knives. Granier pressed himself deeper between the wet roots, his binoculars unwavering as he counted targets. "Thirty-two guards visible," he whispered. "Eight in the towers, rest on patrol."

Beside him, Spitting Woman's pencil moved across her waterproofed notebook with surgical precision. "The northern tower is blind to the fuel dumps," she murmured, sketching rapid lines. "They rely too much on their wire."

The depot's perimeter gleamed with professional pride - triple-layer razor wire catching the artificial light, machine gun nests placed with mathematical precision, guard dogs pacing their runs in mechanical circuits. Two scouts materialized from the darkness. "Eastern approach is mined," one breathed in combat French. "New work, Chinese pattern."

The second scout's hands sketched shapes in the darkness. "Western gate is soft. Guards smoke there, cluster in the light. Dogs kenneled after midnight."

"Three ammunition bunkers," Granier said, his eyes never leaving the binoculars. "Two fuel dumps. Enough to feed a division for two months." He paused, watching a guard's pattern. "They fear the dark places."

More scouts emerged from different directions, each carrying pieces of the depot's puzzle. "Radio checks every hour," one whispered. "Commander sleeps between 0200 and 0500." Another added, "Machine guns have 1,000-round belts. Guards rotate every four hours."

Through their rifle scopes, they studied their prey - professional soldiers who didn't yet know they were being hunted. The guards below continued their patterns, oblivious to the predators above calculating their deaths in whispers.

"The new moon comes tomorrow," Spitting Woman said, closing her notebook. "We strike then?"

Granier nodded slowly. "When the clouds cover the stars." He watched a guard light a cigarette, its ember glowing like a target. "They've forgotten what mountain people can do."

The scouts melted back into the darkness as the first hint of dawn threatened the eastern sky. Granier and Spitting Woman memorized their notes before burning them, watching the ashes scatter on the mountain wind. Below them, the depot's lights carved white wounds in the dark while its guards walked their patterns, unaware that death's own hunters were preparing to teach them why some wars are won by ghosts who remember when all killing was done with patience and silence and the absolute certainty of the grave.

The attack came in false dawn, that treacherous hour when guards dreamed of warm beds and blood ran slow as winter sap. The dogs died first, poisoned darts finding their throats with a precision passed down through generations of mountain hunters. Then the shadows grew hands.

Four guard towers fell silent, their sentries dropping without sound as synchronized shots found their marks. In the central bunker, the Chinese commander heard boot steps on concrete before Spitting Woman's blade opened his throat with surgical precision. His body hadn't finished falling when her team seized his radio, his maps, his codes.

"Clear the fence," Granier whispered, and two men with wire cutters made quick work of the perimeter. The raiders flowed through like mist, their weapons speaking only when necessary.

A Chinese ammunition patrol died in three seconds, their blood staining the resupply forms they carried. The fuel depot fell next, shaped charges placed with mathematical care while the team moved through their rehearsed roles in death's choreography.

"They're bringing up the machine guns," someone hissed, but Vietnamese marksmen had already found their positions. The gunners died with their hands still on unfired weapons. Those who tried to run found Claymore mines waiting in the darkness.

The demolition teams worked with cold efficiency, setting charges in ammunition bunkers and linking det cord between fuel tanks. "Radio building's down," came the whispered report. A Chinese officer attempted to organize resistance, but Spitting Woman's rifle cracked once and he joined his scattered command.

The quick reaction force arrived in two trucks, professional soldiers about to learn how quickly training could fail. The commandos met them with pure violence, killing from angles no manual had ever covered. Twenty elite troops became twenty corpses in under thirty seconds.

Charges set, the commandos pulled back into the jungle. Granier and Spitting Woman followed when they were sure nobody was left alive to follow their team.

Then the depot's heart exploded. The first ammunition bunker went up like an angry sun, throwing steel rain into the chrome sky. The fuel dump followed, chain reactions of flame speaking in dragon tongues. Fire reached into the morning sky, writing revolution in smoke and spark.

Two kilometers out, they paused to watch their handiwork paint the clouds orange and black. "Forty-seven Chinese dead," Granier counted quietly, checking his team for casualties. "No losses except powder burns."

Spitting Woman watched the flames, her face illuminated by destruction's dirty light. "They'll send investigators," she said softly. "They'll find nothing but ash and brass and fear."

The team moved out through the morning jungle, leaving fire and death behind them. They had become the nightmare Chinese soldiers whispered about in midnight barracks, death's own chorus singing war's oldest song. Behind them, the depot burned like the funeral pyre of China's dreams.

Spitting Woman took four men north along the supply road, their packs heavy with mines and triggers while depot flames still painted dawn clouds crimson. She chose her team for their hands steady as mountain stone, their minds cold and certain.

The Chinese would need this road soon to feed their war machine, and she meant to teach them why mountain people should be feared. They worked with mechanical grace, setting their gifts in ground that hungered. At the bridges first, shaped charges placed exactly as her grandmother had taught her to set snares. The Chinese would rebuild, but rebuilding took time, and time was another kind of weapon.

The road itself came next. They laid anti-tank mines in patterns that spoke of professional training but carried mountain wisdom beneath. The obvious ones they wanted found. The real killers lay deeper, quieter. When Chinese engineers swept for mines they would find enough to think themselves thorough. The rest would wait.

Old Tran set booby traps with an artist's precision, having learned demolition from the French. His wire vanished in morning light, connected to things that belonged in nightmares. He spoke in combat French, teaching the others death's mathematics, how physics loved sharp edges, how motion became mortality. They mined culverts with German Bouncing Betty's pulled from forgotten caches. The road's shoulders sprouted toe poppers hungry for feet. Every rest stop, every shade tree, every place a tired driver might pause became death's garden.

They worked silently, their hands speaking older languages. The younger men learned quickly why Spitting Woman placed charges like a mountain cat placed its feet, learned to think like prey to trap predators.

When finished, the road had transformed. Any convoy passing would learn new lessons about dying. The Chinese would eventually cut different routes through mountains that rejected them, but that meant time, meant supplies, meant frontline hunger, meant soldiers waking from dreams of roads with teeth.

Spitting Woman led her team east through paths older than maps. They moved like smoke through trees, leaving behind a road. The Chinese would come, would die, would learn why mountain people marked certain trails. She thought of their engineers with their metal detectors and procedures, their professional pride, how they would discover some wisdom predated war.

The team advanced through morning mist carrying empty packs and heavy knowledge. Behind them the road waited, patient as mountains, eternal as death. They moved to rejoin Granier, their minds holding maps of metal teeth sleeping in red earth. The war would flow around them like water around stone, but for now this road had become death's own hymn, written in wire and want and ways of dying.

Granier found her kneeling before the rifle like it was an altar, the weapon stripped and gleaming in pale starlight. Her hands moved across metal with practiced devotion, each gesture precise and purposeful. He settled beside her on the damp earth, letting the night wind carry acrid depot smoke across valleys where their enemies tried to find sleep.

"More guards at the western depot," he said quietly in combat French, watching her hands never pause in their ritual. "Twenty more at the northern complex. They're reinforcing everything now."

"Good," she replied, the single word carrying satisfaction. The silver length of her cleaning rod caught starlight as it slid through the barrel. "More men watching supplies means fewer men pushing south. Let them build their fortresses. We'll learn to be better saboteurs."

"Chang will change the routes," Granier said finally, naming the Chinese commander. "New protocols, new thinking. He's learning about roads that grow teeth, about shadows that kill. His men wake screaming now."

"Then let him change them," she murmured, reassembling the rifle with swift, sure movements. "Every truck will need escorts. Every convoy will crawl like a wounded thing. Their war machine slows, bleeds, dies by inches."

In the valley below, a dog began barking, the sound carrying clear in the still air. They both tensed, but it was only night's ordinary fears. Spitting Woman's smile gleamed briefly in the darkness, all predator's teeth and ancient knowing.

"Listen," she whispered, nodding toward the distant sounds of the Chinese camp. "They're doubling the guard again. Building higher walls. But walls only mean they're afraid, and afraid men make mistakes."

"Two weeks," Granier said, watching the last depot fires paint the clouds crimson. "Two weeks until their army is fully reinforced. Two weeks to bleed them."

"By then they'll believe in ghosts. Their soldiers will jump at shadows, waste ammunition on darkness. Pride breaks differently in the mountains."

Down in the valleys, they could hear vehicles moving, commanders already calling for more reinforcements, more guns, more ways to fight enemies they couldn't see. But ghosts didn't die like men, didn't bleed like men, didn't stop until their work was finished.

"They're sending another convoy at dawn," she said softly, sliding the rifle's bolt home with a final metallic click. "Let them come. Let them build their towers. Let them learn what we've always known. Some wars," she stood, shouldering the weapon, "are won by whispers in the dark."

Granier watched her melt into the shadows, knowing soon he would follow, knowing the night still held secrets to teach their enemies, knowing that fear was a weapon older than gunpowder. The darkness wrapped around them like a shroud, patient as death, eternal as mountains.

The raiders took what they could carry. Ammunition. Weapons. Fuel. The rest they burned. Let smoke rise like signal fires to tell Chinese commanders why their men went hungry. Why their tanks went dry. Why some supply lines could never run secure.

Through days and nights they struck. Hit fuel dumps. Ambushed convoys. Raided ammunition stores. The Chinese changed their patterns. Added more guards. Sent out more patrols. Started moving supplies at night. Added armored vehicles to convoys. Posted more sentries. Changed their routes. The raiders adapted faster. Learned the new patterns. Found the new weaknesses.

Spitting Woman's rifle dropped officers who tried organizing resistance. The raiders' captured machine guns turned the road into butcher's yard. The surviving drivers abandoned their trucks. Tried running back north. The jungle accepted them. Kept them. Added their bones to its collection.

The raiders learned to shake pursuit. Learned to vanish into mountains that had swallowed three armies. Learned to pick their battles with a hunter's patience. Behind them they left burning trucks. Burning depots. Burning everything that fed China's war machine.

The Chinese troops grew hungry. Their tanks ran dry. Their guns fell silent for want of shells. The raiders kept striking. Kept burning.

The killing changed as days burned into weeks. Each day brought China's finest - elite troops with eyes like frozen lakes and hands that never trembled. They moved through jungle shadows with lethal grace, having learned to hunt ghosts, to watch darkness, to die with professional dignity.

Nhat died first, on a raid that went wrong in the dying light. "Three more," he gasped, blood bubbling from his throat, his rifle still smoking. "Three more for the ancestors." They carried him through mountain darkness, his body growing cold against their shoulders. They buried him deep where no enemy would find him, leaving only his knife, his medals, the three spent cartridges that marked his final kills. No tags, no letters, nothing to mark his passing except the mountain's long memory.

"The Chinese learn quickly now," Granier said one night, watching depot lights through his scope. "See how they watch the high ground, how they've positioned their guns."

"Learning carries its own price," Spitting Woman replied softly. Two nights later, she proved her words true when an elite Chinese squad followed their trail into a narrow valley. None walked out. Their bodies they left as warnings, their weapons they took as tribute, their deaths became whispered stories that made soldiers check shadows twice.

Khac died next, taking half a dozen Chinese with him. The explosion painted dawn clouds crimson, his final gift to the enemy who'd put a burst through his chest. They buried his detonator with him, honoring his right to choose his own ending.

The Chinese brought new weapons then - helicopters that cut through darkness with infrared eyes, dogs that could smell fear, men who'd tracked tigers through Siberian snow and thought human prey would prove easier quarry. "The tigers could have taught them better," Spitting Woman murmured, watching the searchlights sweep the canopy.

Duc they lost to a Chinese trap, one they'd taught the enemy too well. His last act was to pull a grenade pin, denying them even his corpse. "For the mountains," he screamed, and the explosion echoed through valleys.

Each depot became a fortress ringed with razor wire and fear. Every road became a gauntlet, every shadow held death's promise. The team learned to strike like lightning - there and gone before thunder's roar. Khan died covering their retreat, his machine gun singing war songs until Chinese commandos finally silenced him. They recovered only pieces, burying what they could find along with his victory.

"We're becoming something else," Granier said one night, watching his remaining men clean captured weapons with mechanical precision. "Something more than soldiers, less than human."

"We become what the mountains need," Spitting Woman answered, her eyes reflecting starlight. "What the war demands." She taught them her ancient wisdom - how to make each bullet write poetry, each explosion speak prophecy, each death become legend.

They lost Chen to a sniper's geometry, Vinh to a trap's cruel timing, Wu to a night that grew too many teeth. Each they buried with their weapons and their right to choose death's hour.

The Chinese brought more men, more guns, more ways to die in mountains that thirsted for blood. But the team had become death's own children, war's dark whisper, everything that made enemy soldiers wake screaming.

"Tell me," Granier asked Spitting Woman as they watched another depot burn, "does it end?"

She touched the rifle that had belonged to two dead men before her. "It ends when the mountains have drunk their fill," she said. "When the Chinese learn what their ancestors knew – don't underestimate the people of the hills."

They bled but never broke, died but never surrendered, killed but never stopped. Above them, the mountains watched with ancient patience as modern men learned old truths about death and fear.

The scouts came at moonset. Their feet made no sound on the earth. The first dropped to one knee beside Granier while the second whispered coordinates into Spitting Woman's ear. She marked them on the map with a stub of pencil.

"Twenty tanks," the first scout said "Maybe more. Armored cars too. Chinese made a motor pool in the valley where three ridges meet."

Granier shook his head. "Not enough charges. Maybe three tanks if we're lucky."

Spitting Woman touched the spot on the map where the depot's fuel dump sat. "They keep gasoline in those tanks. The trucks need it. The generators need it." She looked at the first scout. "How big are the tanks?"

"Three of them. Big ones. Each one could fill

hundreds of trucks."

"Show me where the tanks are," she said.

"Don't forget the armored cars," said the scout.

"Let's not get greedy. The tanks should be our focus."

"Okay." The scout's finger traced a line beside the depot wall. "They're on the opposite side of the compound from the fuel tanks."

"We'll need to figure out a way to carry the fuel we need," said Spitting Woman. "There should be some fuel cans nearby."

Granier understood. "If we get enough gas into the tank hatches. If the ammunition cooks off in the heat." He studied the map again. The risk measured itself against the reward.

"It'll work," Spitting Woman said. "Steel burns if you make it hot enough."

"Okay, what about the guards?" Granier said.

"Four towers. Two men each. Dogs along the fence. But the north ridge comes within 200 meters. Good angle down into the compound," said the scout.

Granier studied the marked position. The north ridge would give them sight lines into the heart of the depot. Good place for their sniper rifles if they had enough rounds. Bad place to be if the Chinese had night vision.

"Show me the approaches," he said.

The scout's finger traced paths through the valleys. "Here. And here. But they've mined everything else. Found three dead deer this morning. Pieces of them anyway."

Spitting Woman looked at Granier. In the dark her eyes were black as gun oil. They had eighteen men left. Enough to hurt the depot but not enough to hold it.

But twenty tanks. Twenty tanks would bleed the Chinese advance for weeks.

"The dogs," she said.

"We can handle the dogs," the second scout said. He patted the crossbow slung across his back.

Granier nodded once. The risks lined up in his mind like brass on a bandolier. Too many ways it could go wrong. But twenty tanks. He touched the map where the fuel tanks waited. "Show me the fence line. Every detail."

The scouts bent close. Their whispers carried death's coordinates across the damp night air while overhead the moon set behind clouds thick as smoke.

Eighteen raiders and Spitting Woman moved through dark. The moon cast no shadow. No sound but boots in wet earth and the soft click of metal against metal. Not enough explosives. Not enough thermite. Just fire and whatever luck the night held.

Assigning himself overwatch, Granier lay beneath a fallen tree on the north ridge. The bark felt wet against his chest. Through his scope the depot spread out below like a map drawn in steel and shadow. He counted guard towers. Four of them. Two men in each. Their cigarettes glowed red when they smoked.

The tanks sat in neat rows. Twenty armored hulls black against gravel. Fuel tanks were one hundred feet away against the western wall. Three of them. Big ones. Dogs paced the fence line. Four of them. German shepherds with heavy chains that scraped concrete.

The barracks squatted dark near the eastern gate. One red light burned above the door. Two guards walked their rounds. Boots scraping gravel. Every ten minutes they passed the fuel depot. Like clockwork.

Like men who had grown comfortable. Like men who would die tonight.

He shifted the scope to the command post. Three men inside. Radio operator hunched over his desk. The compound lay quiet under stars. Too quiet. Too easy. Nothing was ever this easy.

The wind changed. Brought diesel smell up the ridge. Brought sound of dogs and men who thought they were safe behind wire. Brought promise of what would come with darkness.

Ming found the wire on the perimeter fence. His knife worked silent against steel braids. The gap widened. The raiders slipped through one by one.

The dogs, roaming free in a pack, caught their scent. Four black shapes moved in the dark. The crossbows thrummed. Each bolt found its mark. The animals died with quiet whimpers.

Quy and Kiet took the eastern guard tower. Two soft cracks from their suppressed pistols. The guards fell forward onto the rail. Blood dripped onto concrete below.

Granier watched two Chinese guards walk their rounds. Boots scraping gravel. Rifles slung careless over shoulders. Twenty meters to the fuel tanks.

Spitting Woman lay flat in shadow beside three raiders. Her hand rose. The crossbows lifted silent in dark. Four bolts took the first guard in chest and throat. He died without sound.

The second guard turned at the soft thud of body hitting earth. Bao's knife caught him under the chin. Blood ran black down his collar. He tried to scream but only bubbles came. Tran caught him as he fell. Dragged him into shadow.

More guards walked the fence line in pairs. Pairs of

raiders waited in their path. Each kill came quiet. Bodies disappeared into dark. The depot slept unaware that death walked its grounds.

When the last pair of guards fell the raiders gathered their weapons. Eight men who would never finish their rounds. The war's arithmetic written in blood on cold ground.

The fuel tanks loomed black against stars. Bao found the empty cans stacked neat beside the pumps. The raiders worked in pairs. One held the hose while the other filled cans. The gasoline splashed quiet in the dark.

Lin and Mai carried the first load to the tanks where the second team waited.

Granier watched them work through his scope. Each man climbed the armor with a full can. They poured gasoline through turret hatches into crew compartments and into the engine compartments. The smell rose sharp in night air.

The barracks sat dark except for the one red exit light. Tran pressed against warm brick and peered through the window. Twenty soldiers slept on bunks arranged in rows. One man rose, walked half-asleep toward the latrine. His bare feet made soft sounds on concrete.

The raiders took positions. A men at each window. Two at the doors. Each carried grenades and submachine guns they had taken from dead Chinese patrols. Mai checked his watch. The time had come.

"Now," Tran whispered.

Pins pulled in unison. The grenades arced through windows and doors. For one moment the barracks lay silent. Then the world turned white.

The blast lifted the roof. Fire filled every corner.

Those who made it to doors met rifle fire. The killing was quick. Precise. When it was done the barracks burned orange against black sky. Inside lay those who would never wake. The cost of war written in flesh and flame.

Tran turned away. No pleasure in it. Just necessity. The raiders disappeared into shadows carrying weight of what they had done. Behind them the flames rose higher. War offered no clean victories.

A spool of home-made fuse, soaked in gun oil and caked with gunpowder, snaked from tank to tank. Twenty armor hulls strung together like steel beasts waiting slaughter. When the last can emptied Granier lit the fuse with his Zippo lighter.

The fuse flashed white. Fire bloomed inside the first tank. Orange flame roared from hatches like dragon breath. The heat drove men back. Then the second tank caught. Then the third. Fire poured from each hull in sequence.

The explosions came like a giant's hammer as ammunition cooked off inside each tank. The turrets lifted on a pillar of flame then crashed back. Then the next tank died down the line. Each explosion shaking the earth. Steel screamed. The depot turned bright as day.

Granier counted tanks burning. Twenty hulls became funeral pyres. The Chinese war machine had lost some teeth tonight.

The Chinese patrol came from the east. The sound of the barracks exploding had drawn them back. Sixteen men moving fast through trees.

The first burst caught Tran in the throat as he reached the perimeter fence. Blood sprayed black in the dark. Tran fell tangled in steel mesh. The night erupted. Muzzle flashes lit the compound in strobe flashes. Return fire cut red lines through dark.

Granier saw the Chinese from his position on the ridge. Through his scope their shapes moved black against burning tanks. He steadied his breath. The first shot took their sergeant through the throat. The second dropped a machine gunner. His weapon clattered on stone.

"Move," he called to Spitting Woman. She led the raiders toward the gap in the wire, but Chinese fire had them pinned. Rounds cracked past their heads. Sparked off metal. More Chinese joined the fight. Rounds cracked closer. Ming took one through the shoulder spun but kept moving. Two more raiders fell and lay still.

A spotlight snapped on from the command post. White light pinned them against steel. Granier's rifle cracked three times. The light died. Others followed. The night turned bright as day.

Spitting Woman's rifle spoke single shots. Each one found a target. Taking out lights. Taking out gunners. Buying time they didn't have.

Oanh died. The bullet took him in the spine. He screamed once. The sound carried over gunfire.

Granier's rifle spoke again. And again. Each shot precise. Each shot buying seconds. A Chinese soldier tried flanking the raiders. Granier's bullet took him in the chest. He folded against a burning tank.

Spitting Woman's team reached the wire. Fifteen meters of open ground between them and jungle shadow. The Chinese patrol fired from cover. Keeping them trapped against burning steel.

"Cover," Spitting Woman shouted. The raiders turned. Their rifles spoke as one. Chinese soldiers died in the crossfire. Granier's shots came steady. Clearing the way.

They broke through the wire. More Chinese rounds followed. Mai took one in the leg. Sam and Bao dragged him into trees. Granier fired his last three rounds. Three more soldiers fell. The rest stayed down.

When the raiders disappeared into dark Granier shouldered his rifle. Below the tanks burned. The compound had become a crematorium. Behind him Chinese reinforcements were coming. Time to fade away. Time to count the cost.

Tran had a letter in his pocket for his mother. The paper was soaked with blood. Ming's shoulder would never work right again. In the east the sky grew pale. Time to disappear. Time to try again another night. The war would need more from them. It always did.

Through the trees they heard the quick reaction force coming. Engines grinding up the valley. Too late to save their tanks. Too late to catch the raiders. The night belonged to those who moved like smoke through dark. The day belonged to men who would count the cost in burning steel and cold flesh.

Vengeance

General Chen stood before the war room's sprawling maps, his shadow falling across supply routes that burned redder with each passing day. The smell of cigarette smoke hung thick as morning fog while operations officers shifted nervously in their chairs. His fist crashed against hardwood, making coffee cups rattle like artillery shells.

"Eight depots in twelve days," he growled, his voice low and dangerous. "Enough ammunition to feed a division for months. Enough fuel to drive our tanks to Hanoi. All gone, turned to smoke and scrap and stories that keep our soldiers awake at night."

His commanders remained motionless, knowing how rage made the general's punishments surgical and precise. Only the scratch of pencils broke the silence as staff officers marked another supply route lost.

"The Vietnamese army grows stronger while we bleed," Chen continued, tracing lines that had become death's own signature across the map. "These raiders, these mountain devils - they cut us with paper cuts while our enemies gather strength."

Colonel Wu cleared his throat. "Sir, about our advance—"

"Exactly!" Chen's voice cracked like a whip. "Our advance dies like a snake with a broken spine. No fuel means no tanks. No ammunition means no artillery. No food means no fight." He jabbed a finger at the southern sectors where war had become whisper. "This Frenchman and his woman they turn our size against us, make our strength weakness, our pride prison."

The room held its breath as Chen's mind worked like tank treads crushing options. Finally, he spoke: "Bring in the Fourth Special Operations Group. All of them."

His commanders exchanged glances. Eight hundred elite soldiers who tracked commandos for pay bonuses and killed shadows for pride. Colonel Wu dared speak again: "Sir, the fuel requirements alone—"

"Will be met," Chen cut through the words like a blade through flesh. "Strip the reserve tanks if you must. I want them hunting those saboteurs within forty-eight hours. I want these raiders found and eliminated from my battlefield."

He turned to his intelligence chief, a thin man with wire-rimmed glasses. "Give them everything - every report, photo, rumor. These devils think they hunt us?" His finger stabbed the map where depots had become debris. "Now we show them what real hunting means."

The room emptied quickly, leaving Chen alone with his maps and rage. Somewhere in those paper peaks, the Frenchman and his woman were planning their next raid, their next lesson in fear. "Let them plan," he whispered to maps. "Let them think they're the hunters."

The Fourth Group had hunted Mongol raiders and Siberian wolves, had tracked tigers through snow until the great cats died of exhaustion. They would find these wraiths, these teachers of fear. Would show them China knew old magic too, had written its own books about making warriors wake screaming.

"Let them come," Chen murmured, watching night gather outside his windows. Eight hundred hunters were coming to teach them why some predators hunt in packs, why some wolves wear uniforms, why some nightmares come in daylight wearing Chinese stars.

In the valley's black throat, the depot's lights burned too dim, its guards too obvious, its weaknesses laid bare like invitations. Granier crouched in the shadows, his old wounds aching with storm-sense, with warning. "Something's wrong," he whispered to Spitting Woman. "Too easy. Too clean."

"You're getting paranoid in your old age," said Spitting Woman with a sly smile.

"Yeah, you're probably right. Let's go."

They moved through darkness anyway, their team flowing like wind between the trees. The first guards died quietly, professionally, their blood painting wet circles on the packed earth. Everything unfolded with perfect precision, which was exactly why Granier's hands trembled on his rifle.

The night exploded. The team laying charges never heard the shots that killed them, their bodies crumpling like abandoned prayers into the dirt. Chinese commandos rose from spider holes they'd waited in for days, their weapons speaking a language of coordinated death. Half the team died in the first thirty seconds, learning too late how quickly hunters become prey.

"Back!" Spitting Woman's voice cut through darkness, her rifle already answering, already sending three Chinese soldiers to whatever gods handle prayers of the overconfident. "It's a trap!"

They scattered in pairs, but the Chinese had planned for this, had learned the hunters' ways. The western escape route became a geometry lesson in intersecting bullets. Two more raiders died learning how professionals calculate murder. Then the real trap sprung - the blocking force rising from camouflaged positions, their interlocked fields of fire turning night into death.

"Left flank!" Granier shouted, but three more raiders became statistics before his words faded. No time for clean kills now, for professional pride. Just the raw arithmetic of survival.

A bullet shattered Granier's left arm, the pain blooming like fire flowers. "Keep moving," he snarled, killing three Chinese soldiers before finding cover, two more leaving it. His rifle clicked empty, became a club.

Spitting Woman materialized beside him, her blade dripping black in the starlight, her eyes burning with hell's own fury. "Five left," she hissed. "We need space."

The night burned with muzzle flashes and screaming. They ran, crawled, swam through death's watershed, leaving blood trails their hunters would follow, leaving brothers they couldn't bury, leaving pieces of themselves they'd never recover. The Chinese pursued with mechanical precision, with the patience of wolves who smell wounded prey.

"No time," Granier gasped as they broke contact.

"Just move."

They flowed through jungle like water through stone, teaching muscles new languages of survival. Four hours later, three raiders waited at the rally point, their eyes obsidian, their hands empty. Spitting Woman appeared last, half-carrying Granier, his shattered arm leaving drops of life behind them.

"North," she commanded as she quickly patched Granier's arm and made him a sling. "Through the night."

Five survivors. They moved through mountain darkness where shadows grew fangs. Behind them, eight hundred Chinese commandos followed their trail like wolves scenting dying deer.

"They'll expect us to go deep," Granier mumbled through pain.

"Then we go deeper," Spitting Woman replied. "I remember older paths."

They disappeared into peaks that had swallowed armies before them. The night consumed them like darkness consumes shame, leaving only whispers for their hunters to follow.

Granier sat in the damp darkness, cleaning blood from his last magazine retrieved from his rucksack. Ten rounds remained - barely enough for a proper death. Every movement sent daggers of pain through his shattered arm. Five raiders survived, two wounded, all of them stripped of explosives and options, running only on desperation.

"By morning," he said quietly, "they'll find us." His voice carried the weight of certainty. Eight hundred Chinese hunters had learned their methods, their tactics, had learned how they could bleed.

Spitting Woman watched moonlight filter through

bamboo leaves, her face carved with shadow. "We can't fight them," she said in combat French, "not with empty rifles, not with broken bodies."

Young Bao spoke then, his voice soft as falling leaves. "My grandfather worked a French mine, two valleys east. Phosphorus." He paused, eyes distant with memory. "Deep pit with white walls that burned men who touched them."

Granier's head snapped up, pain forgotten. Chemistry awakened in his mind, oxidation becoming possibility, becoming salvation. "Show us."

They moved through darkness, finding the pit as if guided by the dead. White rock gleamed beneath starlight, decades of exposed phosphorus waiting patient as judgment. But problems surfaced in Granier's mind - no explosives to expose fresh phosphorus, no detonators, no way to ignite a reaction.

Then he saw them - old mining machines, bleeding rust into night. The equation crystallized: iron oxide plus phosphorus equals inferno. Simple chemistry becoming complex vengeance.

"There's a tunnel at the bottom of the pit," Bao said, pointing to the flooded shaft. "Colonial engineering. Could shelter us from the reaction, if we time it right."

"Then I time it right," said Granier

Spitting Woman read his intention like reading old scars. "It's suicide," she said flatly.

Granier smiled, teeth flashing silver in moonlight. "Only if I get the chemistry wrong. Only if I forget how elements love each other." His fingers scraped rust from ancient metal, feeling it come away like blood from dying things. "Tomorrow we teach hunters why some prey is best left alone.

"And if you're wrong?" she asked.

"Then we die anyway," he replied. "But we die teaching them why these mines were abandoned by men and claimed by darker gods."

They worked through night's remaining hours, scraping rust, preparing ground for reaction. Granier explained the chemistry in whispers, how iron oxide would marry phosphorus, how thermite would birth inferno.

"If this works," Spitting Woman said, watching him measure rust with precise hands, "they'll never forget."

"That's the point," he replied. "Sometimes victory comes from empty guns and broken weapons." He looked up at the moon, nearly full above them.

They continued their work, making peace with whatever gods handle prayers of desperate men.

The white stone walls of the abandoned phosphorus mine caught the first gray light of dawn. Inside the pit, five raiders worked with the delicate precision of surgeons, their knives scraping rust from ancient French machinery. The sound whispered across the stone like departing souls.

"Gentle now," Granier murmured, watching Bao struggle one-handed with his blade. The young man's right arm hung useless, punctured by Chinese bullets three days before. "Too much force creates spark and we all burn."

Red oxide gathered in small piles around their feet, dusting the phosphorus-rich ground like bloodied snow. Spitting Woman moved between the workers, her voice low and steady. "The wind must come from the east," she said, gesturing to the walls. "The rust must fall in lines, like temple prayers."

The morning sun crept higher, making the white stone walls gleam like polished bone. Granier stripped to his waist, taking a knife between his teeth. "I'll check the tunnel," he said. "If it's blocked, I'll need another way."

He slipped into the flooded passage, the mountain water seizing him with brutal familiarity. His wounded arm blazed with protest as he pushed deeper, fingers reading the stone like ancient text. Twenty meters in, he found what he feared - mining equipment wedged like bones in the earth's throat, massive machines abandoned when the French empire retreated.

Breaking the surface, he spat water and truth: "Dead end."

Spitting Woman nodded, unsurprised. "Sometimes fate gives only one door," she said, "and it opens into fire. What are you going to do?"

"We both know there's only one way out of this thing," Granier said.

"I should do it."

"Save your breath. That's not going to happen. Besides, this is how legends are made. Make sure your people remember my story."

"They'll remember. I'll make sure of it."

They worked through the growing heat with reverent care, preparing the iron oxide with ritual precision. The raiders understood what was coming - eight hundred Chinese hunters who would fill this pit with their pride and patience, never suspecting they entered their own funeral pyre.

Granier studied the tunnel mouth, calculating. Three seconds to dive deep when the reaction began. The water might boil, might steam, might become his personal hell. Everything depended on molecular bonds.

When the preparations were complete, Spitting

Woman touched his face with butterfly gentleness. "See you in whatever waits," she whispered.

He smiled. "Either at victory's celebration or Hell's reunion."

The raiders melted into the mountain paths, leaving their work behind - rust patterns like fresh blood on white stone, science transformed into desperate hope. Granier checked the tunnel one final time as the sun climbed and wind whispered warnings. He moved behind a rusted tractor, metal thick, good cover. He used his rifle's scope to survey the mine's rim above him. If Spitting Woman and the raiders were successful that is where the eight hundred would arrive.

Hidden in trees near the rim, two of the raiders too badly wounded to join the others in luring the eight hundred. They would wait in silence.

Through green shadows Spitting Woman and the three raiders moved. Not running. Walking slow enough to leave signs. Broken twigs. Scuffed earth. A spent cartridge dropped just so. Behind them eight hundred Chinese hunters followed like wolves on a blood trail. Two kilometers to the mine.

Old Kim touched her arm pointed to disturbed moss. "Scouts. They are close." His whisper barely stirred the air.

"Good. Let's hope they follow." She kept walking measured steps that left just enough trace. The morning heat pressed down through the canopy made their clothes stick to skin.

Mai limped ahead favoring his wounded leg. Blood had soaked through the fresh bandage marked their path like paint. He stumbled caught himself against a tree. The bark held his bloody handprint.

"Keep moving," Spitting Woman said. She helped him up kept him walking. His blood would draw them sure as bait draws fish.

They crossed a stream walked through the water thirty meters then back to shore. An obvious trick. One the Chinese would see through would follow their true trail on the bank. Let them feel clever.

The Chinese colonel was good. Kept his men back. Sent scouts ahead in pairs. Professional. Careful. Dead if he followed far enough.

Kim looked back through the trees. "They spread wide. Try to circle ahead."

"Good." She adjusted the strap of her sniper rifle. "They think we run to escape their grasp."

The white stone cliffs rose ahead. The mine's rim caught the sun like old bone. Mai's leg gave out again. This time he stayed down. "Leave me. I slow you."

"You die here if you don't get up. We need them fast and hungry." She got him up kept him walking.

Closer now. The Chinese moved quiet, but 800 men make noise no matter their skill. Boots on earth. Metal on metal. The sound of breath and effort and men who thought themselves wolves.

The mine waited. White walls rising from green jungle like ancient tomb. Two hundred meters out Spitting Woman stopped them. "Now we run. Let them see us panic."

They crashed through undergrowth like frightened deer. Let branches whip loud behind them. Let their boots strike stone. Let 800 hunters hear prey running scared.

The Chinese shouted orders. The pursuit quickened. The sound of 800 men rushing forward filled the jungle like storm wind.

Spitting Woman and the raiders reached the mine's edge disappeared into predetermined cover. Behind them 800 hunters followed victory's scent. None looked up to see the other raiders in the trees. None looked down to see the red dust scattered just so across white stone.

They stopped at the edge of the mine and searched the area with their eyes. The raiders had vanished.

In the bottom of the pit Granier took aim.

A shot rang out and the soldier next to the commander dropped dead with a bullet through his heart. The commander signaled his men to descend into the pit and find the raiders.

The Chinese commander's voice echoed against the walls. "Secure the perimeter. Cover every angle. No raider escapes today."

The 800 rushed into the mine leaving only a small rear guard to protect their exit. Their boots left bloody prints on rock dusted with rust. Chinese spread through the pit like water seeking its level.

At the bottom, Granier felt the iron oxide shifting under his boots. The chemistry waited, patient as a coiled serpent. The commander stepped forward, satisfaction gleaming in his eyes as their distance closed on Granier's last position.

"You led us on a good chase, Frenchman," the commander said in perfect French, each word precise as a bullet's path. "But the chase ends now."

As the first Chinese soldiers closed in on him, Granier pulled his Zippo lighter from his pocket. With a flick of his thumb he ignited the wick, then dropped the lighter on to the ground into the iron oxide, into chemistry's congregation. Time froze. The universe caught its breath. At first nothing happened. The flame was not enough to ignite the thermite. Granier waited, not panicking, time running out. Then physics wrote its name in fire.

The chain reaction raced across the pit floor in beautiful, deadly fractals. White flames erupted as phosphorus met iron oxide, their marriage an inferno that consumed everything it touched. Chinese soldiers screamed as the white light consumed them.

Granier dove for the tunnel mouth as Hell bloomed behind him. Men tried running but found only more fire. Others attempted to climb the walls but discovered they burned too.

The water at the tunnel entrance boiled as Granier plunged in, holding his breath while physics finished its work. Through the steam he heard sporadic gunfire as the few who reached the rim met Spitting Woman's and the raiders' waiting rifles.

Spitting Woman's voice carried across the inferno, singing ancient songs in her hill tribe dialect. The phosphorus burned for days, creating clouds visible from thirty miles, turning day to night.

When the fires finally died and chemistry declared its peace, she found Granier half-drowned in the tunnel, his skin blistered, his lungs raw from steam. They stood together watching the smoke reach for the sky.

"This is how you kill 800 men," she said quietly. "This is how you teach hunters that some shadows bite back."

Behind them, white smoke rose like angry spirits while Chinese generals calculated their losses and tactical experts wrote new manuals based on the trap.

Mai moved through the stream checking her fish traps the morning sun hard on the water. The woven baskets sat deep in the current where she had placed them three days past. Her father had shown her how to weave them tight enough to hold catfish but loose enough to let the current flow through. She pulled the first trap finding two catfish thick as her arm writhing in the mesh. The trap went into her satchel with the fish still moving inside.

"Good eating tonight," she whispered working downstream to the next basket. The water ran cold around her calves catching morning light like hammered metal.

The snap of a branch made her pause. Three shadows moved through the trees with measured steps. Their rifles caught morning light. Chinese uniforms clean and pressed marking them scouts not deserters. The leader stepped forward moonlight showing a face young as her dead brother.

"You there girl. Show your hands."

Mai turned slow the satchel at her hip heavy with wet fish. Three rifle barrels pointed at her chest. "Stand still," the leader said. The second soldier moved to her left trying to box her in.

"What village," the leader demanded.

"No village," she said. "Just fish traps. Just food." The lie tasted metallic like blood in her mouth. The knife pressed cold against the small of her back where she had tucked it that morning.

The third soldier spoke quick in Chinese. The leader nodded. "Search her."

They moved closer boots falling in the measured steps of trained men. The fate that had followed her all morning drew tight as a snare. The fish in her satchel thrashed once hard splashing water across the leader's boots. He looked down. Half a heartbeat.

"What's in the bag," he started to say.

Remembering all that Spitting Woman had taught her, Mai moved. The knife came clean from her waistband caught the first soldier beneath his jaw. For a moment nothing happened then the blood came and he tried to raise his rifle, but she had already moved past him had already reached the second man. The blade went in below his ribs angled up found his heart. His breath came out all at once hot against her neck.

The third soldier got his rifle up. "Stop," he shouted, but Mai took his legs with a sweep. When he hit ground she drove the knife through his throat pinned him to earth. His hands came up, tried to find the blade but touched only his own blood. His eyes went wide then empty.

"You should have kept walking," she told the corpse. She retrieved her knife wiped it clean on the dead man's sleeve. The whole thing had taken less than five seconds. The bodies lay in spreading darkness that soaked into ground. She took their ammunition their weapons their canteens. Waste nothing. She left the rest for whatever comes in night to feed on fallen things.

Walking home Mai moved like any other morning like the ground hadn't just drunk deep of stranger's blood like her heart wasn't singing war's song. The fish still thrashed in her satchel. The rifles felt heavy across her back. Behind her three men who'd thought her a simple girl lay cooling in dawn's first light. The stream ran on carrying their blood north toward China.

Mai walked through the village gate arms heavy with

captured rifles fish still writhing in her satchel. The guards gathered close as she dropped three sets of web gear and ammunition pouches onto the packed earth. "Three Chinese scouts by the stream," she said. "They tried to take me. The jungle has them now."

Old Minh picked up one of the bloody rifles checked its action found it clean. "Good," he said. "Their weapons will serve us better than they served them." He barked orders to the other guards. "Get Grandfather Vu. The elders need to hear this."

They gathered in the temple while afternoon heat pressed against the walls. Mai stood before them told how the scouts had moved like hunters how their uniforms marked them professionals not deserters. Grandfather Vu's face went hard as stone. "How far from the village."

"Three miles east by the deep bend," Mai said. "I left them for the jungle."

"Scouts mean more behind them," Elder Tran said. "They search for something."

"Or someone," Elder Binh added.

Grandfather Vu studied the captured rifles. "These are not common infantry weapons. See the optics. The special grips. These men were trained hunters." He looked at Mai. "You did well, girl. But their commanders will notice when they don't return."

"They'll send more," Elder Tran said. "Send them soon."

"Then we'll kill more," Mai said, but Grandfather Vu shook his head.

"Pride kills quick as any bullet child. We must warn Granier and Spitting Woman. Must prepare the defenses." He turned to the guards. "Double the watch. No one leaves the village alone. And girl," he said to

Mai, "next time check your traps with a rifle in your hands. The Chinese won't make the same mistake twice."

Mai nodded knowing he spoke truth. The elders talked into evening planning how to face what must come. Through the temple walls came the sounds of women cooking, of children playing, of life that must go on even with death walking the jungle paths. But Mai saw how the guards checked their weapons, how the villagers watched the treeline, how everything normal had edge like knife waiting to cut.

The morning came too quiet. Mai watched from the watchtower while Chinese soldiers emerged from jungle shadows and took positions around their walls. No shots came. No orders to surrender. Just the weight of waiting while sun climbed higher while hearts beat time against ribs.

Old Tran touched her arm pointed up. The sound came distant at first like angry wasps. Through breaks in clouds she saw them. Chinese aircraft circling high as hunting birds. The first bombs fell without warning split air like thunder. The walls shook. Fire bloomed where Le's house had stood. More planes came screaming low their guns turning ground to iron rain.

Children ran for the shelters while bullets chewed wood to splinters. Someone screamed. The bombs kept falling kept turning homes to smoke and flame kept teaching them why armies bring steel wings to simple fights. Through gaps in burning walls Mai saw Chinese soldiers advance with the patience of men who knew victory came certain as sunrise.

Grandmother Dao found Mai in the smoke. "No choice now," she said. Her words carried weight of knowing why some battles ended before blood touched ground. "No choice except who lives to remember."

They gathered in the square while planes circled, while smoke rose, while around them everything burned. Mai watched their gate swing open watched Chinese soldiers enter with rifles held ready. Their commander spoke through a translator. His words fell flat as spent brass. Surrender or burn. Simple as planting. Final as harvest.

Dao stepped forward raised her hands. Others followed. The soldiers moved among them with rope with purpose with the kind of mercy that makes prisoners count breath like counting coins. Mai felt hemp bite her wrists while behind her their home turned to ash while above them aircraft drew circles in sky like writing fate with wings of steel.

Through smoke Mai watched their flag come down, watched Chinese soldiers raise their own, watched everything simple and good turn to memory. The commander spoke again. The village was now under Chinese protection. All weapons would be surrendered. All rice would be counted. All people would learn new wisdom about armies and empire and what happens to those who dare stand against iron maps.

They spent that night in their own temple while guards walked the walls while smoke hung thick as grief. Mai touched the space where jade had hung, remembered other armies that had come, remembered how villages survived when warriors fell. The darkness pressed close while children cried while old ones whispered prayers while everyone learned why some victories came measured in who lived to plant next season's rice.

The raiders knelt in predawn darkness, cleaning their weapons with practiced ritual. Metal scraped against metal as they prepared for the next raid, the next lesson in making an army starve.

Young Hue burst from the jungle shadows, his feet leaving bloody prints through shredded sandals. He collapsed at Spitting Woman's feet, words rushing out between desperate gasps for air. "Chinese soldiers came in night," he choked. "Professional troops. Not bandits." His hands shook as he gripped her sleeve. "They took everyone. Headman first. Then teachers. Children."

Granier saw the weight of screams in the boy's eyes. "They kill one at dawn," Hue whispered. "Say they wait for you. Both of you. Say they kill all if you don't come."

Spitting Woman's face hardened into something ancient and terrible. Her hands moved over her rifle with mechanical precision, checking everything except her heart, which had already chosen. "These are my people," she said first in her hill dialect, then combat French, then in a voice that carried centuries of grief. "They raised me when I had no one. Gave me home when I was nothing."

The raiders watched fate draw its bloody map across her face. Granier turned to his sergeant, speaking with the gravity of three wars lived and too many deaths counted. "The supply lines must be cut," he said. "The snake must starve."

"We will make them bleed," the sergeant replied, sharp as a blade's edge. "Make them count supplies in drops of blood."

Spitting Woman touched Granier's arm, brief as a shadow. "You don't have to come," she said. "Your war is here."

Granier smiled in the growing light. "My war has always been where you are."

The sergeant barked orders, sending raiders melting into jungle shadows. They would keep burning depots, keep teaching the Chinese army the lessons they needed to learn.

Granier checked his rifle, his blade, everything. They moved through morning mist while behind them the raiders disappeared into war's shadows. Ahead, their village waited like an open grave.

"We bring hell," Spitting Woman said, her face carrying mountain's patience and ancestral wisdom.

Granier looked at her then, understanding finally that what he'd thought weakness - his love for these people - had become strength deeper than any empire could break.

In the gray dawn, Granier lay among bamboo shadows, watching Chinese patrols trace their mechanical paths across ground his people had walked free mere weeks before. The village rose behind fresh walls like some architect's nightmare - all sharp stakes and deep ditches that spoke the cold language of modern warfare.

Spitting Woman pressed herself beside him, her breathing so controlled the leaves stayed motionless. Young Bao melted into the earth on their left.

"One hundred twelve on the walls," Granier whispered, scope pressed to his eye. "Thirty-eight in the courtyard. Machine gun nests at north, east, south corners." He counted them like counting mortal sins, each number bringing them closer to an ugly truth.

The Chinese had transformed their home into a fortress. Sandbags piled high, machine guns positioned with mathematical precision, professional soldiers moving with the careful choreography of men who knew their deadly craft.

"Watch," Spitting Woman breathed as a patrol checked the minefield. Their metal detectors swept over innocent grass where hundreds of mechanical flowers waited to bloom in fury and flesh.

Another team walked the palisade walls, morning light catching their rifle barrels like snake scales. No villagers were visible, but cooking smoke rose above the walls. A child's cry carried across what had once been the market square, where women had laughed and old men had recounted their lives in the shade.

Spitting Woman's fingers dug into the earth. "One hundred fifty," she whispered like a prayer, like a curse. "One hundred fifty." Her voice hardened with the certainty that they could not take this place alone.

Bao touched her arm, a gesture heavy with shared knowledge. They needed more - more men, more rifles, more ways to turn Chinese pride into Chinese graves. Most of all, they needed a plan.

She rose like quicksilver, eyes cold with calculation. "The other villages made blood oaths," she said. "Swore on ancestors' bones to help when needed. Time they remember what such promises mean."

"They'll come?" Granier asked.

"They'll come. Such debts are paid in blood and brass and broken things that used to be soldiers."

He watched her fade into the jungle shadows, revolution burning in her heart. Behind the palisade walls, Chinese soldiers followed their clockwork patterns, never knowing they had become numbers in an equation older than their empire - the human need to reclaim what was stolen.

"How long?" Bao whispered.

"Two days," Granier replied. "Two days to gather the villages. Then we unleash Hell."

In a smoke-filled hut, twelve village elders sat rigid as temple statues in flickering candlelight. Their faces bore the deep grooves of men who had watched three wars devour their sons. Spitting Woman stood before them, her shadow dancing against the walls like some ancient spirit of vengeance.

"Remember," she said in dialect older than any man present, "how your fathers met French guns with hoes and sickles. How your grandfathers made Japanese soldiers fear our jungle paths. How your own hands taught American soldiers that they were not gods."

The elders shifted uneasily. Grandfather Vu ran gnarled fingers over rifle scars that mapped his arm. "The Chinese bring tanks," he whispered. "They bring mortars that turn brave men to mist."

Spitting Woman's laugh cut sharp as a blade. "And we have mountains," she spat. "We have memory. We have ten generations of fathers who taught us how to make invaders become ancestors."

She paced before them, naming their dead - sons lost to French guns, brothers buried in unmarked graves, daughters who died running from American napalm. Then she named their living - children who would speak Chinese, wives who would serve foreign masters, elders who would watch their culture die.

"Your walls will not save you," she said. "Your silence will not protect you. Your fear will not feed you. They will come with their tanks, their mortars, their modern ways of making warriors into meat."

The elders watched her turn history into weapon, memory into ammunition, shame into something sharper than any blade. By midday, 117 warriors gathered in jungle shadows, their eyes hard with remembering why their fathers swore blood oaths, why their mothers taught them to die standing.

Granier watched them transform from farmers to fighters. They wore ammunition belts like funeral shrouds, handled rifles like ancient hatreds made metal. Spitting Woman touched his arm, brief as a butterfly's landing.

"Keep them angry," she said. "Keep them ready. The army commander waits with promises written in brass and blood."

She melted into jungle shadows, revolution burning in her steps, certainty hardening in her bones. Behind her, warriors cleaned weapons and checked ammunition, becoming something their ancestors would recognize.

"They look ready," Granier said to no one in particular.

An elder nodded. "They remember now. Remember why their grandfathers taught them to kill before they taught them to plant."

The day burned toward darkness like a slow fuse. The fluorescent lights hummed overhead like dying insects, casting sickly shadows across the commander's office. Maps spread before him told stories of defeat in red arrows and blue lines, each mark another calculation of loss. Colonel Nguyen's shoulders carried the weight of ten thousand dead men. "The Chinese armor comes like a river of steel," he said, voice flat and final as a tomb door closing. "They grind our northern positions to dust."

Spitting Woman stood rigid as a blade before his desk, her shadow stark against the wall. Her eyes held memories of children playing in village dust. "We need only weapons," she said, each word measured. "Let us fight them our way, in our hills."

The colonel's laugh scraped metal-harsh against the silence. His fingers traced the map's blue defensive lines that grew thinner with each passing day. "Fight them? With what? Hanoi keeps our tanks and artillery in reserve to defend the capital. My men die by hundreds while Chinese tanks roll through our bunkers like they're made of paper. Ten thousand of our soldiers bleed into mud, and still they come."

"Then give us the means to make them bleed slower," Spitting Woman said, switching from plea to demand quick as a snake strike. The colonel's head snapped up at her tone, but she held his gaze. "The villages remember how to kill. We've taught three armies why our mountains are filled with their bones."

"Memories don't stop tanks," he said, but his hand moved to a drawer, hesitated. "The army has protocols. Proper channels. Ways of measuring what each village is worth in bullets and blood."

"And what is my village worth?" Her voice could have frozen flame.

The colonel opened the drawer slow as opening a grave. Two green metal boxes emerged, ammunition meant for rifles that once belonged to dead American soldiers. "This is all I can spare. Ammunition for your sniper rifles," he said. "Use them well. With luck you can build your own arsenal from your dead enemy's weapons."

Spitting Woman lifted the boxes, felt their weight

settle into her bones like prophecy. In these simple green containers lay mathematics simpler than army calculations - how many bullets it takes to stop a soldier, how many soldiers it takes to make an army hesitate, how many hesitations it takes to keep a village free.

The colonel watched her move toward the door, his eyes heavy with knowing how many villages he'd already sacrificed to buy time. "We can't hold them forever," he said to her back. "Some ground must be surrendered so other ground can live."

She paused at the threshold, half-turned. "Not my ground," she said. "Never my ground." The words fell between them like stones into still water.

Outside, darkness gathered thick as smoke from burning homes. Each step away from the colonel's office made the ammunition boxes grow heavier, as if they contained not just bullets but the weight of every ancestor who had died defending this soil, every child who would live or die by how well she used these too-few rounds.

The night wind carried scents of gunpowder and burning diesel from the northern front. Somewhere in that darkness, Chinese soldiers prepared tomorrow's attacks.

The jungle drew its shadows close as Spitting Woman found them gathered in the hollow, warriors quiet as hunting cats in the darkness. Granier sat cross-legged on wet earth, his hands moving across his rifle with the precise tenderness of a man remembering old lovers, old wars, old deaths dealt in other shadows. When the green ammunition boxes hit dirt they rang hollow as temple bells in abandoned shrines.

"Two hundred rounds," she said in combat French, her voice barely stirring the night air. "That's what the army measures as our village's worth." The warriors drew closer, moonlight catching their eyes in ways that made them look like creatures born of older, darker ages. Some still carried wounds from the temple battle, half-healed reminders of what modern weapons could do to ancient courage.

Granier's hands never stopped moving across the rifle, but his eyes found hers in the darkness. "Not enough," he said. "Not nearly enough." His fingers traced the weapon's scars like reading prophecy. "But we'll make do."

The warrior chief, Tran, touched the rifle that had been his father's, that had killed French and American soldiers before coming to rest in his hands. "They have helicopters," he said, voice soft as falling leaves. "Have tanks. Have things that turn night into day and men into meat."

"They have pride," Spitting Woman answered, and her smile gleamed sharp as a knife catching moonlight. "Have protocol. Have everything that makes soldiers walk the same paths at the same times thinking shadows will never know."

"We need to draw them out into the jungle. We own the jungle. We fight on our ground, not theirs," said Granier.

He scraped a map in the earth with a stick worn smooth from drawing other battles, other ambushes, other ways of turning enemy strength against itself. The warriors gathered closer, their breath mixing with night mist as he showed them how Chinese patrols moved, how modern armies wrote their death warrants in predictable patterns.

"Every soldier carries 200 rounds," he said, each word measured careful as ammunition. "Every patrol becomes our supply line." His finger traced paths through the dirt map. "Here, they'll walk proud. Here, they'll walk tired."

Old Minh, who had fought three armies from these hills, spat into the darkness. "But their guns reach further," he said. "Their grenades turn earth inside out. Their bullets don't care about ancient ways."

Granier's laugh came soft as blood soaking into soil. "We have what they can never have," he said. "We have ten generations of turning invaders' pride into invaders' graves."

Spitting Woman moved through the warriors like smoke through trees, touching shoulders, whispering old words. "First their weapons," she said. "Then their ammunition. Then their lives. Then everything they thought they could keep." Each word fell between them.

Understanding bloomed in the warriors' eyes like night flowers opening to moon's touch. They had heard stories from their grandfathers, stories of how hills people turned French rifles against French soldiers, turned American bombs against American troops, turned every army's strength into that army's weakness.

By dawn they would begin writing legend in blood and brass and borrowed weapons. The night wrapped them in shadow while they planned how to make Chinese soldiers donate their rifles to village victory, how to make modern army become an unwilling quartermaster.

They had become something older than metal, older than gunpowder, older than anything except the need to defend what was always theirs. The jungle watched with ancient patience while they prepared to teach Chinese soldiers why some victories are written in weapons that change hands like changing fate.

In the distance, a helicopter's searchlight swept the valley like a dying star, never knowing it illuminated its own future grave. Tomorrow would begin the revolt. But tonight belonged to the shadows.

As dawn broke, Granier, sun to his back, wedged himself into the fork of a massive ironwood eighty feet up. The ancient branches held him like a cradle of stone. Through his scope he watched the walls where Chinese soldiers moved in patterns shaped by protocol and pride. One hundred rounds lay cool against his chest. Each one a promise each one a death if his hands stayed steady.

"Let's begin," Spitting Woman, also carrying one hundred rounds, whispered from the teak twenty meters left. Her voice carried just enough. A soldier stepped into view checking his sector the way they had trained him. Her shot cracked and he went down thrashing.

Inside the fortress hundreds of soldiers moved with purpose. Granier picked his targets. An officer shouting orders fell quiet when the bullet took his jaw. A machine gunner died adjusting his weapon. A radioman dropped with his handset still raised. Each shot precise. Each shot measured. Each brass case falling through leaves.

The Chinese commander grabbed his lieutenant spoke sharp and angry. Through his scope Granier watched them gesture toward the jungle's edge. The sawing started then. Steel teeth cutting through wood.

The timber groaned gave way birthed a hole big enough for men to slip through in the palisades near the back of the village.

"Thirty men," Spitting Woman said. "Moving fast. Professional." Her rifle cracked again and a soldier on the wall fell inside. More brass falling through leaves. More promises kept.

"Let them come," said Granier.

"If we don't move our firing positions, won't their commander suspect something?" said Spitting Woman.

"I doubt it. He thinks we're farmers and don't know the ways of war," said Granier.

The lieutenant led his platoon through the gap. They flowed into jungle shadow. Their training made them dangerous. Their pride made them dead.

Camouflaged eyes watched as the Chinese soldiers moved below while death waited above.

The platoon moved through jungle like men who knew their business. Their boots found clear ground their eyes swept shadows their rifles stayed ready. Professional soldiers who had no way of knowing they walked a path shaped by older wisdom. The first man died when his foot found a trigger he never saw. The punji pit opened beneath him and he fell screaming onto bamboo points smeared with poison.

The platoon scattered for cover, but cover had been chosen for them. More traps. A snare took a soldier by his ankle hauled him up and slammed his body against a tree trunk covered with spikes. Trip wires sang their steel songs and men fell clutching wounds that would not clean would not heal would not be anything except what village wisdom made them… death.

The lieutenant feared moving his men further

through the jungle. He considered his options, but he was too late.

With the platoon now immobilized the warriors came. They flowed from high ground like water finding low. Their spears flew straight and true. Blowguns and bows launched their arrows. Metal sparked against metal as Chinese rifles tried to answer but jungle knows its own and warriors moved too fast too far too deadly for modern weapons to matter.

A Chinese sergeant went down with three arrows in his chest. A radio man died with a dart in his throat his voice gone before he could call warning. The lieutenant shot two warriors before a spear took him through his back.

When silence came the warriors moved among the dead. They took rifles took ammunition took everything empire had donated to revolution's cause. Their own dead they carried deep into the jungle. The Chinese they left for whatever comes in dark to feed on fallen things. The jungle would keep their bones like it kept all the bones of men who thought numbers alone made victory.

The warriors disappeared into shadow carrying captured steel and bullets. They left brass scattered like copper coins left blood soaked into earth left markers for others to read.

The Chinese commander stood at the map table when the scout came through the hole in the back of the palisades. The young soldier's uniform hung in tatters. Blood ran from a dozen thorn cuts across his face. He tried to salute, but his arm shook too bad.

"Report," the commander said.

"All dead, sir. The whole platoon. We found them

scattered through the trees. Thirty men striped of their gear and weapons."

The commander's hand moved to his pistol. The weight of it steadied him. "How?"

"Traps first, sir. Pits and snares. Then the savages came. Too many footprints to count. A hundred maybe more. Spears and arrows. The lieutenant he tried to—" The scout's voice cracked. "They took the weapons, sir. Every rifle. All the ammunition."

The commander's fist came down hard on the map table. The scout flinched. Outside the walls the morning heat pressed down and somewhere in the shadows death waited with scavenged steel and stolen brass and patience older than empires.

"What of the snipers?" the commander said.

"No sign, sir. But the warriors they came from high ground. From the trees. Maybe that's where—"

"Get out."

The scout fled. The commander stood alone with his maps and his pride and the knowledge that thirty of his men lay dead in jungle shade while their weapons now armed the enemy outside the wall.

Siege

Morning mist clung to the valley like sacred smoke while the young boys and girls from the village followed Old Tu to gather water and fish from river traps. Two Chinese guards escorted the children and old woman to the river. Behind the fortress walls, Chinese soldiers gripped modern rifles, watching these primitives with their baskets and jars.

Hidden, Bai watched from the high grass while old Tu led the children to the river. Eight of them carrying clay jars that had held rice now empty would hold water. The two Chinese guards followed lazy in the heat their rifles slung watching children they thought no threat.

Tu knelt at the water's edge showed the children how to rinse the jars. Her ancient hands moved with purpose while the guards stood in shade.

One guard lit a cigarette. The other leaned against a tree. Their eyes had stopped watching, had grown soft with morning heat with duty that felt more like rest than war.

The first stone caught the smoking guard in the temple. The sound it made was like a finger snapping. He fell without noise blood painting the ground where he dropped. The second guard had time to reach for his rifle before Bai's stone launched from his sling crushed his throat. He died trying to breathe trying to understand why death had come from empty air.

The guards on the wall didn't notice anything amiss as the two guards died silently.

The children stood frozen while Bai came down to the water. He took the rifles the ammunition the canteens. The bodies he rolled into deep water let the current take them.

The baskets they carried came from grandmother's hands, woven strong with patterns older than gunpowder. Old Tu had stayed up three nights weaving the slings, her gnarled fingers remembering motions taught by her grandmother's grandmother, when weighted cords could turn distance into death.

Tu reached into her basket pulled out slings woven from twine. She handed them to the children one by one. Her fingers lingered on each showing them how to hold how to load how to make simple cord become weapon.

"Not these." Bai kicked aside rough stones on the water's edge. He walked upstream chose others. Bai knelt in wet sand, his fingers moving across river stones like a blind man reading prayers. Each rock he chose had to be perfect - smooth as aged bone, heavy as destiny, balanced. "Like this," he whispered to the others, holding up a stone that seemed to hum with its own weight. "Feel how it wants to fly."

The children collected stone showing Bai to ensure they passed his inspection. Within a few minutes they had filled two baskets with the ancient ammunition. Once the baskets were filled with stones, the children filled the remaining jars with water and the baskets with wiggling fish from the traps in the river.

Satisfied with the haul, Bai and Old Tu led the children deeper into the jungle. They would not return to the village, not until the Chinese soldiers were dead and the villagers were free. They would live with the warriors now and learn the ways of the jungle.

Before joining their new caretakers, Bai swung around the jungles edge keeping everyone out of sight of the soldiers manning the watchtowers and walls. He came to a section of open ground in front of the palisades. He knew the area well. He had planted the mines that had protected the villagers, but now protected the Chinese soldiers from a surprise attack.

"Watch," Bai said, loading his sling while others gathered close. His movements came fluid as the river itself, each gesture precise as ritual. "Let the stone become bullet, let the cord become rifle, let simple things remember why they were first made for war."

Bai's first cast arced high against gray sky, stone singing ancient song through morning air. Seeing the young warrior at the edge of the jungle using the ancient weapon, the Chinese soldiers laughed behind their wall until the explosion bloomed like a dusty flower, one of their precious mines becoming smoke and shrapnel.

"Now, you try," Bai called, while rifles cracked from the walls, their bullets wasteful and wild against distance. The children stepped forward out of the treeline with their slings and river rocks. More stones flew, more mines bloomed, more paths opened through death's garden. Each explosion wrote revolution's name in dirt and fire.

Behind the fortress walls, soldiers counted detonations with growing unease. These were not the weapons they had trained against, not the threats their modern manuals had prepared them for. These were older things, simpler things, deadly things.

"They think their guns make them gods," old Tu said, handing Bao another basket of smooth stones. "They forget that rivers remember longer than armies, that some weapons need no powder to speak death's truth."

Through morning they worked, letting river stones teach Chinese mines about gravity, about impact. Not many mines died this way, not many paths opened through the killing ground, but enough to show how patience could turn minutes to hours, turn stones to shells, turn ancient ways into modern victory.

The river gave up its ammunition smooth and deadly and patient as time. Young boys and girls who had never known war without gunpowder learned why their grandfathers had taught them to swing stones before holding rifles.

Behind their walls, Chinese soldiers watched and measured and never understood why some of their mines now refused to wait for human feet, why simple rocks could make modern weapons betray their makers to paint battle's face bright and burn war's heart black.

As the afternoon sun sank towards the horizon, Granier and Spitting Woman sat in their respective trees watching. There were few targets now, sometimes only one ever couple of hours. Patience and discipline were required. The Chinese had learned not to break cover while veteran snipers lurked in the jungle. But killing Chinese at this distance had little risk and only cost them precious bullets which they never wasted.

Through scope glass Granier watched Chinese soldiers die one clean shot, one brass case, one lesson at a time. The sun cast long shadows across the killing ground, turning each figure into a dark smear against the pale earth. Spitting Woman lay twenty meters left, her hands steady as mountain stone, her breath measured between heartbeats between kills between ways of making soldiers fear sunlight.

The Chinese soldiers moved like wary animals below, keeping close to the walls, peeking only through gaps in the wooden poles, their eyes scanning the treeline where death waited patient as centuries.

Another Chinese soldier died watching through spaces in wooden walls, his body jerking once before folding in on itself, fell back like a puppet with cut strings while companions learned nobody was safe.

"Clean," Granier murmured. He worked the bolt on his rifle, the metal whispering against metal, the empty brass casing flipping into the air and landing on the earth below.

Another soldier died from Spitting Woman's barrel thinking distance meant safety, thinking the afternoon sun would blind the pair of snipers. Blood painted the hut wall behind him in abstract patterns.

Through glass they read fear blooming in enemy eyes, watched it spread like infection through the ranks. Modern warfare broke against their patience like waves against stone. No food came in, no water came fresh, no supplies reached men who thought themselves hunters but learned about being prey. A sound rose from behind the walls, something between a moan and a prayer.

"They're starving in there," Spitting Woman said, adjusting her scope with careful precision. "Listen to them. Even their prayers sound hungry."

"Their fortress has become their prison," said Granier always keeping his eye search for targets through his scope.

The Chinese commander tried moving men at night, tried shifting positions, tried teaching soldiers how to stay below wood's cover, but always someone grew careless, always someone stood too tall, always someone died learning why snipers remember every shot they take. A third soldier fell reaching for his canteen, his last thought spilling red across parched ground.

The Chinese commander watched his men distribute the day's water ration. One cup per villager no more. The well still ran clear, but they couldn't risk letting the hostages gather too much. Might hide it might store it might plan something. Better to keep them thirsty keep them weak.

Through gaps in the palisades wall Chinese sentries scanned the jungle. Their rifles stayed ready their eyes searching shadows where death waited. Three men had died yesterday when they grew careless. Single shots clean through the head. The snipers never wasted ammunition never missed never showed mercy.

Inside the village hall the Chinese had converted to their command post Lieutenant Wu marked another day on his chart. Eight now since the siege began. "Water holding steady," he told the commander. "Rice for one week maybe less." He didn't mention ammunition. They all knew those numbers. Knew how the snipers were bleeding them round by round man by man.

Old Tran watched the Chinese ration out the morning rice. His granddaughter clung to his leg eyes blank with hunger. Half a bowl each now. The children got no extra. The soldiers took the most kept their strength while the village grew weak. Through gaps in the walls he could see jungle thick and green. Could hear birds calling soft as memory. Somewhere out there the warriors waited. Patient as mountains.

The Chinese had learned to stay low stay in shadow stay away from gaps in the walls. The snipers knew every angle every line of sight. When men died they died clean one shot one brass case one lesson about Chinese vulnerability. The jungle held its own mathematics its own ways of counting coup.

Mai gathered her family's water ration watching the Chinese guard measure it careful as counting gold. Her daughter's lips had cracked from thirst. The soldiers kept most of the water for themselves. Used it to make tea to wash their clothes while children grew hollow-eyed with need.

Through the day heat pressed down like a weight. The Chinese rotated positions keeping low where bullets couldn't find them. Four-hour shifts they worked always watching always waiting.

Lieutenant Wu moved along the wall checking his men. His rifle stayed ready against his shoulder. They had learned to recognize death's angles. Where shadows grew teeth where jungle turned men to meat. Some called the snipers ghosts though never where the commander might hear.

The cooking fires burned low through midday. The village women stirred pots where rice cooked thin as water. The soldiers watched them careful making sure nothing disappeared nothing hidden nothing saved.

The hostages ate in the square where guards could watch them. Could count spoonfuls could keep hunger's mathematics precise.

At the temple the Chinese had stacked their medical supplies. Bandages ran low. The iodine bottles stood nearly empty. Three men had died of infection this week. The jungle taught its own lessons about modern medicine and how some wounds refuse to heal clean.

The afternoon brought heat that made air shimmer. Sweat soaked through uniforms leaving dark patches. The soldiers passed a single water bottle between posts. Two swallows each no more. Above them the sun moved like a torch across empty sky. No clouds no rain no relief. It was as if nature itself was conspiring against the invaders.

In the command post the commander marked positions on his map. Four hundred meters of wall to defend. Ninety-eight rifles spread across the positions. Not enough to cover every angle. They rotated the gaps hoping the snipers wouldn't find the weak spots. Hoping supply lines would reach them before ammunition ran too low before food ran out before the jungle's patience outlasted them.

Night brought its own rhythm. The hostages gathered in family groups sharing what little they had saved from their rations. The guards watched them careful as counting coins. Someone hummed an old song soft enough the commander couldn't hear. Couldn't stop. The music carried like prayer across darkened streets.

Through darkness Chinese patrols walked the walls. Their rifles ready their eyes searching shadows. The snipers were out there. Waiting. The soldiers had learned to count success in surviving one more watch one more night one more moment between bullets.

Dawn came gray as gunsmoke. Another day began. The hostages lined up for water for rice for measuring life in spoonfuls. The soldiers took their positions watching jungle that waited thick and green. This was how siege worked. Not with glory but with patience. With counting ammunition like counting heartbeats. With holding on until something broke. Until pride or hunger or the jungle proved stronger.

The days ticked away. The siege held. No rain. No relief. The villagers gathered in the temple court while morning heat pressed down. Their faces had gone sharp with hunger. Children cried for water that wasn't there. Through his scope Granier watched the Chinese soldiers across the yard looking just as hollow, just as dry, just as close to breaking.

Old Lien came out with his last jar of rice wine. He poured measures small as mercy into tin cups. The wine went to the children first then the old ones then the rest of the villagers. Each sip just enough to wet throats gone raw with thirst.

"Three days," Tu whispered. Her voice cracked like dry earth. "The well runs red with rust. The jars stand empty."

Little Dao huddled against his mother. His lips had cracked and bled.

Through the walls came the sound of Chinese voices. They spoke of water of food of everything men think about when hunger burns away discipline. A soldier tried to drink his own urine. Others watched him with eyes gone dull with need.

No one spoke of giving in. The villagers had eaten the last rice eaten everything that could be boiled soft enough to swallow. But the villagers would not give way to thirst or hunger. They had something armies forget. This was their ground, their home, their place that remembered them.

Granier watched a Chinese soldier collapse from heat. Others dragged him into shade. The villagers watched and said nothing and knew that thirst would drive the soldiers out or kill them where they stood. Either way the ground would remember who it belonged to.

"How many rounds?" Granier asked, watching brass shine dull as old coins in morning light.

"Enough," she answered. "Enough to teach them why walls work both ways."

"Soon, their commander will swallow his pride and radio for reinforcements."

"Good. We need more weapons."

Behind fortifications Chinese troops stayed low, stayed hungry, learning when pride becomes preview of funeral. The sun moved overhead like counting days while brass cases fell like counting coins.

"Look," Spitting Woman whispered, a smile sharp as knife edge touching her lips. "They're burning their dead now. It won't be long."

"The villagers suffer along with the Chinese."

"Yes. But they know why they suffer. They're tough. They'll outlast their captures."

Dark clouds rose above wooden walls, carrying scent of defeat on morning wind. They had become something older than war, something that turned daylight into darkness. Victory would taste like ash and knowing that hunger kills slower than bullets but just as sure.

Through night dark the scout came silent as prayer spoke quick as dying told how China wrote its name in diesel smoke and truck wheels and soldiers racing toward dawn's appointment. Sweat ran down his face, clothes torn from running jungle and mountain paths, eyes wide with urgent news. "Fifty more men and supplies," he said, voice carrying weight of iron wheels on mountain roads. "Coming up the south road. Heavy trucks. Machine guns mounted."

Granier and Spitting Woman stood in shadow, their eyes meeting knowing some battles choose themselves. The jungle air pressed close around them, thick with night moisture and the scent of coming violence. "The trucks would come fast," the scout said, chest still heaving. "Would come heavy. Chinese infantry with fresh ammunition."

"How long?" Granier asked, already checking his rifle's action.

"By morning. Maybe less," the scout whispered. "Every truck but the lead truck drive without lights, but I heard them."

"Some must stay here and keep the Chinese pinned down in the village. We cannot allow the siege to be broken," said Granier.

Granier and Spitting Woman gathered their hunters, warriors who had learned to kill clean, who had learned to make night into weapon. Through dark they moved, bare feet finding silent purchase on wet ground.

"Here," Spitting Woman said, touching earth where mountain road cut sharp. "Where trucks must slow, where drivers must gear down."

Through moon dark the warriors shaped earth into dragon's teeth, steel spikes driven deep, angled sharp, waiting patient as graves for truck tires. The jungle night pressed close around them, alive with cricket song and the quiet sounds of men preparing death's garden. Granier moved among warriors, his whispered instructions barely stirring the heavy air. "Here," he said, "and here."

"The first truck must die there," Spitting Woman said in her hill tribe dialect, pointing where road curved sharp against mountain. "The others will pile up behind it." She worked alongside them, teaching angles, teaching timing, teaching ways of making soldiers die in precise orchestration. Her knife caught moonlight as she trimmed wire to lethal lengths.

The zigzag trench cut the road like a serpent's spine, like fate's own signature. Young Tran dug deep, sweat gleaming on his shoulders despite the night's chill. "Will they see it?" he asked, voice tight with anticipation.

"Too late," Granier answered. "Far too late."

They worked silent as ceremony, laying gifts in ground. Trip wires thin as mercy stretched between shadows. Punji pits lined with bamboo spikes waited beneath innocent earth, their tips smeared with things older than gunpowder. "Grandfather's recipe," Old Wei whispered, applying dark paste with practiced care. "Makes even small wounds speak with death's tongue."

The warriors moved through dark like specters through dreams, placing Chinese-made Claymores stolen from dead patrols and supply depots, positioning death just so, just right, just where soldiers must walk when trucks meet dragon's teeth. "Make every tree a weapon," Spitting Woman instructed, showing them how to turn jungle itself against their enemy. "Make every shadow a kill zone."

"No cover," she whispered later, marking where Chinese troops must cross. "They will come proud of their training and weapons," she said, checking sight lines through her scope. "They will die professional."

Through night they worked, through shadow they shaped, through darkness they built. The air grew thick with purpose, with certainty.

Granier touched earth, touched wire, touched everything that would turn soldiers into statistics. "It's good," he said finally, watching warriors disappear into foliage, into shadow, into whatever darkness birthed vengeance.

"The first truck," Granier said, positioning his men in shadow, "must die here. The others will have nowhere to turn."

Spitting Woman spoke soft in hill dialect translating for Granier. Her hands moved swift and sure, setting charges.

Down valley, they heard the first distant growl of engines. Trucks came carrying the battle's next chapter, written in diesel smoke and dragon's teeth. "Now," Spitting Woman whispered, "we wait. We watch. "

"No choice," Granier said, checking fields of fire, measuring angles, calculating how to turn truck column into metal coffins.

"No choice," she answered, her voice carrying certainty harder than the bullets they'd use.

They waited in dark, while truck sounds came, while diesel engines wrote their own obituaries. The night air grew thick with anticipation, with knowing fifty soldiers rode toward whatever gods handled prayers of men who die.

"Listen," Spitting Woman whispered. " They make noise enough to wake our ancestors."

The trucks came fast and heavy.

Positioning himself up on a knoll above the road, Granier felt his pulse steady, felt time crystallize into perfect moment of knowing. He waited while engines grew louder, while fate grew closer.

Through his scope Granier watched the lead truck's headlights sweep the mountain road. The driver hunched forward squinting at sharp curves up steep slopes that forced the trucks to grind up in low gear. The soldier next to him held a map with a flashlight trying to read terrain in dark.

"It's too late for that," said Granier covering the light with his hand. "They'll be here soon enough."

The driver saw the dragon's teeth too late. His headlights caught the jagged trench across the road ahead and he yanked the wheel left, but the truck was already moving too heavy too fast. As the front of the truck sank into the trench, the front tires exploded. Metal shrieked as spikes ripped through the undercarriage. The truck slammed sideways blocking the road.

Behind it brake lights flared red as the convoy tried to stop. Three trucks crashed into each other accordion-style. The fourth truck managed to halt five yards back.

Soldiers poured from the vehicles shouting orders. They took up defensive positions used the trucks for cover tried to secure the area. A lieutenant got them organized into fire teams. Their flashlight beams cut through dark as they began searching the jungle edges. And still nothing happened.

Granier steadied his breathing. Through the scope he watched soldiers move in practiced patterns. He kept his finger off the trigger waited for the ambush to fully develop. Fifty men bunched between the trucks exactly where they needed them to be.

The lieutenant sent two fire teams into the tree line. That's when the claymores detonated. The blasts caught the soldiers in crossfire sprayed steel balls through their ranks. Men fell screaming.

Spitting Woman fired a tracer round into the lead truck's gas tank. The gas tank exploded painting the night orange and illuminating the Chinese soldiers. Perfect targets.

The warriors opened fire from the high ground. Their rifles spoke in controlled bursts. Soldiers died trying to find cover died trying to return fire.

The lieutenant rallied his men behind the second truck. Granier put a round through his chest. Seeing their commander dead, the soldiers broke then ran for the jungle. Trip wires caught their legs. Punji stakes found their flesh. The warriors kept shooting kept killing kept turning the road into a slaughterhouse.

The remaining soldiers ran for the dark tree line. Their boots slipped in mud as rounds kicked up dirt around them. A private went down screaming with a punji stake through his thigh. His squad mate tried to help him caught a bullet in the throat.

"Into the trees," the sergeant shouted. He fired blind at the hillside where muzzle flashes marked the warriors' positions. Twenty men left. More dying. They crashed through undergrowth while more bullets snapped past their heads.

Three soldiers hit trip wires at once. The explosions lit up the night. Body parts rained through branches. The sergeant stumbled on something soft that had been a man moments before. More shots came from the flanks now. The warriors had them surrounded.

A soldier stopped to reload. An arrow took him in the chest. He pulled it out died clutching the shaft. The others kept running leaving him there. A grenade exploded somewhere behind them. Someone screamed for his mother in Mandarin.

The sergeant found himself alone. His men were dead or scattered. He ran until his lungs burned. When he stopped to get his bearings a blow gun dart caught him in the neck. He died trying to understand how fifty professional soldiers had become prey so quickly.

Only four made it into deep jungle. They ran until their legs gave out. When they stopped to rest spears came out of darkness. The warriors took their weapons their ammunition left their bodies to the night.

When the shooting faded to nothing Granier counted bodies. Fifty men lay scattered across the road between burning trucks and in the jungle. The warriors moved among them taking weapons taking ammunition leaving everything else for the jungle to claim.

Granier examined each truck searching for more weapons. He found a mortar with wooden boxes filled with shells and two light machine guns with tripods. He knew firsthand the power of artillery and heavy weapons how they created chaos even against an enemy with superior strength.

As dawn approached, Spitting Woman and Granier led the warriors back toward the village. After four miles the warriors stopped in a clearing to give their legs a rest and examine the loot they had claimed from the dead Chinese soldiers. Four warriors guarded the perimeter.

Through jungle shadow they spread war's bounty across damp earth, rifles and shells laid out like sacred artifacts on banana leaves and woven mats. The mortar lay clean as sin between them, its dark mouth promising high angles and death. Warriors moved with quiet purpose in the heavy air thick with gun oil and revolution's sweat, cleaning captured weapons.

"Here," Spitting Woman said, her fingers dancing across a Chinese rifle's action, scarred hands moving with mechanic's grace. "Listen to how it speaks." She worked the bolt, metal whispering against metal in the humid air. "Different from Soviet guns. Looser. But it kills just the same." Her eyes caught morning light filtering through the canopy, sharp as the knife at her belt.

Granier knelt beside wooden boxes of mortar shells, their Chinese markings stark against dark wood, counting their weight in brass. Sweat ran down his neck as he measured each box, feeling the heat of the day building. "Enough to reach the village," he said, measuring distances in his mind, reaching the guards who thought themselves safe behind the wooden wall. "Enough to break through the palisades."

"More than enough," Chi said, his young hands moving swift across a captured machine gun, oil-stained rags turning metal mirror-bright. His eyes held hunger, the look of a boy given his first man's weapon. "How many mortar shells for each box?"

"Twenty," Granier answered, lifting one shell to catch jungle light on its brass case. The shell felt heavy with purpose, with everything that turned simple metal into judgment.

Spitting Woman moved among the men like a priestess among acolytes, adjusting grips, correcting stances, teaching the language of captured weapons. Her voice carried weight of vast experience. "Hold it tight against your shoulder," she told Ming, watching him struggle with an unfamiliar stock, his arms still bearing scars from their last battle. "Let it become part of you."

The mortar tube caught filtered sunlight between broad leaves, metal gleaming with deadly promise. Old Wei studied the sighting mechanism with careful eyes, his weathered face reflecting memories. "Like the French ones," he said, fingers tracing familiar curves. "From when I was young. But Chinese make them heavier."

"Pride makes the best weapons," Granier said, stacking another crate of ammunition beside the growing arsenal. Brass shells caught jungle light like fallen stars. "Pride and arrogance and thinking technology alone wins wars." His hands moved across captured guns, reading their stories in scratches and wear and the marks of men who died holding them.

Through afternoon they worked in rising heat and falling light, cleaning and counting. Young Bao mastered the mortar while others practiced with captured rifles until metal spoke smooth as mother tongue. Night came slow through jungle canopy, bringing cool air heavy with promise of rain and the soft sounds of nocturnal things waking to their own hunger.

"Even with these, we still don't have enough weapons for everyone," Granier said, watching warriors pack their deadly harvest into cloth and canvas, weapons disappearing like snakes into shadow.

"Our people are dying of starvation. We are out of time."

"Tomorrow then."

"Tomorrow," Spitting Woman agreed. "Tomorrow

we show them why death speaks clearest through China's own guns." Her eyes held certainty hard as the brass shells they'd counted, bright as the muzzle flashes that would paint tomorrow's dawn.

Moonlight caught the metal pole in Mai's hands while she waited behind the temple. The night air hung thick with humidity and wood smoke. Through gaps in the wall she watched the Chinese guards walk their rounds precise as ceremony. Twelve shadows crouched beside her each one holding tools they had kept hidden since surrender. Hoes and scythes and the long poles they used for harvesting fruit. Simple steel that remembered how to kill.

The guards passed marking time with boot steps that echoed off stone. Mai counted heartbeats. The women had learned the pattern of the patrol over three days of watching. Twenty steps then turn. Fifteen more then check the gate. Simple as tending rice.

She touched Lin's shoulder once. They moved through shadow through smoke through spaces between moonlight. Their feet found earth silent as cats while behind them the guards kept walking kept counting kept measuring night with steps that meant nothing against women who had learned to hunt before they learned to hide.

The first wire sang when Mai's pole lifted it. They crawled beneath it one by one while metal whispered against cloth. The second barrier came harder. Hong's hoe caught the wire wrong made a sound like fingernail against teeth. They went still as death while above them a guard turned raised his rifle peered into dark.

When his back turned they moved again. Poles and tools lifted wire while women flowed beneath it like water finding low ground. Mai went last made sure the wire settled silent behind them. They crossed the killing ground between barriers and jungle in seconds that felt like seasons.

The forest wrapped them in shadow in shelter in everything that made women stronger than soldiers. They moved without sound without mercy without looking back at walls that had become prison. Mai led them along paths her grandfather had taught her. The warriors would be waiting. Would be watching. Would be counting breaths until women became weapons.

When they found the warriors the night had turned toward dawn. Mai stood straight while around her twelve women who had been prisoners became hunters. When she spoke her voice carried weight of knowing why some fights started with tools that remembered blood. "We've come to kill them," she said. The warriors nodded while night turned toward morning while women became what mountains needed them to be.

Home

Before dawn, Granier, Spitting Woman, and the warriors arrived in the jungle surrounding the village. The children woke and ran to Spitting Woman grabbing her hands, touching her clothes like some magic would rub off on them. Spitting Woman gently touched each child saying their name perfect and precious.

Old Binh approached Granier and spoke in French, "Nothing has come in or gone out since you left. The siege still holds, but our people suffer."

"Not for long," said Granier reassuring him.

"You were successful?"

"Yes. But we are still short on weapons. Those without rifles will wait in the cover of the forest until one of our warriors goes down, then they will pick up his weapon and continue the assault."

"It will be done as you say. We attack tonight?"

"No. We attack now. As soon as the men are in position."

"It will be daylight."

"Yes. We will have clear targets should they fire on our warriors from the walls or watchtowers as they advance."

"But so will they have clear targets."

"Yes, but I think our aim will be more accurate than theirs."

"This will be a bloody battle."

"Hopefully more their blood, than ours."

Granier turned to the warriors. "Set up the mortar and machine guns where I showed you. We will attack the wall and gate at the front of the village."

In morning light, the radio spoke in crackling bursts, its voice carrying news of fifty men becoming meat in mountain shadows. The Chinese commander stood rigid in his office, sweat dark on his collar while beside him his lieutenant's voice shook reporting losses. His face twisted as each detail struck him, each burned truck, each broken body, each failure.

Through village streets he moved with fury's own purpose, his boots marking earth like measuring graves. The hostages huddled against temple walls, their eyes carrying weight of knowing what came next. He watched them while morning sun cast long shadows, while birds fell silent, while air grew thick with coming violence.

Young Yen stood among them, her wedding flowers barely wilted on the altar at home, her hands still hard from working rice fields before China came claiming ground. The commander's hand found her hair, fingers tangling like fate's own grasp. "This one," he said, voice flat as slate, empty as shell casings.

Through the village they went, her steps steady despite his pulling, despite knowing death walked beside her. His men watched with faces carved from stone, some turning away, some watching with hunger's own eyes. The hostages wept quiet tears that watered earth already drunk on sorrow.

Spitting Woman lay on the ridge above, scope glass cold against her eye, hands steady despite the rage burning in her chest. She watched Yen walk, remembering the child who once brought her flowers, who danced at harvest festival, who represented everything the village had tried to protect from war's hunger. The front gate opened and Yen stepped out alone.

Spitting Woman and Granier watched looking for a shot at her captor. There was none.

Hidden behind the swinging gate, the commander's pistol came clean from leather, metal catching morning sun. Yen stood straight, her eyes finding horizon like seeking tomorrow's dawn. The shot cracked across valley walls, echoing like fate's own laughter. She fell without sound, without fear, her blood running black across the ground.

Through scope glass Spitting Woman watched, her tears falling hot as rifle brass, each drop carrying weight of vengeance yet to come. They left Yen's body there, morning sun painting her skin gold, making her more than corpse, more than warning, more than whatever measures distance between living quiet and dying loud.

Spitting Woman counted breaths until rage turned cold as gun metal, until fury became calculation, until grief became weapon sharper than any blade. The sun burned while Yen's blood soaked into earth.

"Remember," Spitting Woman whispered to the wind, to the mountains, to whatever gods handle prayers of those who kill for love, not hate.

"Remember what they've taught us about cost. About price. About why some deaths can only be answered by burning everything China built thinking walls alone make a fortress."

In the morning mist they gathered beneath trees older than empires, Granier and Spitting Woman standing close enough that their shoulders touched, their breath mingling. Around them the warriors moved like wraiths through shadow, checking weapons. The coming battle hung between them heavy as a stone, its weight pressing against their skin like a physical thing.

"No words for victory," she said in the hill dialect that flowed from her tongue like water. Granier touched her arm once, a gesture brief as a butterfly's landing but carrying the permanence of a scar. They both knew some fights couldn't be won, only survived.

The captured Chinese rifles gleamed dully in the twilight as the warriors checked their stolen ammunition. The Chinese had weighed everything except a warrior's courage, which sat in their bones heavier than death itself. Dawn would come soon, painting the sky in color.

They spoke of village life, of fishing lessons, of simple things that felt like prayers against the darkness. Neither mentioned how many would die before the walls fell, before the hostages breathed free air again. "No retreat," Granier said, his fingers moving across his rifle like a blind man reading fate. "No mercy," Spitting Woman answered, her eyes black pools that reflected Yen's death and the hostages' terror.

The warriors gathered close, their captured guns held like talismans against the night. Spitting Woman spoke in dialect old as the mountains themselves, "The coming day carries weight. It carries cost. It carries knowing that some battles end only when the last warrior falls or the last wall breaks."

"We go together," Granier said, the words coming heavy with choices made long ago.

"We die together," she answered, and sometimes truth needed no more decoration than that.

They moved through darkness like incense through temple halls, checking weapons one final time while dawn approached on feet soft as a tiger's. The jungle held its breath around them as fate measured the narrow distance between living and dying. There would be no surrender, no retreat, no victory measured in anything except complete possession or absolute destruction.

The warriors understood this truth deep in their bones, carrying it like extra ammunition, like a weapon itself. When dawn finally came it painted the sky red as a wound. Some fights could end only one way, and they all knew which way this one must go.

The first mortar shell screamed through the darkness like a demon unleashed, its arc perfect as an engineer's dream. When it struck the fortress wall the explosion bloomed orange and deadly. More shells followed, their steel voices carrying revolution's judgment into the predawn air.

Through the jungle's black throat hundreds of flaming arrows rose like fireflies gone mad, their burning tips seeking the wooden palisades that had once been trees. The flames caught and spread, racing along the walls while Chinese soldiers scrambled in confusion, their shadows dancing grotesque against the growing inferno.

Granier's rifle cracked once, precise as a surgeon's knife. A soldier spun away from the burning wall, his chest blooming red, his eyes already seeing whatever waits beyond duty. Twenty meters left, Spitting Woman's rifle spoke three times in rapid succession, dropping soldiers who thought protocol meant something against a warrior's fury.

On the edge of the jungle, Mai stood in predawn shadow the weight of the chain heavy in her hands. Her fingers traced the cold links remembering how she had worked these same fields in peace had planted rice where now mines slept beneath innocent earth. Around her fourteen women waited their breath mixing with morning mist their hearts beating time against ribs. Through gaps in the trees she could see the village walls where Chinese soldiers walked their rounds where home had become fortress.

The chain lay coiled at their feet like an iron snake waiting to strike. Mai remembered Spitting Woman's words about how to sweep it how to clear the killing ground how to make safe passage through death's garden. The metal felt strange against her farmer's calluses different from hoe handles different from the weapons of peace.

Hong touched her shoulder once quick as bird's wing. No words needed between them. They had rehearsed this in darkness had practiced the movements had learned how to dance with death. Mai nodded and they lifted the chain together fifteen women becoming one body one purpose one force against empire's teeth.

Fifteen young women emerged from the shadows dragging a heavy chain between them, their faces set with ancient purpose. Their eyes read the earth like blind men reading fate, knowing where death slept beneath the innocent grass. The chain swept forward, hungry as a serpent, hunting for the mines that lay waiting.

Granier and Spitting Woman increased their rate of fire, protecting the women as they advanced toward the palisades. Chinese soldiers firing from the top of the wall were quickly dealt death's blow, the survivors diving for cover behind the wooden wall.

The first sweep brought thunder. Earth fountained and smoke rose while shrapnel sang past their heads. Mai felt the chain jump in her hands as mines awakened. Through drifting smoke she saw the walls where Chinese soldiers stood rifles ready. A bullet cracked past close enough to stir her hair. More shots came but warriors in the jungle answered and more Chinese soldiers fell.

They moved forward step by careful step letting the chain find its prey. Another mine erupted and Quynh screamed as fragments caught her. Her body rose and fell like a broken doll blood painting morning air. Mai wanted to help her, wanted to comfort her, wanted everything except what war demanded. But the chain needed pulling, needed moving, needed hands steady as mountain stone. She kept pulling the iron links.

Duyen took Quynh's place fingers finding the chain without hesitation. Above them machine guns hammered from the jungle keeping Chinese heads down. But some soldiers braved the bullets stood tall took aim. Three more women fell their bodies marking the path forward. Others came from shadows to take their places grief turning to fury turning to purpose.

Each step brought them closer to the walls. Each sweep of the chain cleared ground that had drunk too much blood. Thu stumbled caught herself kept moving though red ran down her leg. Mai felt sweat run beneath her shirt felt muscles burn felt everything that made this morning different from all the mornings before.

A mortar shell found the wall and wood exploded outward. Chinese soldiers appeared in the breach their eyes wide their rifles trembling. Another shell landed among them and bodies flew apart. Mai watched them fall watched them die watched war write its story in flesh and bone.

The girls' pace picked up as they closed in on the twenty yards of open ground. More minds exploded. More girls went down. And finally, they made it.

The trench waited before them now deep as a grave its slopes lined with wooden stakes they themselves had placed. Mai let the chain fall drew her machete felt its weight like counting future moments. The blade caught dawn light as she climbed down into shadow. Around her women attacked the stakes clearing the way forward one swing at a time.

Bullets sang past finding flesh finding bone finding all the soft places that make women die. Thu screamed high and sharp clutching her ruined leg. More sisters fell more blood ran more death gathered in the trench's throat. Someone far away shouted retreat, but Mai and the others kept swinging, kept cutting, kept measuring time in chunks of wood falling away. They moved through the bottom of the trench and up the opposite side hacked away the stakes, clearing a path for those that would follow.

She saw the grenades arc over the wooden wall

tumble through morning air saw their dark shapes fall saw everything that came next written in their curves. Five of them end over end eternal as stars falling. Mai tried to shout warning tried to move tried to do anything except watch death descend.

The explosions came as one and fire filled her world. Pain in her side from ripped flesh. Her mind whirled like a tornado. Heat and pressure and the wet sound of bodies coming apart. She felt herself fall, felt others fall on top of her, felt the weight of sister's flesh cover her like burial stones. Blood filled her eyes and darkness pressed close.

The last thing she saw through red haze was Chinese soldiers lining the wall was rifles pointing down was everything she had fought to prevent. Then darkness took her and she fell into it letting her sisters' bodies hide her from those who would count her among the dead. Somewhere beyond the dark beyond the pain beyond whatever waited next warriors carried her sacrifice forward carried her fury carried her purpose toward walls that had stolen home from those who belonged to this ground.

Granier had seen many acts of bravery during his wars, but nothing measured those women. He was stunned.

Spitting Woman let her shock turn to anger and fired at the Chinese soldiers killing one after another. Unyielding.

Having seen their sisters and girlfriends fall, the warriors broke from the tree line at a dead run toward the village walls, scream a blood curdling yell, using the path the women had created sacrificing their young lives. The warriors' rage was unstoppable.

The Chinese commander peered through a gap in

the wall seeing a hundred warriors crossing the open ground closing in on the village walls. There was nothing left to stop them. The mines had been detonated, the trench had been cleared, and the wall had been breached. "Fire, you fools. Fire!" he shouted to his men on the top of the wall.

But whenever a soldier raised his head above the top of the wall, Granier or Spitting Woman would take it off. After a half dozen soldiers fell from the wall, nobody challenged the snipers. It was better to face their commander's wrath than a sniper's bullet.

The machine gun covering one of the watchtowers ran through the last bullet on its belt. The gun fell silent. The loader grabbed another belt and opened the gun's feed tray cover to reload.

On the watchtower, a Chinese soldier took the opportunity to rise up and fire down on the advancing warriors in the open field. One of the warriors tumbled to the ground, dead. The other warriors didn't break stride. They kept running at full speed.

Spitting Woman saw the rifleman on the tower and took aim. The bullet hit him in the stomach. Unable to keep his balance, he fell to the ground and died just as the machine gun began firing again.

As the warriors charged toward the breach in the palisades, the Chinese commander yelled to his men, "Fix bayonets!"

The soldier pulled out their long bayonets and snapped them on to the end of their rifle barrels making them shortened pikes.

The warriors now faced a breach filled with sharp steel. None of them flinched. As the first line of warriors reached the trench they jumped to the bottom and started up the side toward the wall. A warrior in the second line swung a pig's bladder full of rice wine and flung it toward the breach. The bladder landed on the end of a bayonet and tore open sending the rice wine on to the soldiers protecting the breach. Another warrior threw a torch at the breach. The rice wine caught fire and consumed five soldiers in an inferno. They dropped their rifles leaving a large gap in the Chinese defense.

The warriors climbed the trench slope using their rifles to break the last of the wooden spikes, then entered the breach. The fighting was hand-to-hand as the warriors using their knives and rifles as clubs fought to create a foothold inside the wall. More warriors poured in through the breach.

The Chinese were unable to hold back the frenzied warriors fighting for their homes and loved ones. More Chinese soldiers rushed forward with their bayonets, but it was too late. The warriors were inside the hamlet and weren't about to give it back. One warrior pulled the ring on a grenade and threw it. It landed next to the leg of one of the towers. The explosion shattered the wood and tower tipped over, then came crashing to the ground with the soldier standing on the platform.

The warriors poured through the breach like a river that had waited centuries to break its dam, their movements fluid as mercury, deadly as nightshade. Too late the Chinese tried to form their lines, too slow they brought their weapons to bear.

Inside the temple, Young Bao watched the three Chinese guards listening to the battle outside. From where Bao sat against the stonewall the curved knife stayed pressed flat against his spine where he'd hidden it three days before.

The oldest guard's curiosity get the better of him and he walked toward the door to see what was happening outside.

Someone started humming. Low and steady. More voices joined. The sound built like wind through trees. The guards shifted their rifles. "Shut up," one shouted. But the humming went on. Got louder.

Angry, the guards turned toward the sound, ready to bring the villagers to heel. Bao moved. The knife came free silent and clean. He drove it up under the nearest guard's ribs. The blade went into the hilt. Blood ran hot over his hands.

The villagers surged forward as one body. They had no weapons except what rage gave them. They caught the second guard as he tried to turn. Pulled him down. His rifle went off once into the ceiling. Then hands found his throat. Found his eyes. Found all the soft places that make men die.

The last guard got his rifle up. Shot Thu's father through the chest. Then the women reached him. They used teeth and fingernails. Used the rage of mothers who had watched their children go hungry. He screamed once before they tore his throat out. Yen's mother stood up. Blood covered her arms to the elbow. "Our home," she said.

The villagers took up the dead men's rifles. Bao wiped his knife on a guard's shirt. They grabbed weapons stones knives anything that could kill. The temple doors burst open and they joined the fight for the village.

Through his scope Granier counted the falling soldiers like a merchant counting coins, each death marking the rising tide of the assault. Beside him Spitting Woman's rifle fired in precise bursts, her shots spaced as carefully as words in a poem. The warriors moved through the fortress like fate made flesh. The more Chinese that fell, the more weapons the warriors picked up and armed their brothers.

The Chinese commander stood in gunsmoke so thick it turned the morning sun blood-red. He watched his fortress become a tomb as his soldiers died in precise military formation, everything their modern training had taught them worthless against mountain people. An in that moment, the commander learned his final lesson – don't fuck with the hill tribes.

Through that mouth of the breach poured all the rage of mountains that had watched their children, brothers and sisters, their fathers and mothers die. The warriors kept coming, moving through smoke that curled around them like grateful spirits. There was no mercy, just torn flesh and broken bone. The night air hung thick with cordite and the copper smell of blood.

Granier steadied his breathing as he tracked targets through his scope, the borrowed Russian optics turning darkness into ghostly green images.

"Watch the tower," Spitting Woman whispered beside him, her voice low and lethal as a knife against throat. "They're moving up their reserves."

Her rifle cracked three times before Granier could answer. Through his scope he watched the first round catch a Chinese officer high in the forehead, his death almost gentle as he folded backward into shadow. The second shot opened a machine gunner's throat in a spray of arterial red. The third transformed a radio operator into cooling meat.

The warriors flowed across the killing ground like water seeking its own level. Their captured weapons gleamed dully in the firelight as they advanced through the village. They found the command hut and rushed in.

Private Chen died first, his young face surprised as a long knife found his throat. Captain Wu followed, his commands cut short by a warrior's bullet in his left cheek.

His remaining men fell like dominoes, dying in perfect rows as if their orderly deaths might somehow deny the chaos consuming them.

"They're bunching by the eastern wall," Granier murmured, adjusting his scope. "Getting ready to counter."

Spitting Woman's rifle spoke twice more, and the gathering counter-attack dissolved into screams and confusion as two more soldiers fell from bloody headshots. The remaining soldiers dove for cover sealing their fate as warriors approached with their long knives.

"Like hunting tigers," Spitting Woman said, her voice carrying memories of older wars. "You don't count the cost until the kill is made."

Granier's rifle answered methodically. The heavy machine gun position died first, then an officer whose rank meant nothing to the bullet that claimed him. Through it all the warriors kept moving, kept advancing, kept turning captured weapons against their former owners.

"They're breaking," he said, watching the Chinese lines start to waver.

"For Yen," Spitting Woman whispered, her rifle claiming another life. "For all of them."

The smoke from burning huts and palisades filled the village. Granier and Spitting Woman could no longer identify their targets. "Screw this," said Spitting Woman jumping up.

Her face transformed like something ancient and terrible woke in her eyes. She became what the mountains had birthed - not a woman but vengeance given flesh. When she moved it was like smoke torn loose from fire, like a river breaking its banks.

"No!" he screamed, but she was already gone. His voice was lost in the thunder of his rifle as he laid down covering fire, trying to keep death away from her while she sprinted across the blood-soaked ground.

She ran with inhuman grace, floating between bullets like a ghost through gravestones.

Granier's rifle cracked again and again, dropping Chinese soldiers before they could draw a bead on her. Each brass case that fell from his weapon counted down the moments until she reached the walls.

When the smoke swallowed her, when the fortress walls claimed her, Granier felt something tear loose inside his chest. His rifle fell silent, the last brass case spinning away. He could no longer simply watch. Some battles demanded more than observation - they required blood sacrifice.

He broke cover and ran, becoming something beyond mere soldier, beyond simple warrior. Chinese bullets sought his flesh but found only empty air where his body had been a heartbeat before.

Through fire and smoke he ran, carrying the battle's final chapter written in his bones. He moved like fate itself, like death made of flesh.

When he reached the breach he disappeared into it like smoke into sky, became everything war needed him to be. He fought close enough to feel the enemy's dying breath, close enough to taste their fear.

In the end, it wasn't even close. Pride fell before determination, walls crumbled before will, and China learned why some earth remembers who it truly belongs to. The night filled with smoke and the screams of the mortally wounded.

Through the evening mist they gathered their dead, gleaning a bitter harvest while dogs howled at nightmare's edge and crows circled black. The villagers moved in solemn lines, carrying fallen warriors to ground that would remember them, while others dragged Chinese bodies into pyres that painted the night's sky the color of old blood.

Granier watched smoke rise, thinking how death smelled the same in any language. Behind him, men with faces carved by war sorted captured weapons into piles, counting the coins of victory. Women came through the temple door carrying water, washing blood from ancient stone, trying to cleanse walls that had seen too many wars, scrubbing at memories of violence that would stain the floors forever.

Spitting Woman moved among them, touching shoulders, speaking soft words in dialect that was ritual, was a way of making people forget what they had witnessed. The children helped as children do, carrying brass cases like fallen stars while their mothers tried to shield young eyes that had already seen too much.

Spitting Woman moved through morning smoke that hung thick as grief over the killing ground. Bodies lay scattered across earth that had drunk deep. The trench waited black against dawn sky a wound carved in soil that held too many daughters. She climbed down into shadow her feet finding purchase where hours before sisters had died clearing the way.

The first body she touched was Lin face turned skyward eyes gone empty as abandoned bowls. She lifted her gentle as handling newborn, laid her aside, spoke words in dialect older than any war. Thu lay beneath arms still wrapped around her ruined leg. More daughters waited in soil gone muddy with blood. Spitting Woman's hands moved steady and sure though inside something broke with each sister lifted with each weight settled aside with each face that would never again know morning.

She found Hong next, remembered teaching her to weave, remembered her laugh, remembered everything war had stolen. The bodies lay three deep in places where grenades had done their work. Her fingers traced paths through tangled limbs through flesh gone cold through all the ways young women become memory.

Something moved beneath her hands. A sound came soft as dying wind. She went still as a hunting cat, listened with ears that had learned death's every voice. Another sound somewhere between breath and prayer. Her hands moved faster now pulling bodies aside letting morning light touch faces that had seen their last dawn.

Mai lay at the bottom blood painting her black in the shadows. A bubble formed at her lips broke red against morning air. Spitting Woman's fingers found her throat felt life flutter weak as moth's wing. "Mai," she whispered though inside her heart hammered though inside hope burned fierce as signal fire. "Mai, child of my heart, wake now— wake and live."

Mai's eyes opened though one was swollen shut though blood ran from places that should hold no wounds. Her lips moved, shaped words that carried no sound. Spitting Woman gathered her close as gathering scattered rice, as gathering broken prayers, as gathering everything that makes life worth the pain of living. "Help," she called and her voice carried command carried need carried 10,000 years of women protecting their own. "Bring bandages, bring water, bring everything."

Warriors came running through smoke their rifles still hot their hands still remembering how to kill. But now those hands turned gentle, now those hands carried Mai from shadow, now those hands helped death wait its turn. Above them morning sun painted clouds gold while somewhere past the walls birds began singing while beneath the blood Mai's heart kept its rhythm kept its count kept its promise to see another dawn.

They carried her home through morning light through smoke through everything war had tried to take. Spitting Woman walked beside her speaking soft words in dialect that had survived three empires that had survived this morning that would survive whatever came next. Mai's blood marked their path, but her breath came steady now, came stronger now, came carrying promise of days yet to be lived.

"It hurts," Mai mumbled.

"Hurt is good," said Spitting Woman. "It's life."

They laid her in her bed, treated her wounds, soothed her suffering with ancient song and prayers. Night fell and Mai slept.

By morning the temple walls shone wet with water and memory while smoke from soldier pyres rose straight as accusation into the sky.

Granier found Spitting Woman next to the river, her hands red with other men's blood, her eyes heavy with knowing some stains never wash clean.

"I have to go back," he said, his voice soft as mercy but sharp as a blade. "Have to finish what we started. Make the supply lines bleed until their army starves."

She didn't turn, didn't speak, didn't need to.

"The warriors," he continued, "some will come with me. Help cut China's legs from under it. Make Chinese soldiers count cost in hunger, not just blood."

Her hands moved against the stone around her like reading braille, measuring the distance between duty and desire.

"Stay," he said. "Protect them. Help them remember why villages survive when armies fall."

Still she didn't turn, but her shoulders carried the weight of mountains, the certainty of rivers, knowing why some choices are made before words speak them.

When time came she touched his arm once, light as shadow. "Come back, my love," she said in French.

He left as he had come - smoke through shadow.

Repercussions

The sun had vanished behind smoke when the Chinese tanks started their final push. Vietnamese Colonel Van crouched in the forward bunker. The Chinese tanks came through morning smoke like iron beetles. Their treads left deep scars in wet earth. Van watched them through field glasses while blood ran down his sleeve. The shrapnel in his shoulder meant nothing now. His radioman called coordinates in a voice gone raw from smoke.

"Tank down on the left flank. T-59 burning. Two more pushing through the gap." The boy's words carried over the thunder of guns.

Van touched the bandage at his neck. "Tell Third Company to hold that ridge. They cannot lose that ridge." He watched Chinese armor roll forward in perfect lines. The tanks kept coming.

A shell landed close enough to shower them with dirt. Through his binoculars Van watched Chinese armor roll forward in perfect formation. Twenty tanks, then thirty, then more emerging from the smoke. His men died in neat rows trying to hold their lines. The Vietnamese bunkers collapsed one by one.

"Sir." His radioman's voice cracked. "Third Company reports no ammunition for the mortars. Fourth Company lost their heavy guns. Fifth Company..." A shell burst cut his words short. When the smoke cleared the radioman lay dead throat torn open by shrapnel that cared nothing for youth.

The Chinese guns found their range. Started walking shells across the Vietnamese positions. Broken wood and broken men fell together.

Captain Phan crawled through the connecting trench. His uniform was black with other men's blood. "They broke through on the right," he shouted above the explosions. "Nothing left to hold them with."

"What about the anti-tank teams?" said Van.

"Dead. All dead." Phan spat red dust. "The men want to know if Hanoi has abandoned us."

Van grabbed a working radio. Tried raising command. Got only static. More tanks appeared through the smoke. Endless steel. Endless guns. Endless death coming in waves. A young lieutenant stumbled into the bunker. "Sir. The Chinese infantry. They're moving up behind the tanks."

"Tell the men to fix bayonets," Van said. "We die here if we must."

Then a new sound cut the morning. Jet engines screaming low. The ground shook as sonic booms cracked the morning air like thunder. "Aircraft," someone shouted. "Vietnamese aircraft."

The MiGs came in fast and low. Their missiles streaked down like divine judgment. The first tanks died in blooms of fire. Steel coffins burning. Behind them trucks appeared on the ridge. Green Vietnamese army trucks packed with men.

Captain Tran grabbed Van's arm. "Sir. Look." He pointed south where dust clouds rose. "The forces from Cambodia. They made it."

Van snatched up the radio. His voice rose strong and clear. "All units. Counterattack. Counterattack now." His remaining men fixed bayonets and rose from their holes. Started forward through smoke and shell bursts.

The Chinese lines wavered. Their tanks tried to turn in the churned earth. Found their treads had no purchase in the red mud. They slid sideways crashing into each other.

More Vietnamese aircraft appeared. Dropped their loads precise as butchers.

The Chinese artillery fell silent as Vietnamese counter battery fire found their positions.

Through the smoke Vietnamese armor appeared. T-54 tanks moving in formation like an iron tide. Their guns spoke in unison. Started killing Chinese machines with mechanical precision. The tank commanders stood in their turrets. Waved their men forward.

"Look at the bastards run," Phan shouted. The Chinese lines had broken. First in fragments then all at once like ice giving way. Their soldiers fled north. Left their equipment burning. Left their wounded screaming.

A sergeant ran up. His rifle was slick with blood. "Sir. They're falling back across the whole front."

Van nodded. Watched through his binoculars as the Vietnamese army pushed forward. Bayonets fixed. Blood on their boots. The Vietnamese aircraft kept up their ground assault launching missiles, dropping bombs, strafing trenches. The Chinese retreat had become a rout.

"Send all units forward" he said. "Don't let them regroup. Push them all the way back to China."

The sergeant grinned. His teeth were white in his smoke-blackened face. "With pleasure, sir."

Captain Phan touched the crucifix at his neck. "The politicians said we couldn't stand against Chinese armor. Said their army was too strong."

"Politicians." Van spat the word. "They don't know what Vietnamese soldiers can do."

They stood together and watched their men advance through the wreckage. Burning tanks marked their progress north like cigarette burns on green cloth. The battle had turned. Had become the thing that made history.

Behind them more trucks brought more men. More tanks rolled forward. More planes screamed overhead hunting Chinese columns that fled without order. The Vietnamese army had come to take back its ground. To show China that some soil remembers who has bled most to keep it.

The Vietnamese MiGs rose through clouds dense as memory, their wings catching the light. Lieutenant Minh felt the familiar shudder of missiles nestled beneath, each one a promise written in steel. His weapons officer Tran worked the radar scope, fingers dancing across switches while dawn bled across the horizon. Chinese fighters appeared high above, arrogant in their approach, ignorant of the history written in Vietnamese skies.

"Contact, bearing zero-three-zero," Tran called, his voice steady despite the g-forces. "Four bandits, maybe more behind them."

"Let them come," Minh said, easing his stick right, feeling his fighter respond like an extension of his own body. "They think height makes them gods."

The first missile launch came without warning, a Chinese Sidewinder burning through cloud, seeking Vietnamese heat. Minh rolled left, deploying flares, watching death pass close enough to paint his canopy in fire. Behind him, Tran swore softly.

"These children think they own our sky," Minh said, bringing his nose up, letting his own missile systems acquire lock. "Time to teach them about inheritance."

The radio crackled with a voice he recognized - Captain Nguyen, flying lead in the second element. "For my father who died fighting French planes, for my brother who fell to American bombs, for every ancestor who bled defending our sky." Then Nguyen's MiG tore through the Chinese formation, leaving two burning fighters in his wake.

"Fox Two," Tran called as Minh squeezed the trigger. The missile leaped away, hungry for Chinese metal. Through his windscreen, Minh watched it connect, watched pride become flame.

"They're breaking, they're breaking," other Vietnamese pilots called, their voices carrying victory's edge. The surviving Chinese fighters turned north, leaving their dead behind in contrails of smoke and shame.

Minh banked his aircraft in a final victory roll, watching the enemy retreat. Below, the border stretched like a scar across earth, before men learned to make sky itself into battlefield. But some lessons, he knew, could only be taught in Heaven's vault, written in falling fire and broken wings.

"Good hunting," Tran said quietly as they turned

for home. Behind them, the clouds swallowed wreckage.

The Chinese tanks stopped retreating, regrouped, and turned back on the Vietnamese forces that had been chasing them. The valley lay dark as a grave until the guns spoke.

Colonel Van stood on the ridge, watching Chinese armor crawl through mountain shadows like steel centipedes. Behind him, artillery crews worked their weapons with the precision of men who had learned war's discipline in American fire.

"Range confirmed at two-eight-zero-zero meters," Lieutenant Tran called from his position by the forward gun.

"Open fire," Van ordered, voice quiet as prayer. "Let them know we will not yield."

The first barrage came like apocalypse, shells arcing high through night sky before finding earth that hungered for metal. Chinese tanks died in pairs, in trios, their turrets thrown skyward by explosions that turned valley floor to hell's own garden.

"Adjust fire left two-zero meters," Sergeant Minh called from his observation post. "They're trying to shift formation east." His voice carried the calm of a man who had seen three armies die in these hills.

Above them jets dueled like angry gods, their contrails writing war's poetry across dawn clouds. A Chinese pilot's scream cut through radio static as his fighter became flame. Below, tanks burned like funeral pyres.

"Sir," Lieutenant Tran called, "Chinese artillery responding." The words had barely left his mouth when enemy shells began falling.

"Let them waste ammunition," Van said, watching his crews work through the barrage. "They don't understand this our hunger for revenge."

Through smoke thick as history, Vietnamese infantry moved between rocks, their rifles speaking softer deaths. A Chinese soldier screamed as bullets found him, his voice echoing off valley walls that had heard such sounds before.

"Counter-battery fire, right battery," Van ordered. "Silence their guns." The crews responded shells flying true to find Chinese artillery that thought steel shields meant safety.

"Sir," Tran said quietly, "their armor is in full retreat." Through his binoculars, Van watched Chinese tanks withdraw, leaving their dead scattered across valley floor like broken toys.

Dawn came red as victory while shell casings cooled and men counted ammunition.

General Chen sat alone in candlelight that cast shadows like accusing fingers across his desk. Casualty reports covered the wooden surface – 60,000 dead, 200 tanks destroyed, supplies burned faster than clerks could count losses. His fists crashed down on papers that read like funeral rites.

"Impossible," he whispered to empty air. "All that force, all that steel..." A bottle of rice wine stood untouched beside reports of another depot burning, another supply line cut.

His aide entered without knocking, carrying fresh papers that spoke of fresh disasters. "Sir, the 4th Armored Division reports complete fuel depletion. They're abandoning their tanks."

"Abandoned?" Chen's voice cracked like ice

breaking. "The mighty People's Liberation Army doesn't abandon tanks."

"Sir, they have no choice. No fuel reaches the front. These raiders..." The aide's voice trailed off as Chen raised a hand sharp as executioner's blade.

Through his office window, Chen watched dawn reveal his army's retreat. Tanks stood lifeless as monuments, trucks burned precious fuel carrying defeated soldiers north. Radio reports crackled with commanders trying to mask retreat behind words like "strategic withdrawal" and "tactical redeployment."

"Tell me," Chen said to his aide, "how does an army of peasants defeat China's finest?" But he knew the answer lay in burning depots, in hungry soldiers.

Miles south, Granier watched through his scope as Chinese forces withdrew. Beside him, Old Giang cleaned his rifle with methodical precision.

"They leave much behind," Giang said, noting abandoned equipment that would rust into monuments. "Steel gifts for our inheritance."

"Pride makes poor fuel," Granier answered, counting retreating tanks that would never reach home. Through morning mist, Chinese soldiers marched north carrying defeat wrapped in silence, knowing that some battles do end not with gunfire but with slow starvation.

In his office, Chen wrote his final report. His brush moved across paper like knife across throat, each character admitting defeat without speaking its name. Outside, morning sun painted clouds the color of victory, though none could say whose victory it truly was, except perhaps the ground itself.

Dawn broke green and gold through jungle leaves as the warriors returned home. Village children stood at the gate, their eyes older than their years, watching heroes emerge from morning mist.

Granier was met by Spitting Woman, noting how her face softened with each step closer to peace. "You came back," she said with a soft smile.

"Where else would I go?" he replied.

Little Diep ran forward first, carrying wild flowers, a gift for her saviors. Other children followed, surrounding warriors who had left as farmers and returned as legends.

The warriors carried captured Chinese weapons toward the temple, their bare feet finding familiar earth again. Old Tran met them at temple steps, burning incense that curled like prayers into morning air. "Welcome home, children," he said, though some who left would never return. The warriors laid their weapons before the stone statues of the old gods, steel offerings to peace bought with blood.

"The ground remembers," Tran said, touching temple walls where bloodstains still marked Chinese occupation. "It remembers who defended it."

Through afternoon they buried their dead, thirteen graves for thirteen heroes. Women keened ancient songs while men laid brothers in earth that had demanded such sacrifice.

"Was it worth it?" Granier asked Spitting Woman as they watched children playing in the village square again. A cooking fire's smoke rose straight as incense, carrying scents of normal life returning.

"How could it not be?" she said, gesturing to women washing clothes, to men repairing hut walls, to all the simple things that peace allows. "This is what we fought for. This is what our ancestors demand we defend."

Evening brought celebration quiet as temple prayers, fierce as memory. Warriors who had dealt death now passed rice wine, shared stories, became farmers again. Through temple doors came sounds of children learning lessons that had nothing to do with war.

"They'll come again someday," Granier said as night fell soft as mercy across mountains.

"Perhaps," Spitting Woman answered, watching peace walk familiar paths. "And we'll fight again if we need to. But let's not think of that now. Let's enjoy the peace as long as it lasts."

Stars emerged while village life flowed like ancient rivers, while victory transformed into something sweeter than mere survival, while peace proved itself worth every drop of blood spent defending it.

Northern Vietnam

Tuan came through the morning mist rifle still slung across his backpack still heavy with army gear. The rice field spread green against dawn cloud and through the rows someone moved slow and careful pulling weeds from between young shoots. His feet found the path without thought found the dike walls found the edge of the paddy where morning light caught figures working in wet earth.

He saw her then, knew her even stooped, even moving with the careful rhythm of one whose wounds still sang with each motion. Mai worked the rows her hands finding weeds her body reading earth the way it had before war came, before blood came, before everything changed. The bandage at her side showed dark where morning damp had soaked through.

She did not hear him approach did not see him until his shadow touched her. When she looked up her face carried new scars carried marks war had written carried everything that made her more than simple farmer's wife. For a moment neither spoke. The silence held weight of all the days apart all the battles fought all the blood spent finding way back home.

"The weeds grow whether we fight or not," she said. Her voice came rough from where grenade fragments had torn her throat. She tried to rise, but her legs betrayed her and she started to fall.

Tuan caught her held her, felt how her body had changed, how wounds had reshaped her, how war had marked her deeper than skin. But her hands found his chest touched the jade pendant still hung there touched everything that remained same between them.

He breathed in the smell of her, the earth, the growing things, the life that had refused to die. Then his mouth found hers and they came together like rivers joining like earth meeting sky like everything that makes peace worth the blood spent keeping it. Her arms went around his neck pulled him closer while morning wind moved through rice shoots, while birds called, while somewhere past the fields life went on as it always had.

When they broke apart Mai's eyes held tears, but her smile carried light he remembered from before war came from before blood came from before everything changed and nothing changed between them. "Grab a hoe," she said though her hands still held him though neither moved to break apart. "These weeds won't pull themselves."

He smiled. She was still his Mai. They worked through morning her showing him which weeds needed pulling, which shoots needed tending, which things needed their four hands working together. The sun rose higher and sweat ran down their backs but neither spoke of battles or wounds or all the days spent apart. They had become farmers again, had become husband and wife again, had become everything the ground demanded of those who belonged to it.

When noon came they sat in shade sharing water from a clay jar that had survived the battle. Mai's fingers found his, touched calluses that spoke of rifles, touched changes that war had written, touched everything that made him more than soldier now. "Next season will be better," she said. "The earth remembers how to grow rice even if we sometimes forget how to live in peace."

Tuan watched her hands move across earth, watched how even wounded she read soil like reading fate, watched everything that made her stronger than any army. They had survived, had found each other, had come back to ground that remembered them. The rice grew green against blue sky and they worked together while peace walked familiar paths between them.

Beijing, China

General Chen stood rigid beneath fluorescent lights that cast shadows like dancing ghosts across the politburo chamber. Cigarette smoke hung thick as morning fog while twelve men in identical suits watched him with eyes pale as cave fish. Chairman Hua sat center, tapping ash with deliberate precision.

"Tell us again, General," Hua said, voice soft as an executioner's whisper, "about this victory you claim in Vietnam."

Chen's medals gleamed dull against his uniform. "Sixty thousand casualties inflicted," he began. "Infrastructure destroyed, villages—"

"And yet," Hua cut through his words like knife through throat, "Cambodia remains outside our influence. Our primary objective, abandoned for your... what did you call it? Teaching Vietnam a lesson?"

The general's mouth worked like a dying fish. Overhead fans stirred stale air while committee men watched with eyes that had seen other generals fall, other failures justified, other defeats masked as strategic withdrawal.

"We bloodied them," Chen tried again. "We showed them China's strength—"

"Strength?" Hua's laugh came sharp as broken glass. "You showed them our supply lines could be cut. You showed them our modern army could be starved into retreat. You showed them China's strength had limits."

Through smoke thick as history, Chen saw his fate written in twelve expressions carved from stone. "The terrain was difficult," he said. "The guerrilla tactics—"

"Guards," Hua spoke quietly, and they appeared like ceremony given flesh, like judgment made manifest. Their hands fell on Chen's shoulders while his medals - three decades of service to empire - were cut away, falling like tears against marble floor.

"Please," Chen whispered as they led him toward steel doors. "I served faithfully—"

"Yes," Hua said, lighting fresh cigarette. "You

served. And now you will serve as reminder why failure cannot be hidden behind victory's mask."

The cell door closed with precision of prophecy fulfilled. Through years that followed, Chen learned new mathematics of loss, of pride, of why some failures cost more than mere freedom. While above him, politburo men chose new generals, planned new ventures, wrote new chapters in China's endless book of ambition.

Northern Vietnam

Temple smoke curled thick as memory while villagers gathered beneath ancient beams. Grandfather Chi moved through shadow carrying a bundle wrapped in cloth old as mountains themselves. Incense coiled between carved pillars that had witnessed 10,000 prayers, 10,000 blessings, 10,000 passages from stranger to brother.

"Kneel," Grandfather Chi said to Granier, voice soft as temple bells. "Let the ground know your weight." Granier sank to stones polished by generations of supplicants while children watched with eyes bright as flame, while women burned herbs that spoke to older gods than any empire knew.

Spitting Woman stood at temple's edge, her warrior's hands clasped before her. "He comes to us from far," she said in ritual response, "but his blood now knows our soil."

"How does soil know blood?" Grandfather Chi asked the ancient question.

"Through defending," the villagers answered as one voice. "Through sacrifice. Through giving what cannot be measured."

Grandfather Chi unwrapped the cloth bundle, revealing a sash woven with patterns older than written words. "Once we were strangers to each other," he said, draping it across Granier's shoulders. "Now we are bound by things stronger than birth."

"I am not worthy," Granier whispered, but Grandfather Chi's hand touched his shoulder.

"Worth is measured by deeds," the old man said. "By choices made when death watches close. By standing with brothers when foreigners come calling."

Through firelight, children began singing songs of when mountains were young, when ceremonies spoke in whispers, when worth was measured in wisdom not weapons. Women wept silent tears while men nodded, their eyes carrying weight of knowing why some outsiders become more than mere allies.

"Rise now," Grandfather Chi said, "no longer stranger but elder. Rise now, carried by ancestors who choose their own children. Rise now, bound to this ground by things deeper than blood."

Granier stood, feeling weight of ceremony settle across his shoulders like morning mist, like destiny, like everything that happens when village claims warrior as its own.

"The ground remembers," Grandfather Chi said finally, touching earth that had drunk blood of three empires. "It remembers who defended it. It remembers who became more than simple soldier."

They celebrated through night soft as prayer, fierce as memory. Stars watched while mountains waited while peace walked ancient paths.

Other Books By Author

Author's Biography

Born in 1958, David grew up on a horse ranch in Northern California, breeding and training appaloosas. He has had all his toes broken at least once and survived numerous falls and kicks from ornery colts and fillies. David started writing professionally as a copywriter in his early 20's. At thirty-two, he packed up his family and moved to Malibu, California, to live his dream of writing and directing motion pictures. He has four motion picture screenwriting credits and two directing credits. His movies have been viewed by over fifty million movie-goers worldwide and won a multitude of awards, including the Malibu, Palm Springs, and San Jose Film Festivals. In addition to his twenty-four screenplays, he has written fourteen novels. He developed his simplistic writing style after rereading his two favorite books, Ernest Hemingway's *The Old Man and the Sea* and Cormac McCarthy's *No Country For Old Men* An avid student of world culture, David lived as an expat in both Thailand and Mexico. At fifty-six, he sold all his possessions and became a nomad for four years. He circumnavigated the globe three times and visited fifty-six countries. Known for his detailed descriptions, his stories often include actual experiences and characters from his journeys.